Whose Names Are Unknown

Whose Names Are Unknown
A Novel

Sanora Babb

University of
Oklahoma Press
Norman

Also by Sanora Babb

The Lost Traveler (New York, 1958; Albuquerque, 1995)
An Owl on Every Post (New York, 1970; Albuquerque, 1994)
The Dark Earth (Santa Barbara, 1987)
Cry of the Tinamou (Lincoln, Nebr., 1997)
Told in th Seed (Albuquerque, 1998)

This book is published with the generous assistance of the Wallace C. Thompson Endowment Fund, University of Oklahoma Foundation.

Library of Congress Cataloging-in-Publication Data

Babb, Sanora
    Whose names are unknown : a novel / Sanora Babb.
        p.   cm.
    ISBN 0–8061–3579–4 (cloth)
    ISBN 0-8061-3712-6 (paper)
    1. Farmers—Fiction. 2. Oklahoma—Fiction. 3. California—Fiction. 4. Labor camps—Fiction. 5. Depressions—Fiction. 6. Rural families—Fiction. 7. Migrant agricultural laborers—Fiction. I. Title.

PS3552.A17W47 2004
813'.54—dc22

2003060395

The paper in this book meets the guidelines for permanence and durability of the Committee on Production Guidelines for Book Longevity of the Council on Library Resources.

9   10

To the people who do the work of the western valleys

Foreword

Arid Cimarron County, Oklahoma, 1936. A featureless man, accompanied by two small children, leans into a thick wind, hunched over and looking down, as he walks toward a desolate, shabby outbuilding half-buried in sand. When Arthur Rothstein, a photographer from the Farm Security Administration, staged his subjects and snapped this now-famous picture, "Fleeing a Dust Storm," he created perhaps the most enduring visual image ever of the environmental hardships faced by depression-era farmers of the High Plains. What kind of people, the photo challenges us to ask, live in such a place? How do they survive? And what will become of them?

With a clarity and sympathy born of her own experience as a child in the dryland farm region that would become the dust bowl, Sanora Babb begins *Whose Names Are Unknown* in the bleak landscape of 1930s Cimarron County, the western end of the Oklahoma Panhandle. The novel's second half renders, with equal authenticity, the migrant labor camps of California. Written more than sixty years ago, her stunning story—perhaps the most famous unpublished novel of the thirties—is a narrative companion to Rothstein's portrait that makes vivid and real the people who inhabited this region. It is a novel that interlinks the indignity of poverty with the dignity of the impoverished.

Historian Donald Worster has called the 1930's dust storms that swept over the southern plains "the most severe environmental catastrophe in the entire history of the white man on this continent."[1] *Whose Names Are Unknown* assumes little of the epic scope suggested by Worster's pronouncement, dramatizing instead the human dimension of this ecological nightmare. Focusing on the family of Julia and Milt Dunne and a small community of fellow farmers, the novel is an intimate account of the daily struggles of simple people. And in their very simplicity lies the story's brilliance. In an age when concept novels and blockbusters dominate best-seller lists and much serious fiction is tainted by relentless invention and self-conscious wordplay, Babb returns the reader to a reassuring lineage of fiction built on a subtle delineation of characters who, though faced with seemingly insurmountable obstacles, find their meaning in the ordinary activities of their lives. Failed pregnancies, suicides, dust storms, the threat of tornadoes, labor violence, all are subsumed by the mundane, more powerful drama surrounding the characters' day-to-day activities: how to pay bills, afford groceries, help needy neighbors, get work, plant crops, keep a house clean, take care of children, find the gas for transportation. Babb lyrically captures the moment-by-moment ordinariness, even drabness, of poverty and labor. The documentary quality of her sensibility adds artistic weight to the commonplace. The result is a novel more intimate and familiar than allegorical, symbolic, or grand.

What elevates *Whose Names Are Unknown* above the level of a merely well-crafted story is its willingness to cast a reflective eye on so many conventional (if problematic) pieties of American identity: the near-sacred status of the yeoman farmer, the benevolent bond between nature and her human benefactors, the lure of the West as a wellspring of opportunity, the inexorableness of upward mobility. Most important, without a trace of self-righteousness or rhetorical excess, Babb upends the kinds of myths about poverty that allow the more well-to-do the illusion of their own essential superiority. Readers are provided no mental cushions that might grant them a comforting buffer from the afflictions of the book's poor folk. They are not foreign born, nor uneducated. They are families who bear the burden of children and the elderly. They are proud upright people who work hard. They are more honest and reliable than the institutions, whether banks or government camps, on which they must rely. "No disgrace to be poor," as Mrs. Starwood says, "but cussed unhandy." Were Babb to bring home one point above all others it is that such people—even amid dispossession, deprivation, and squalor—still find room to be generous and compassionate. Babb is alert to the effect of small kindnesses. Poverty does not make her characters forfeit their humanity. Wanting more than "bread and sleep," they are denied, by their reduced circumstances, the luxury of engaging in nonutilitarian contemplations and therefore denied the very basis of meaning in their lives.

No writer of the era was better poised to write about her subjects than Sanora Babb.[2] She was born in 1907 in an Otoe Indian community in Oklahoma Territory the year Oklahoma became a state. Her family moved around at the whim of her restless father, settling for a time on an eastern Colorado broom-corn farm where they lived in a dugout homesteaded by Babb's grandfather. The farm was a failure, so the Babbs moved to the Oklahoma panhandle where Sanora graduated from Forgan High School. In a 1970 memoir, *An Owl On Every Post*, that became her best-known work, she chronicled the challenges of growing up in the kind of places where crops rarely made it and neither firewood nor schools could be found for a hundred miles. From her earliest days, Babb exhibited a genuine talent for adapting to personal hardships by turning them into words. When combined with her finely tuned intellect and a keen sympathy for the struggles of the underprivileged, her writing ability made a career in journalism an obvious choice. A printer's devil at twelve, a reporter in Garden City at sixteen, a writer for a farm magazine, and a rural schoolteacher, Babb moved to Los Angeles in 1929, at the age of twenty-two, to become an Associated Press reporter. She recalls that, just as the *Los Angeles Times* was about to hire her, the stock market crashed.

Nearly always broke and for a time homeless, she honed her writing skills by cobbling together an unusually broad range of articles, stories, and poems in Left-leaning little magazines, literary journals, popular magazines, and newspapers, which brought her some distinction but no steady income. It was in this environment that in 1938 she went to work as a volunteer for the Farm Security Administration in the San Joaquin and Imperial Valleys, helping organize camps for the dispossesed farmers, many of whom hailed from towns in or near where she grew up. By day she helped set up tents and attend to the needs of the community, and by night she wrote. Fueled by what she described as "an essential interest in the farmers who were done dirty,"[3] she both kept a diary of her experiences and began a manuscript of her first novel, which would become *Whose Names Are Unknown*. While writing, she received a letter from her mother that was a long account of the horrible dust storms afflicting western Kansas. Sanora imported the account into her manuscript almost verbatim, and it became the symbolic and dramatic centerpiece of the novel, Julia Dunne's wrenching entries of coping day after day with dust and blackened skies. It would be these storms that would seal the Dunne family's fate and drive them west.

One of Babb's closest contacts was Tom Collins, the founding manager of the Weedpatch migrant labor camp in Arvin and a tireless advocate on behalf of the migrant population. Collins asked Babb to keep notes and later was impressed enough by the results to request a copy of them for another writer who was visiting the camp to research a novel. That writer was John Steinbeck, whom Babb reports she met twice. Whether Steinbeck read her notes can only be speculated. Babb herself does not know. However, given the two writers' shared political affinities, Steinbeck's reliance on Collins as an invaluable source, and his general habit of relying on documents like the one Babb supplied as tools in his writing arsenal, it is easy to imagine that her notes helped in some way fuel his imagination.

In an act of naive audacity, in spring 1939 Babb sent four completed manuscript chapters of her novel to Random House, a publisher of such distinction it rarely gave agentless manuscripts a second look. Nonetheless, cofounder and eminent editor Bennett Cerf liked what he saw, mailed her a check, and asked her to come to New York City for the summer to complete the novel. When she finished, what she gave to Cerf, on which he bestowed high praise, is the same work, with only minor alterations, that is featured here. However, whatever grand plans Cerf had for publishing her "exceptionally fine"[4] novel disappeared the moment *The Grapes of Wrath* hit the shelves and sold 430,000 copies the next five months. "What rotten luck," Cerf wrote her, that *The Grapes of Wrath* "should have so swept the country! Obviously, another book at this time about exactly the same subject would be a sad anticlimax!"[5] Still convinced of her talent, he paid her an advance for a future novel and reassured her that her manuscript might some day find a home. After receiving similarly kind rejections from editors at Scribner's and Colliers, as well as a letter from Steinbeck's own editor at Viking, Pascal Covici, indicating no interest in publishing a novel that would compete against their star writer, Babb accepted the inevitable, put the manuscript in a drawer, and resumed writing other things.

Babb was accorded overdue recognition in 1958 when she published a well-acclaimed novel entitled *The Lost Traveler*. More than a little autobiographical, it focuses on a nomadic gambler and his wife and daughters in the Kansas-Oklahoma region during the depression, displaying throughout the novel characteristic insight into the dynamics of family life. Conscious of the implications of gender roles, Babb also quietly anticipates later feminist dialogue. The past decade has seen the publication of two story collections and a book of poetry. Still living in the same Hollywood home she and her husband, James Wong Howe, moved into over five decades ago, and describing herself as "pathologically independent,"[6] Babb remains an articulate primary source of dust-bowl-era history.

What finally makes *Whose Names Are Unknown* a novel worth reading after all these years? In a country increasingly molded by its migratory and dispossessed populations, this is a story that has not lost but has gained relevancy over the years. Other writers have addressed the hardships of living on the Great Plains during the depression. Lawrence Svobida's account *Farming the Dustbowl* and Frederick Manfred's 1944 novel, *Golden Bowl*, join recent works such as Karen Hesse's 1998 adolescent verse novel, *Out of the Dust*, Carter Revard's 2001 memoir, *Winning the Dustbowl*, and Carolyn Henderson's newly edited *Letters from the Dustbowl* to represent a small sampling of comparable works. Even in the face of such renewed interest, Babb offers something genuinely new. As a novelist, her firsthand experience as both itinerant daughter of the plains and observer-participant in California migrant camps is unrivalled. A woman writing about migration, she sets her representation of the experience in domestic terms—as a challenge to creating a sustainable family and community—and thus departs from the more politicized narratives of her male counterparts. Her elemental familiarity leads to a haunting, evocative sympathy for her characters that has neither Steinbeck's condescension toward the Joads nor the veiled scorn that Erskine Caldwell exhibits toward his Georgia sharecroppers.

In a sense, *Whose Names Are Unknown* is very much a contemporary novel to the extent that it deviates from earlier realist literature produced by reform-minded outsiders looking in. By aligning herself instead alongside a powerful new generation of chroniclers of the poor, Babb joins writers such as Dorothy Allison, Kaye Gibbons, Carolyn Chute, and Roxanne Dunbar-Ortiz. And as with them, the basis of her vision is a deeply personal knowledge of her subject as harsh as it is artful.

LAWRENCE R. RODGERS

Notes

1. Donald Worster, *Dust Bowl: The Southern Plains in the 1930s* (New York: Oxford University Press, 1979), 24. Worster's work joins another volume, James N. Gregory's *American Exodus: The Dust Bowl Migration and Okie Culture in California* (New York: Oxford University Press, 1989), as definitive accounts of the milieu about which Babb writes.

2. Details concerning Babb's biography have been culled from several sources: Rodgers, phone interview with Babb, May 28, 2003; Sanora Babb, *An Owl on Every Post* (New York: McCall, 1970); Alan Wald, "Introduction," *Cry of the Tinamou*, by Sanora Babb (Lincoln: University of Nebraska Press, 1997), ix–xvi; and Douglas Wixson, "Sanora Babb: A Brief Overview of Her Life," unpublished ms, November 2002. As Babb's biographer, Wixson has played an important role in providing helpful information about her and her work that must be acknowledged.

3. Rodgers interview with Babb.

4. Letter from Bennett Cerf to Sanora Babb, July 27, 1939, copy in possession of author.

5. Letter from Bennett Cerf to Sanora Babb, August 16, 1939, copy in possession of author.

6. Rodgers interview with Babb.

Author's Note

The title of this book is taken from a legal eviction notice: *To John Doe and Mary Doe Whose True Names Are Unknown.* The time is the 1930s, the time of the Great Depression and the dust bowl disaster. Earlier the government had opened the dryland grazing plains of buffalo grass to farming; one could obtain 320 acres for "proving up" the land by living on it, building a home, and working it. It was a mistake to plow the plains in a land of little rain and wind, wind, wind, and the mistake resulted in dust, which covered fields and buildings, killed people and animals, and drove farmers out with nothing.

Part I
Oklahoma Panhandle

One

Although the old man had raised a fair crop of broomcorn that summer and the price per ton was better than usual, by the time the year's debts were paid and a little money kept back to send to the mail order houses for winter needs, nothing was left. This was the way every dry farmer lived from year to year, earning only enough for food and clothes and little enough of these. Good seed must be bought for the next season, and taxes were due. Taxes were a yearlong ogre and, more often than not, the crop did not yield enough to keep them paid up.

Milt Dunne wanted to change crops, but his father, the old man, held back reluctantly. It was better to be safe with a little. Milt had grown up in the corn country, working on farms until he learned the baker's trade. He dreamed then of the wheat country farther west, and when he was older, wandered about in those regions. Now this land lay on the western edge of the wheat country, but many farmers around were trying wheat. Brownell had raised it for years. The average for any crop in this drought country was two out of every four or five years, the rest being outright failures or just enough harvest to get by with pinching.

There was an early freeze and a good snowfall, and Milt wanted to try winter wheat. They could spend the early fall days planting, and during the winter he would have a crop to watch, and a green pasture for the cow and the horses.

The old man finally gave in. Life could not be any harder than it was or money more scarce. It might be a way to keep up a little better with the big farmers who could afford irrigation for alfalfa and who made money raising hogs. Not that he cared about keeping up, but the well-to-do ones made it hard on the poor ones, buying up their land for past-due taxes, and renting it back out to them. Brennermann, just to the north of him, owned thousands of acres he had bought up from farmers who had proved up government land. Brennermann was also a power in the Flatlands Bank, which held the farmers' loans.

When old man Dunne first filed his claim on a half-section of "farmland," he found it to be a piece of flat grassland in the midst of thousands of acres of free range. He broke sod and planted row crops, and the lean range cattle overran his fences and devoured his crop. In the winter when they drifted with the storms, sometimes the cattle came through his fences and hovered about in the slight windbreak of his dugout and barn. Then, as more men filed claims and crops began to appear in the range country, a fence law was voted, and the cattlemen had to keep their herds on their own land. There was a great and angry to-do among the ranchers. Many of them refused to fence for a long time, and on the sparsely settled plains no one enforced the law favoring the farmers.

The old man recalled vividly the first year he raised broom-corn, how he made himself two sturdy hand-wired brooms, one for the dugout and one for sweeping the bare yard around the door. Now he was going to venture winter wheat because his son Milt said there was more money in it.

With the money that had been put away for winter clothes, Milt and three other farmers, Hull, Gaylord, and Starwood, drove to Riding and bought seed. Milt's wife, Julia, wrote to a cousin in Virginia, asking for any old clothes they might give away that winter. In a little while, the cousin sent a box that caused a lot of excitement when it came. It contained a red coat that could be made over for Milt's daughter Lonnie, a pair of leather house slippers with soft pom-poms like puffball weeds (an elegance never worn), an old beaded party dress that perhaps could be traded to one of the Brennermann girls, some worn underwear, and a pair of long silk mesh gloves. Everything but the red coat looked very strange in the little dark house. Milt put the fragile mesh gloves on, tearing them with his chapped hands, and wore them while Julia was getting supper.

"You see," he said, "this is the kind of stuff your relatives give you." He spread his hands on his overalled knees. "Not worth a damn."

4

"But the coat is mine," Lonnie said. "I'll wear it to town." She ran her hands possessively along the soft bright wool. "I hope the girl didn't die," she added soberly. Lonnie was five, with silky white hair and an inward-looking, almost sullen face, silent and aloof, caring only about Milt.

"What do you get out of this, Myra?" Milt asked his older daughter. Myra was seven, brown-skinned, with an unruly mass of dark curly hair, wild, friendly, and easily hurt, almost a bully like Milt was sometimes.

"I want the box to keep my hen in."

"What hen?"

"Old Pet. I tamed her. She lets me pet her on the nest. Lonnie has tamed Dove."

"You let the hens alone when they're on the nest. They'll hide out and lay."

"She won't. She talks to me, and she drinks water out of a spoon."

"All right then."

Milt squared off with his fists in the lacy gloves and slapped the old man lightly on the side of his head. The old man stood up and struck him back, and the two of them boxed all over the room, knocking over the chair and the boxes, and shaking the small stove filled with fire. The little girls climbed onto the bed-rail and watched, Lonnie taking sides with Milt, and Myra with the old man.

"We'll make a lot of money next summer, old man," Milt said when they stopped. He pulled off the gloves and dropped them onto the beaded dress.

The old man was breathing hard. "Nothing risked, nothing gained," he said resignedly, but he was secretly pleased.

"You can get a square meal on that monkey stove, then, Julia." Milt lay down on the big bed and put his feet on the end rail. "If we get a good crop I'll put that land of mine in wheat."

"That land is nothing but a gold brick," the old man said gaily. "It's nothing but high range."

"We'll see," Milt said, seeing the wheat wave on the high plateau of land that was his.

Two

In September the winter wheat was planted. Milt and the old man rose every morning at daybreak. Julia was up before them, building the fire and getting the coffee and oatmeal ready. While they were eating the oatmeal, she fried them each two eggs and gave them thick pieces of the bread she baked one day in the week. There was butter, but not to be used generously or it would not last until the next churning. In the dugout it was still dark, and the men ate by lamplight. When they came up into the yard, the sharp high air of western autumn came into their noses, penetrated their clothes, made them go about their chores briskly. Each morning they felt renewed in themselves, and a clear unknown excitement sprang up in them with the sense of the new season. They looked at the land they had planted the day before, and the land they would plant this day, and they felt a sense of possession growing in them for the piece of earth that was theirs. But these unformed thoughts never came to words. The men spoke of the wheat, of the weather they needed. A freeze. Snow through the winter, to lie on the fields, to sink into the ground below the roots so the young plants could withstand the dry summer days. A little spring rain. No hail. No hot winds. No year would be as certain and perfect as this, but every season the dryland farmers hoped for one thing, feared another, and breathed again in relief if the crop was still safe.

They got up at daybreak and went to bed at dark. The days passed like this, each one so much alike that time broke only at the seasons. The wheat came up and lay like a green carpet over the level prairies. Where miles of short curled buffalo grass separated the farms, the land was gray and dry.

Sunday, Milt and the old man walked over their field, as every other farmer did on that day, watching the new leaves grow, kicking the dry clods apart. Every morning, every night, they looked at the sky to see the coming weather. Then the long cold winter set in, and the wheat acres lay growing under the snow. When the field was uncovered the horses and cows grazed on the wheat.

Late snow melted under the tepid spring sun, the rutted byroads held muddy brown water for days, and the yard was wrinkled deep with wagon tracks and pocked by dog paws and animal hooves. The pure white world of winter—with its noble stillness, its grand and awing beauty, its mighty storms—slipped deftly into a wild and windy spring. Moisture blackened the earth deeply beneath tender green wheat that leaned far over under a lashing wind. The tracked yard hardened into a mask. The old man walking against the wind saw the chickens scratch determinedly on the drying crust of earth, trying to reach the worms below. He watched them brace themselves as their feathers blew backwards, and he spoke softly to himself, "When it comes in like a lion, it goes out like a lamb."

Then the gusty spring passed into the dry hot days of summer, the wind died into a breeze save for the occasional sandstorm that swept across the plains. The wheat was strong and growing tall. Milt and the old man tended it, walked through it, watched the sky for rain, and waited. Milt was afraid of hot winds. Some days the fear was real and close, when here and there in the field the leaves burned crisp and pale. Great white clouds lay in a clear blue sky and at night they drifted away. Far off, low on the horizon, lightning winked with promise from the dark banks. Sometimes a curtain of rain spread nearer and hope flew into their talk and patience returned. Then suddenly and swiftly when hope was almost gone, clouds blackened the sky, churning and threatening, riding closer on a slight rising wind, perfumed with the fresh sweetness of rain. The men stopped their work and stood in the yard watching for signs of wind or hail. Heat lightning flashed wide and harmless, receded, and the quick forked bolts snapped brilliant and close. Mountainous thunder roiled through the heavens seeming to shake the earth. An ominous quiet cupped a hollow over them. In the strange electric light, objects miles away appeared in dreamlike clarity. Brennermann's tall white house looked like a staid woman in a long white dress. Starwood's simple farmhouse sat clear and bright like a toy that could be held in the hand. Each post in the long fences binding the farms stood out in unreal definition. The dark swooped down like a hawk in the rising crescendo of the storm, and the rain broke and crashed through the charged air, down upon dry and waiting fields. It came down in a heavy drenching flood, and the storm was over. Julia and the little girls, Milt, and the old man stood in the yard after the rain began, then seeing it would be a steady rain, they went into the house, listening happily to the even thudding on the roof. Milt went out often, to look at the clouds and sniff the air for hail, and contented at last with the rain he went to the barn to feed the horses, feeling almost giddy with relief.

The violence and magnificence of storms came again and again during the hot summer months, but when the wheat was gold ripe with very little burned, waving lazily in a warm wind, the heads fat and whole, Milt arranged for the Brownell boys to help him cut and thresh the grain. They came with their tractor, combine, and truck. Milt hauled the grain away from the combine and when he was back, the bin was full again. He looked at the yellow wheat and he felt good. For days the lusty rhythm of the machines hummed over their acres, and the combine laid the field bare to gold stubble and wide lonely reaches again.

This was a good harvest. One or two of the late harvesters were hailed out, but for most the crops were saved. Nothing could keep these new wheat farmers from planting wheat. The big wheat farmers near the state line had long been eyed with envy. Now these smaller farmers tried the crop and succeeded. They tended their row crops, the feed for their stock, but wheat was their crop. They never tired of speculating what they would get the next year and the next, weather willing, prices steady.

The old man paid his taxes. Milt gave Julia money for some clothes for winter—coats, underwear, shoes, stockings. They paid the grocery bill. They gave themselves a few "feasts," and afterward life lapsed back into the same pattern, with little money left over until next harvest. There was not enough that year, or the next, to plant the land Milt had bought fourteen miles away. It lay unfenced and unproductive, eating up taxes. The old man wanted him to sell, but raw land would not bring much, and Milt was sure someday he would improve the place and farm it. In the meantime, a little pasture rent helped pay the tax.

Three

The sound of a motor could be heard in the late summer dusk long before it reached the half-mile stretch of fence along the Dunne farm. The little girls were standing on a box at the window watching the truck. It seemed like a friend, and they felt excited and warm in their hearts for this noisy machine bumping along the road. The lights came on as if the thing was suddenly looking at them, and they jumped a little but resumed their curious watching. The lights came closer, making all the country around them darker and lonelier. Then the truck turned into the gate. The little girls leaped from the box and cried out in fright.

"Mama, it's turning in!" They withdrew together against the wall so that Julia was between them and the door. She was cooking a kettle of potatoes and onions for supper.

"Whoever it is won't eat you," she said, smiling at them, but their faces were tight and curious and they only looked and waited. The lonely years on the farm had made them as shy as cottontails. She studied them a moment through the steam from the kettle. They had grown taller but their bodies were thin and fleet and their skin brown with the sun. It had been two years since their wheat crop, two summers of dust. They were almost eight and ten now but they looked younger.

Voices could be heard mingling with those of the old man and Milt at the barn. In a little while all the footsteps came together on the hard bare yard toward the house, and the screen door opened. They all came down the steps, crowding into the little room. The old man put his head in first and said to Julia, "The Brownell boys."

"Hello, Max. Hello, Pete," she said. She was glad to see them. The old man went over to the little girls and prodded them with his long hard fingers.

"Look at my grandchildren," he said, as if they were people in their own right, and they longed to go forward and say something, to live up to their grandfather Konkie's compliment. "Growing like weeds!" The boys shook hands with the little girls, who looked up quickly, then down, and their hands trembled and felt cold in the big hands of the boys. Myra said hello; Lonnie withdrew her hand politely, unable to squeeze a single word from her tight aching throat. She sat down on the box by the stove. Both girls felt wretched and watched the nice young men when they were talking to the others, hoping they would stay, wishing they would leave. Myra looked at Konkie to see if they had done wrong, but his eyes were kind, proud even, and she sighed and sat down by her sister. When Myra was too young to talk plainly she had named her grandfather Konkie and since then they all called him that at times.

"How did your trees stand the dust this summer?" Julia asked. "I always said I'd like to steal your trees."

"If you plant trees right away and then live here as long as Mom and Dad have, you'll have some too. They dug them up along the creek and set them out around the house," Pete said.

"And watered and coddled them like stray calves," Max added. "Mom said she couldn't live here without trees. She said when she first saw this country and not a tree in sight as far as she could see she thought she'd come to the end of the world. She's worried now because the dust hurts them but they're still alive."

"When the dust stops, now that we have a well . . . " said Julia, not finishing, dreaming already of the tall cottonwood trees trembling their shining bright leaves in the wind.

"We had a lot of fun helping with the well, didn't we?" Pete said. "Well drillers are over at Starwoods now. Old man Brennermann finally had to put a well on that place. Starwoods have rented it for years and hauled water five and a half miles. Finally Mrs. Starwood had a showdown with Brennermann. She didn't let him alone till she got that well."

"She's a caution," Julia said, laughing.

"I'd been aiming to get a well for years," the old man said, "and finally we made 'er. Next thing's a house if the dang dust don't blow next summer. Mine's about the only dugout left in this country; everybody else has got an adobe or a rock house. I kind of take to this cement block they're using too, if I can build a stone."

"When we were trying to decide between a well or a house," Julia said, "we took the well so we could have a garden and thought if we'd stood this place so far we could wait another year, and look what happened. No garden this year for the dust even when we got water. But the creek's drying up so I guess it's best we got the well."

"One big wheat crop will start us a house," Milt said. "But that wheat would have to cover the state to get all the things we need." He laughed good-humoredly. The good smell of onions cooking filled the room, and he felt gay and eager to talk with these friends. "Why don't you boys stay to supper with us?" he asked, and looked at Julia to second the invitation. Her gladness at hearing the words and the laughter in the room struggled with the fear of having too little to offer. They were having only potatoes and onions themselves, and there was nothing else unless she made biscuits hurriedly. She smiled quickly and asked them to stay. Before they could answer Milt started for the door.

"I'll kill a chicken. One thing we have, plenty of chickens." The little girls felt a silent panic. Something fluttered in their breasts like the very wings of the chickens they loved. Each bird had a name, each one was a friend. They grieved when one was killed.

The boys halted him at the door, laughing. "No, really, we've got to get home to supper. Next time we'll stay but Mom is making supper for us."

"If you don't mind us in your way, Mrs. Dunne," the other one said, "we'll stay and chew the rag awhile. The real reason we stopped by from town was to ask you folks to come over to dinner next Sunday. Mom says she's getting lonesome to see you."

Julia flushed with pleasure. "We'll come, thank her, if she won't go to a lot of bother."

"It's settled," Pete said. Max was standing in the door leading down the vertical steps of the entryway, the "doghouse," where side shelves served as a pantry for Julia and a store place for the old man's possessions that no one dared touch because he was "particular." There was a jumble of boxes he had made with pegged fasteners, and three thick books leaning in a dark corner. Max slid one of the books into the light and looked for the title, but the cover was worn; he would have to open it to find out. The old man was watching him secretly, and when Max turned back the cover, he rose and took the precious book from the boy, putting it back in its place. No one noticed them. The boy felt offended. The old man looked at him, excluding all the others, and for the first time the boy saw the fierce aliveness in his black eyes. They were as young as a boy's eyes but the flesh around them was old and he thought the old man seemed to hide them.

"Some other time," the old man said as if in confidence, and Max warmed to him again.

Pete went and stood in front of Lonnie and Myra. He gave Lonnie's white hair a gentle tug, and she looked up shyly.

"You girls like to go to school?" They looked down in agony, and their throats quivered with the effort to reply.

"They're taking private lessons from old professor Dunne," the old man said, wanting to help them, giving them a wink.

"That's why we've got all this reading matter on the walls," Milt said, waving at the newspapers. "It's handy. Myra read the papers before she read a fairy tale." The little girls lifted their blushing faces like an offering of two pretty apples to their friends.

"I can read and spell and write and figure, and draw some," Myra said.

"I can read and spell but I don't like 'rithmetic," Lonnie said, and she ran to Milt to hide her face against his leg, laughing in a low sweet way.

"There's some talk of a district school this year if there's money for it. They'll probably build a one-room schoolhouse two or three miles east of you. There's some kids growing up in the neighborhood now and it's too far to Flatlands or Riding without a school bus." Julia turned away from the stove and her face was almost radiant.

"Thank goodness," she said in a voice so relieved voice it was almost singing. The young boys saw the ripening fullness that curved downward from her high breasts to her thighs. They turned back to the little girls.

13

"Can you walk two miles in the winter?" Max asked them.

"Oh, yes," said Myra. "Konkie would take us in the big blizzards. It would be fun to ride on the sled."

"That sled's seen better days," the old man said. "I'll make a new one quick as a wink if they build a school."

"If we know for sure, we'll all make it on Sunday," Pete said. "We'll put real seats on it; can't we, Mr. Dunne?" The old man smiled and nodded.

Julia said, "I think we ought to have a bell on it."

They all laughed and talked about the sled and the school until the boys remembered they had to start home. The old man made a clucking sound with his tongue and his teeth as he watched them drive out the gate.

"Fine boys," he said. "You wouldn't know they'd been away for schooling, would you? No airs. Pete's been to high school in Riding and Max has been to Kansas A & M to study agriculture." The old man had told them these facts many times. "He's as common and friendly as an old shoe. All of us farmers could learn from that boy. He knows what his father taught him here, and he knows the new ideas too—scientific. They're both plum crazy about farming." Lonnie was trying to make a toy bell she had play a little song. While she was busy forcing half a tune, she said soberly, not turning around, "Sunday, we'll get something good to eat."

Four

At the end of the week the days were like Indian summer, and they all walked the mile and a half to the creek to take a bath. The creek was no place so deep that a horse could not walk through it, and some places were now almost dry. In a shallow place behind a clump of willows, Julia and the girls undressed and bathed. Milt and the old man found another secluded place farther down the creek. They spread their towels and clean clothes on the low tree sprouts, along the bank, and passed the bar of soap to one another, rubbing themselves in the cold clear water. It was hardly necessary to seek out a hidden place for bathing, so few people drove along the road, and if a car or wagon were approaching it could be heard a long way in the country stillness.

Julia scrubbed the heads of the little girls, then washed her own hair while they played at catching minnows. Sometimes they stared at their mother's changing body, but they already half understood it from the talk at home. Bossy had a calf when her belly grew big, but it was still something of a mystery since the calf had suddenly appeared in the pen one morning, with the mother cow unchanged except for her deflation. It was never known exactly how the calf got out with its full body and long legs, but they secretly vowed to watch her more closely next time. Whether Bossy was the same as Julia was another question that deepened the mystery. That was something to be contemplated at home when there was nothing else to do. They began trying to catch the slippery minnows again. Now and then water snakes slid out from the shaded bank and fled the commotion.

* * *

Next day the horses were harnessed by eleven o'clock. Heavy comforts spread over dried fodder made a seat in the wagon bed for the old man and the little girls. Julia and Milt sat on the high spring seat.

The Brownells lived over five miles away with the creek running near their farm. The boys had ditched a small field of alfalfa, and in the spring when the water came down from the melting snow in the far away Rockies, some of it poured into their field. The fragrance from the purple blooms drifted sweetly over the farmyard and into the house, and when the hay was cut it sent out another kind of sweet odor, so that almost the year round Mrs. Brownell worked through her long tasks pleasantly aware of good things growing, or the pungent smell of new-turned earth. The deep well watered a kitchen garden to one side of the backyard, and this was Mrs. Brownell's special care. She was sometimes helped by the boys or her husband, but it was looked upon as her garden in much the same way as the flowers she coaxed and nursed in the shelter of the house.

When the Dunnes arrived, Max and Pete were waiting to greet them. They helped unharness the horses and water them, and when they were tied to the wagon wheels the boys brought hay and the horses ate and dozed away the afternoon. Mrs. Brownell was standing in the back door holding the screen open and calling out to them. Julia and the little girls went in through the large kitchen filled with the soft sounds and inviting smell of food cooking. A delicious foretaste of everything went through them for a moment and they knew this would be a wonderful day. Mrs. Brownell beamed on them in a hearty way and made them feel at home at once. She was a large woman whose glowing good health and natural graciousness drew the three quickly into her own warmth. Her shining brown eyes, her wide soft mouth, the black and gray hair wound high and loose on her head, all made a vivid picture in the minds of Lonnie and Myra. This was the first time since the girls had come to Konkie's farm that they had looked upon a stranger without fear. They visited the Starwoods and played with the children, and they liked them, but Mrs. Starwood's sudden loud laughter and her gruff good humor frightened them a little. They also visited the Longs who lived more poorly than they, except that they had more room, but dirt floors. The little twins were always sick and whimpery, and Mrs. Long was always worried and too tired to smile. They had never eaten at either place because the old man told them beforehand that their friends had nothing to spare. In this the Starwoods and the Longs were like the Dunnes, although all of them would make a meal from something if company stayed for mealtime. Mrs. Starwood often invited them but they always went home before supper. The Brennermanns were the most frightening of all. They had more to eat than anyone else but they never asked anyone to stay. One of the grown girls, Frieda, sometimes saved out eggs or garden food and brought it to her friend, Mrs. Starwood, when she could get away without being seen.

Mrs. Brownell was different from all the others. She asked them to dinner, and the whole room was alive with the food she was cooking. There were two large pans of muffins not yet placed in the oven, and the big table in the center of the kitchen was laid with pretty plates and knives and forks without wooden handles. Mrs. Brownell asked them to sit down in the room with her, but finally she permitted Julia to help. The older woman moved about quickly and surely, and just before everything was ready she went out to call the men and brought from the milk house a huge pitcher of milk, which she placed on one corner of the table.

"Well," she said, "I'm having a good time." The men walked over from the barn and washed their hands in the pan outside the door. Pete came in for a clean towel.

"Look at Mom," he called through the screen. "Ain't she having a heyday!" Mr. Brownell came in and stood by Julia.

"I never saw such a woman for company," he said, smiling at her. He put his fingers under his large gray mustache and pushed it away from his lips on one side and then the other. He was watching his wife admiringly, almost forgetful of the others.

The food was put on the table in large bowls and they all sat down and ate eagerly. The boys helped the little girls to plates as full as the others' and they forgot their shyness and ate.

When the meal was over, and Julia was helping clear away the dishes, Mrs. Brownell stopped suddenly in the middle of the room, her hands filled with plates. She looked at Julia's belly and there was anger in her face, but somehow Julia knew it was not against her.

17

"Tell me," demanded Mrs. Brownell, as if it had been on her mind all the time, "how are you going to have that baby in old man Dunne's place?"

The blood flew up to Julia's face, and she said, although she had been wondering the same thing, "It isn't time yet."

"You poor child!" Mrs. Brownell said. "It's a sin people have to live like pack rats. What have you done to deserve this, or what have the children done? It's a sin. The devil is right here on earth somewhere, if we could only lay our hands on him, or it, or whatever he is." Julia looked at her oddly, although she thought it did sound reasonable. Mrs. Brownell laughed a little, but she was still angry.

"My, I do get upset about these things. I hope I haven't said anything to hurt you." She began to wash the dishes.

"I should say not," said Julia. "It is terrible, but I guess a lot of people live worse than we do."

"I should think not much worse," Mrs. Brownell said. "And you all work so hard."

"Don't worry about us, Mrs. Brownell," Julia said patiently. "It can't last forever."

"You don't know that," the other woman said emphatically. "Edgar and I have lived here a good many years. We saved a little money before we came, and we built part of this house and added on later and drilled a good well. We got a small herd of stock and built it up. It's not large, but it brings in some money. We bought a few hogs. There's always been good money in hogs. We raised row crops for the stock, and the hogs ran on a little patch of alfalfa we had near the well. We raised broomcorn. Bad years I helped Edgar in the field. The boys were small then—they helped too. I made myself a garden, and to keep it, I spend half my life taking care of it. We've worked hard all our lives, and I don't say for nothing, because we've sent the boys in town to high school, and Max to college. Pete wouldn't go. He didn't want to be away that long, but he used to read the books Max sent home." She took a deep breath. "My boys love to farm—they dearly love it. I'm so thankful I have good sons, Mrs. Dunne." She was quiet for a moment.

"Oh, yes," she began again, "I was telling you how we keep going in this dry country. We've no complaints, I guess, because we're comfortable, but we daren't let up at all or we wouldn't have this, 'specially since the dust storms these last two years. It isn't enough just to have a nice house and enough to eat and a few little things. The future is a fearful thing when you begin to get as old as Edgar and me. We don't want to depend on the boys; we want them to have their own lives. But we can't work like this always, and we haven't been able to put away enough to be sure of our old age. We don't ever mention these things to the boys, because in the next few years we may be able to figure some way." Her brown eyes that had been so young and full of laughter were serious and perplexed. "This is a terrible way to talk to you. My goodness! You'll think I'm a fine one."

Julia felt pleased that she had spoken so freely. "Don't worry," she said. "I feel that I don't know a thing and I like to listen."

"Well, I've made up my mind to one thing this afternoon," Mrs. Brownell said. "You're to have that child over here when the time comes. I can fix up my sewing room. I'll borrow Max's bed for a few weeks and give him the davenport for his room. I can take care of you easily till you're strong enough to go home. I'll swear I don't know how you're all going to live in that one small room. That's settled, do you hear, young woman?" She began to laugh warmly. "Why, I'll be a grandmother!"

"You don't look old enough," Julia said, and then she remembered that this sounded as if she were accepting. Her face burned again. "I couldn't be all that trouble to you. I don't know how to thank you, but I can't."

"It's all settled. You can't refuse. Edgar and the boys will be tickled pink. What do you and your husband want?"

"A boy," Julia said almost shyly. "Milt's always wanted a boy. We've got him all planned, and we'll name him Tommy. Tommy Dunne. Isn't that nice? It's awful to have a baby when we're so poor, but we can't help wanting him after he's here. I don't know how I can ever thank. . . . " and Julia began to cry, holding the dishcloth up to hide her tears.

"Shush! I'm going to enjoy it more than you," said Mrs. Brownell. Julia laughed at this, and they went on putting the kitchen in order.

"It won't be long," Julia said.

* * *

In the yard the men were sitting on the ground, smoking and talking. Max and Pete were sawing and hammering odds and ends of lumber, putting a wide seat on a sled. School would open for seven months, two miles from the Dunne farm, and the children could walk that distance except in deep snow. There would be eleven pupils in the one-room school, in all grades. Anna Brennermann would be the teacher.

"I suppose you'll be taking the Dunne kids to school when it storms so you can see Anna," Pete said.

"Funny," Max said, ignoring Pete's watchful pause, "why old man Brennermann won't let the girls go with boys. Frieda will be an old maid pretty soon."

"She looks kind of shriveled already," Pete said.

"Anna'll never look that way. Gee, her taffy-colored braided hair is pretty. Think so, Pete?" Pete grunted. "You know," Max went on, "the school's going to have a pie supper once a month on Friday nights and there'll be a couple of literarys during the year."

"How do you know so much?" Pete asked, looking at his brother in good-humored suspicion.

"I saw Anna in town yesterday."

"Cooking up something already, huh? If she hadn't got the school the old man would never let her out." Pete paused. "Be careful," the younger boy said in a wise cool way. "You'll be married before you know it."

"Not too soon for me," Max said, watching the nail heads as he hammered, not looking at Pete.

"Well, jiminy crickets!" Pete moaned and sat down on the sled. "*That* bad!"

"That good!" Max said seriously. "Look at Mom and Dad— they've been married longer than we've been alive. In a year or two I'll have a crop enough for a start."

20 "I'd say that big Anna is a start."

"I like her just like that—big and warm with a soft voice. She's got a mind of her own too." He drove a nail and wanted to be quiet, but there was an urge to talk to Pete who probably would not understand yet. "Sometimes in the morning when I come out to milk I feel good, and I wish Anna was back in the house getting breakfast. Sometimes I drive by Brennermann's and I see her with her clean dress blowing against her, working in the garden, and everything's different for a few days. Think of a girl making you feel like that just to see her a hundred yards away." Max worked awhile without speaking, thinking of Anna. He was saying things in his mind in a way that astonished him, but when he wanted to tell Pete he was awkward and he felt a little ashamed to be talking so boldly about something that belonged to him so privately. Pete listened. He was afraid to joke anymore now and he was curious at the things his brother felt. When Max had finished speaking, Pete felt (but did not formulate his thoughts) that something between them had finished. Everything before had belonged to both of them. Now Max was thinking of getting away from him, being separate, being with Anna. Her wide blond face with the high cheekbones and the clear blue eyes, the thick blond braids coiled around her head, filled Pete's mind for a moment. Before this she was just a nice girl but now she was strange—she was going to be his sister.

"Wait till the girls get after you, Pete."

"I want to go with several before I get married," Pete said, feeling better.

"Don't worry, you will."

"You think so?" Pete asked.

"It's your own fault you don't now."

Pete thought he might take the oldest Gaylord girl to the first pie supper.

Five

The door opened into the great darkness of the prairies, leaving a blade of light on the bare yard. The old man came out making a long shadow, closed the door, and stood for a blind moment. Dimly the barn shaped, then the low wheat-stubbled field spread away faintly under the dark. His feet felt the yard familiarly as he walked toward the fields, swinging his right leg gamely. The words in the house were going around and around in his old head. He ought to be in bed asleep at this hour, forgetting the gnawing in his stomach. *God dang it, a man can't live on his own farm in peace. The moving in wasn't so bad, it's all the dang wrangling.* Five persons eating and sleeping and tramping in and out the same room gave it the smell and the look of being stuffed with life, a little more than it can hold, some of it spilling over in a vague obscene intimacy. He took the cud of tobacco from his pocket and held his finger and thumb close to the edge so he would take no more than a small bite. "God dang it," he said aloud and started back to the dugout. The warm light from the window flush on the ground drew him back, away from the biting night wind. He stopped at the edge of the cane patch to relieve himself.

As he went down the stone steps of the doghouse, he could hear the low voices in the same tone as when he left. He brushed against a dishpan hanging on the wall to make a noise; they might be talking about him. No telling. When he went into the room Julia was filling the lamps and trimming the wicks. It was always the last thing she did at night, must be the storm was over. The old man sat down on his wire davenport in the corner and began to take off his shoes and socks. Myra was already in her grandfather's bed with her head covered away from the light. She poked him gently with her foot to tell him she was not asleep.

Lonnie was asleep in the big bed in the opposite corner. Milt and Julia kept on talking, but it seemed to the old man it was the same thing over again. He sat waiting for the lamp to be turned out. Julia's eyes were red and swollen. She wiped the black out of the chimney with a piece of newspaper and polished the glass, then she set the clean lamp on the shelf above the table. Milt began to undress, and when he was ready for bed he stood by the fireless monkey stove in his underwear. The seat hung down limply away from his flesh and his strong body was lost.

"God, your feet!" he said to the old man, looking at his parchment feet resting on the base of the stove. The old man opened his mouth almost as if he were laughing, but his eyes were dark and hurt. "Why don't you wash?"

"When?" asked the old man. "In front of you all? It ain't warm enough to take a bath outdoors at night."

"Well, you could do it in the daytime when it's hot."

"I could. Just on account of the children. . . ."

"Well, Christ, you could wash your *feet*."

"Oh, shut up!" Julia said. "Haven't you growled enough for one day?"

"It's no mind," the old man said, hoping to end it.

"Dad's dirty," Milt said, as if his father were not there.

"Leave Konkie alone," Myra called from under the covers.

"Ain't it time to turn in?" the old man asked.

"Hurry up, Julie, so Dad can get undressed." Milt pinched his wife under her filling breasts as he went by her, and he got into bed. Julia blew the flame out in the lamp, and she and the old man began to undress in the dark.

"I'm going to town in the morning," Milt said. "Better make up your mind."

"Oh, take it then!" she said and her voice was choked.

"What's that?" the old man said.

"The piano," Milt said. "We've got to get a little money someway. Julie's got to have something better than pancakes and molasses now."

"That's too bad, Julie," the old man said.

"It's too crowded here, anyway," Milt said, "and besides it'll be ruined down here in the ground. You said yourself the keys are all sticking."

"I know. It's just so lonesome out here is all, and it's all the pleasure I have. If I just thought I could get it back sometime."

"We will, don't worry, and we won't be like this all the time." The old man sighed heavily, and they stopped talking.

Milt lay thinking about the money and the long time till next harvest. He did not want to start charging groceries till winter at least. Old man Flanery already had more farmers on his books than he could hold much longer. Milt would have to get a little money for the doctor too. Here in this one room half-buried in the earth, with the two beds and the red mahogany piano bulging from a corner, Julia was going to have a baby sometime in the autumn when it would be getting too cold at night to send the little girls outdoors. The piano would be gone then. *Wonder who'd get it?* As if it were already sold, he remembered the way Julia sat on the round stool, holding her fingers stiffly arched over the keys, playing the old songs by ear. The dolorous strains of one of the melodramatic songs forced into his worried thoughts the sad monotony of verse after verse until he fell asleep. The great stillness of the plains settled down inside the house, only disturbed now and then by the dog barking at a coyote and returning to the barn.

* * *

Next day with the help of two neighbors they loaded the piano onto the wagon and drove to town. Julia went along to see the doctor. The old man sat in back with Myra, and he held one of Lonnie's swinging legs to keep her from falling from her adventurous perch on the piano stool. To part with the piano was like losing a friend, like losing Bossy—or Rusty, who trotted along after the wagon with his tongue dripping sweat. The horses were surprised at the strange pull, and the young one shook his head back and forth almost jerking the lines from Milt's hand, lagging a little in his harness, letting the older mare pull the load. Milt flicked the line on his back.

"Buck is lazy," Milt said. "He always lets Dell do the pulling."

"He don't like pulling with the big mare," the old man called up front. "Ever since Starry died, he lags; he won't work with another mate."

"Well if I can ever get ahead a little," Milt called back, "I'm going to buy a truck. Even the poor farmers got something to drive."

"That's about all they've got," Julia said.

"Consarn it!" the old man said to Myra. "He's selling the piano and talking about buying a car."

"Only rich people have cars," Myra said.

"No, it ain't quite that," the old man said, "but some has and some hasn't".

"Well, why do Brennermanns have two trucks and a car an' we don't have any?"

"They have irrigation too, and we don't," said Lonnie.

"Well, that's the way things go. The world's a hard place. You'll find that out soon enough. Better you don't know every-thing yet."

"Do you know everything, Konkie?"

"Not by a long shot! If I did I wouldn't be in the fix I am."

"Maybe when we grow up we can find out how to fix you," Myra said.

"Maybe so. Maybe so. Maybe you can fix the world. It's out of joint somewheres."

"Maybe if it was fixed there wouldn't be any poor people like us."

"Then I could buy a quarter's worth of candy," Lonnie said.

"I'd build a house on top of the ground," Myra said, "and it would have two whole rooms, and Konkie and me could have a mattress to keep the wires from sticking us."

"Would you still eat hardtack?" the old man asked, laughing.

"Sometimes, because I like molasses, and we'd still have little thistles in the spring, but we'd have more too. Maybe some of the things like we had at the Brownells'."

"Well, you hurry up and bring this about because I'd like to have a piece of lean meat before I die, and plenty of smoking tobacco."

"Well, shut your eyes," Lonnie said, "and when you open them, it will all be right here."

"No sir, I shut my eyes too much already."

They were driving through the edge of town and in a few minutes more they were tying the team in the lot by the store.

Some men were standing in front of the store, and when they saw the piano they came over. Seeing the small crowd gather, men and women further down the main street walked leisurely toward them. Julia got down from the wagon seat and started off with the little girls toward the doctor's office. While she was listening to the doctor, a kindly old man with a good deal of gruffness, she was thinking about the piano.

"Watch your food a little," he said looking at her thin face with concern, "and get some exercise, and you've nothing to worry about." He felt suddenly impatient, not with the woman before him, but with the whole business of watching people live and die and being able to give them very little more than a half-measure of help in either. If he questioned this woman about her diet, he knew what he would find out. It was the same with all of them. No use to ask, when he could not help. He could give them his time, his knowledge, his skill, but he could not give them what they needed. They could not afford to pay him, and the ones who could put him off. More and more the poor farmers brought him eggs or milk or butter, whatever they could spare as a token of their intention.

"Do you drink milk?" he asked her.

"I did at first, but the cow is going dry now, she's calving, and I use what there is for the kids."

"Better try to get some from the neighbors—maybe trade some eggs. You need it for yourself and the baby too."

"I can do that," she said. The doctor was finished and waiting for her to go.

"I want to wait. My husband is coming over with the money; we're selling our piano today, and he'll be here in a little while." She kept swallowing the hard ache in her throat and holding her face quiet from the nervous breaking inside.

"Let it go, let it go," he said. "I did nothing but talk. Better save the money for the big event. Come in and see me when you're in town again." He patted her shoulder and started walking toward the door, talking above her protests. When she was gone he walked quickly into the back room and put a pan of water on the stove. On a round table covered with a heavy old

tapestry were two pipes in a large carved wood pipe rack, several bottles, a number of medicine samples, a plate, a cup and saucer, and a glass. A crystal flower vase held a knife, a fork, and spoons. A half-gallon pail of milk was staying cool in a crock of water. There was another crock with eggs. The bread was in a box on top of a small instrument cabinet on the wall. The boiled-over coffee began to perk on the stove. He dropped three eggs into the boiling water and laid his watch on the table in plain view.

Nights when I was out on an urgent case, I can remember now how she used to act when I came in. She'd lie with her face in the pillow and pretend to be crying because she was lonely. When I smoothed her hair, she'd cover her head and talk to me so low I never could hear. Then she would sit up in bed with her eyes dry and angry, saying anything that came to her mind. It always ended the same. "You work like a common man!" she'd say in scorn. "You work like a horse in harness!" We were never able to get on the same footing so I could make it up to her when we were together.

He sighed heavily and replaced his watch. The eggs were ready. Quickly, he arranged the table and sat down. "How stubbornly I go over these things," he grumbled half-aloud. *Memory is a cruel power, and yet it dulls and enhances. Thank God I am busy with these decent, honest people. They take me for what I am to them. Maybe they love me in their stern, bleak way.*

Before he had quite finished eating, he heard the office door open and close. He stood up quickly, more from habit than necessity, brushed his handkerchief across his mouth, and for the first time noticing the couch on which he slept still unmade, threw the blankets up over the pillow. He washed his hands carefully and went into the outside rooms, pulling the door to firmly. He always thought it better that no one see how he lived. As he closed the door he could see impersonally the whole jumbled intimacy of the room as that of a lonely man. It made him strangely uneasy, this feeling of having left part of his life unlived. *When there are no years left for changing,* he thought, *these disturbing thoughts are only lulled by the attendant weariness and hopelessness of their repetition.*

* * *

Milt met Julia on the way and turned back with her, walking always a half-step ahead of her so she had to run a little sometimes to keep up with him.

"Running from a cyclone?" she asked, and he slowed his pace. The old man was standing by the wagon waiting; the little girls were already sitting at the back with their legs swinging. The wagon yard was deserted, not another farmer's wagon or car was there. Flanery, the storekeeper, was standing out front waiting for the supper trade to begin. The main street of the little town empty of the farmers was now taking on another life with the townspeople going home to meals, stopping to talk on the way, calling out across the street to their friends. Motors sounded clear and friendly. The cooling air brought out the smell of the powdered dust under their feet. Everything appeared in a new clarity.

The old man was watching Julia with his swift black eyes, and when she came up to him, he gave her a quick sidewise nod of sympathy, and his brown sharp face was thoughtful and tender. Milt helped her onto the spring seat, and the old man went to the back of the wagon and sat between Myra and Lonnie. Julia looked at the cans and sacks in the boxes on the floor.

"By God, we'll have a feast tonight," Milt said. "We may not get another square meal. I got the kids some candy too. Myra ate all of hers in the store, but Lonnie ate one piece and hid the rest in her dress. She'll have that candy a month. Where do you suppose she gets that Dutchman's blood?" He laughed, looking back at Lonnie. "Say, captain, why don't you give Konkie a piece of candy?"

Lonnie turned her little white face around, frowning and serious and worshipful. She reached for her candy, but the old man laughed and shook his head.

"My teeth ain't good enough," he said.

"Too bad she's not a boy for you," Julia said, smiling at the boy's cap on Lonnie's small girlish head. Milt backed the wagon, and as they drove past the side of the store, old Flanery raised his hand in the farmer salute that served for greeting and farewell.

Once outside the town they slumped into their accustomed postures, the excitement died within them, and they rode home quietly with the lonesome sounds of the wagon and straining leather in their ears. A pleasant content filled them as the evening deepened, with all its dry odors of grass and weeds and fields.

The clear horizon circled the land as far as they could see, making the earth a world of prairies fenced in by the sky. The hidden sun was spraying up colored beams in the west. The first faint dark was rising like blue dust in the air, the bending sky seemed to lift higher and bluer above them. Rabbits sprang away from the road, and the small owls and prairie dogs sat up boldly together in their little community of mounds. Large owls scooped through the dusk and settled like blossoms on the tops of the frail country telephone poles. All along the road they felt they were going through a lane of owls. Now and then the wires hummed. The owls sat still on the dead poles and watched the people in the wagon go by. When they neared the farm, the little girls jumped from the wagon and listened at the singing poles, imagining they could hear the words. The dog waited with them and they all came into the yard as the horses were being turned loose.

"Better catch yourself a rabbit," Milt said to the dog. "You just chased 'em for fun on the way home."

"He'll wait till morning," the old man said. "He's tired. There may be a scrap for him."

Six

On a warm clear day when the clouds were lying great and white against the blue sky, Julia and the little girls prepared to walk the two miles north to the Brennermann farm to visit a little and buy a gallon of milk. Lonnie had been feeling sick ever since that day in town and could not walk all the way, so Julia and Myra took turns pulling her in an old long-tongued cart. The right wheel squeaked and wobbled uncertainly. It all but threatened to leave the cart. Milt was working on the Hulls' farm in exchange for the help they gave him during the last dusty, failing harvest. About a quarter of a mile down the road, they passed the old man preparing the ground for winter wheat, hoping for moisture. He was coming to the end of a row. They waved at one another, and as he noticed the rickety cart, he hailed them to stop. They waited in the quiet road for him to finish and watched him as he swung his long legs over the fence and strode stiffly through the drying weeds that grew in healthy profusion along the roadside.

"You won't get far, I can tell you that," he greeted them. "The pin's lost from that wheel. Wonder to me you got this far. Get a hustle on, Sprout, out of the cart. I ain't got any time to waste." He knelt in the road and ran a wire through the small hub, securing the wheel.

He nodded toward the syrup pail. "Getting some milk from Mrs. Midas? You better have taken your money along. A good neighbor would spare it, but not that Mrs. Brennermann. Her girls seem likely enough girls. Probably take after their grandparents."

"I'll ask," said Myra.

"You keep still. Come a day when a trap will catch you right on the nose poking it into others' affairs, my lass," the old man said.

"I know that," she said, holding her nose. "It hurts already."

"Let that be a warning to you." He lifted Lonnie into the cart. "Well enough of this tomfoolery. Milt'll finish on the Hull place midafternoon and be home before you," the old man said to Julia. "They say Starwood is two years behind in rent with two crop failures. He's afraid Brennermann will put him off the place if he can't make it next season. Starwood's an easy-going man, but a hard worker. Four young ones, six mouths to feed, keeps a man's nose to the grindstone these days."

"And a woman's too," Julia added.

"That's no lie," the old man said, reluctant to end the talk. Julia wondered at him. For days he would speak no more than necessary, then there would be no stopping him. *Ordinarily, he's a quiet man*, she thought. He went through the weeds again, waving them on.

"I'll get bit by a dang rattlesnake wading through these this-tles." He turned suddenly and called out to them, "Watch out for snakes!"

"You watch out, too," Myra called back to him with affection.

Beyond their own field, the road ran for a mile between a well-fenced pasture on the left and open country on the right. The land sloped gently into a long hollow and up again to level ground beginning with the Brennermann farm. At the bottom of the hollow was a small pond where the cattle and horses drank. Here the road rose with exciting steepness to the tabled plain. Irrigation ditches began with the Brennermann farm, and year round, within their hems, the young alfalfa was green and sweet, purple-bloomed and fragrant, or ripe good-smelling in the stacks. Hogs fed in the green crop, completely hidden in a tender leafy forest. Not many of the farmers could afford irrigation, but everyone knew how come the Brennermanns had it: some said they were so stingy they didn't even give their harvest hands enough to eat. Of course, there was more to it than that. Besides this large farm, they had tenanted farms in three counties and took a percent of the crops each year. Brennermann was on the board of the Flatlands Bank but seldom left this farm except on trips to see his large wheat acreage in other counties. He never went near the rented farms as long as the crop third came in promptly. He oversaw the work on the homeplace, and

31

his wife and three daughters ran the household. His wife was a tireless frugal old woman who worked as hard as her years would let her. She pinched and saved fanatically, much to the dissatisfaction of the two younger girls, Frieda and Anna. Elsa, the oldest, was a queer intensified counterpart of her mother. She seldom spoke to anyone even in the family, worked from morning till night, saved whatever money was allowed her, and invested in hog breeding. She had no life beyond these narrow limits and showed no inclination or desire for one.

Frieda, still in her twenties, had got past the accustomed age for going out with neighboring boys, and she brooded over the possibility created by local custom that she had lost the chance for a husband and a household of her own. Every year she watched more and more of the young men of her age getting married until the bachelor crop was narrowed down to a few peculiar middle-aged ranchers who seemed disinclined toward the help of a wife. Although privately she had not given up the idea of marriage, she concluded a job in town might more surely lead to a solution of what she considered a final problem. She was waiting her time to press her father for a place in the Flatlands Bank. Whatever her father's objections, they might be overcome if the young man were prosperous and steady enough to suit his requirements. Frieda by this time, in a sense of desperation and the fear of continued frustration, was willing to forgo the tender excitement of falling in love. In fact, moved by a wistful envy she did not recognize as such, she considered Anna's secret friendship with the Brownell boy a hasty and dangerous venture. Anna, on the other hand, was determined not to be left "drying on the tree" as she put it, waiting for a young man with crops and money secure in the bank. It was clear enough since the year of the closing of the banks that savings were not always safe in such an institution. It was also clear that most farms were mortgaged and most crop returns passed into the bank to repay loans. She heard her father discussing these things with the bank manager who sometimes took Sunday dinner with them. Few clear titles remained in the possession of the farmers who worked the land. Anna had until the last few years looked upon a bank as a public aid to people who found themselves in need of immediate money until the next harvest. Finally, as she learned more of its various functions and more about the hardworking, sacrificing families involved in its existence, she began to see it as a mercenary business profiting most off the misfortunes and desperate circumstances of others. It seemed now to her, strangely intertwined as it was with her own personal life, a monster gorging itself on the farmlands and crops of the people she knew, who had lost their independence either through accidents of nature or through the fluctuating prices for crops and animals and—in general—the depression. Frieda's longing to work in the Flatlands Bank seemed a distasteful escape to Anna, but she understood the secret desire that urged her sister's ambition. Anna's friendship with Max did not hinge solely on her desire to escape the fate of her two sisters. She and Max were truly in love, and economic requirements to the contrary, she intended to marry him the moment he asked her. Furthermore, it seemed to her that their future would be more secure than most of their neighbors'. The Brownells were not large landowners like her father, but they were sound, scientific farmers who owned their land and machinery, each year added to the comfort of their home, and spent money in experimentation. This last was a concession to the new ideas of Max and Pete.

* * *

As Julia and the little girls came through the yard toward the back door, she saw the look of suspicion come over Mrs. Brennermann's face when she noticed the gallon pail in Myra's hand.

"Good day," Mrs. Brennermann said through the screen door, her greeting half a question.

Frieda came up quickly behind her and pushed the screen open gladly. She brought them into the large clean kitchen and called upstairs in an excited voice, "Anna, come down! Julia Dunne's here!" She turned to them eagerly. "You must be hot and tired after the long walk. Want a drink of cool water? Or, better still, milk?" she said, unable to keep from glancing at the protruding front of Julia's cotton dress. She hurried out to the milk house under the windmill and returned with a pitcher of milk. The little girls drank it shyly but with great pleasure. The old woman spoke

33

of the weather and returned to her baking. On a long table against the wall, golden loaves of warm bread lay on a white cloth cooling, filling the room with a delicious odor that stirred their appetites. Anna came into the room sniffing the bread and greeting them at the same time.

"Oh, Mom," she asked, "can't we have some hot bread? I love bread just out of the oven!"

"I s'pose," said the old woman, smiling warmly at her youngest girl. Anna whetted a long knife on the edge of a crock and sliced the soft loaves into thick uneven pieces while Frieda buttered them. They sat in the kitchen eating and talking until Julia asked them to play the piano and sing together. In the dark, cool, unused living room, they played and sang the whole afternoon. Anna was making a warm dress for school, and she and Julia basted seams as they sang. Mrs. Brennermann finally came in.

"It's getting about supper time. Maybe you folks want to get started home." She went out and came back in a little while. "It's looking stormy out, maybe you ought to get started." Julia would have gone the first time but the Brennermann girls held her back. They went into the kitchen and the pail of milk was ready. The old woman had scalded the bucket and made it shine.

"Ten cents, isn't it?" Julia asked, hoping this was right. She laid the dime on the table.

"Well," the old woman smiled, "ten cents is enough between neighbors."

"Mama!" said Frieda, but she laughed away her intended reproach. The troughs in the milk house were filled with crocks and pans of milk and butter, bedded in cool running water from the well.

"She don't want it for nothing," the old woman said slyly. Julia and the little girls were already on the steps. The clouds were dark and the air was fragrant with the coming rain.

"You should stay," begged Anna, "you'll be caught in the storm." She looked at Julia's swollen belly and then quickly away.

"It's about supper time," Julia said, looking at the old woman. "We can get home before the storm hits. It's just threatening. Maybe it won't rain." The girls studied the sky doubtfully.

"Frieda, if you'll walk down someday, you may have my old songs. I don't need them without the piano." Elsa was coming in from the hog pens, watching the clouds. She wore overalls and walked heavily, freely. She raised her arm to them in a masculine greeting. They turned out of the yard into the road between the telephone wires, walking fast to get ahead of the storm.

They were almost a mile away, walking in the hollow, when the rain began in large slow drops, and the far horizon quivered with sheet lightning. Fork lightning snapped suddenly, splitting the moving clouds, flashing close to the wires. The whole flat world under an angry churning sky was miraculously lighted for a moment. A strange liquid clarity extended to the ends of the earth. Julia saw the trees along the creek and animals grazing far away. The bleak farmyards with their stern buildings, scattered sparsely on the plains, stood out in naked lonely desolation. A sly delicate wind was rising. Their dresses moved ever so little. Thunder clapped and boomed. They were afraid of the electricity that speared into the ground with a terrifying crash after. Julia stopped for a moment to get her breath and look at the approaching storm. Then she took Lonnie from the bumping cart and pulled her along by the hand, while Myra pulled the cart and clung to the pail of milk. They moved off the road away from the wires, going through the open hollow.

"There's wind in the clouds, Mama," yelled Myra. "See them boiling. Does it look like it's making a funnel to you?"

"No, it's only an electric storm. There's no cyclone cloud. It's too late for cyclones. Rain won't hurt us. It's just scary, that's all." Myra was yelling something else. "Now don't talk. Save your breath and hurry." They began to run along the shallow ground, wanting to reach the level road. The rain burst heavily, and they cringed together when the lightning cracked near them, they started on again, their breath cutting like knives in their lungs.

"Leave the cart by the road," Julia called back to Myra. "We'll get it tomorrow." Myra hesitated, then dropped the tongue and ran on. The wind was rising, whipping the rain into a great swishing silver tail that lashed across the plains. It blew against them in sharp little spears and ran into their eyes, half-blinding them. Then it grew gentler and thinner, but the lightning and thunder came with new violence. They bent far forward as they plunged into the strengthening wind. Once Julia slipped on the wet surface of the road and fell on top of Lonnie, and the bedraggled and shaken little girl sat on the wet grass almost crying, waiting for her mother to recover her breath. Julia got up quickly, oddly aware of her unwieldy body, and ran on pulling the little girl along close.

They were going along the level plain for sometime before they saw Milt coming to meet them. He was racing the horses and the clumsy wagon was straining and rattling as if it would fall apart. He turned it around wildly and helped them into the seat. Myra's hands were tight on the milk pail and she almost fell getting in. When Milt saw the whiteness in Julia's face, he stung the horses with the line ends and they leaped ahead through the rain and wind and into the gate so madly that the wagon almost went over. The old man was in the yard waiting. Water was streaming over the broad brim of the old hat he held on against the now driving wind. He helped Julia into the dugout and made her lie down. The room was filled with the strong spicy smell of coffee. He poured a cupful and handed it to her.

"I'll be all right as soon as I rest," she said. The little girls were getting out of their wet clothes and into dry overalls. He poured another cup half-full and handed it to Myra.

"Here, drink it between you. It'll stop your teeth chattering. Now get your mother something dry and put this iron to her feet." He got a heavy cloth from the doghouse. "Wrap the iron in it, and mind you don't burn yourself."

He went out to see about the horses. It was bad to get them so excited; they might have run away. Milt had unharnessed them and was coming toward the house. The horses were standing in the fodder shelter by the granary, still trembling, their eyes wild and their nostrils dilated. The old man went up to them quietly, talking to them, coaxing them out of their fear. When they were quieter, he led them into the barn and rubbed them down until their flesh ceased its spasmodic twitching. The mare was steadier and more plodding. She settled down contentedly to eating her fodder long before the pony stopped swinging his head about, showing the whites of his eyes, and breathing in great gusty sighs.

"You're no plow horse," the old man told him. "You want back with that wild herd. You need breaking to the saddle, but I'm too old to tackle you." One winter that now seemed long ago, he had driven to the cedars for wood when Chip, Dell's mate, was alive, and the old man had caught a sorrel colt, just past weaning, from the herd of wild horses that roamed the forested mountains. These horses had once been tame. They had broken free from their owners' wagons at night or wandered off in too loose hobbles and been lost. As they interbred, the young ones became smaller and wilder. The farmers who went each winter to bring back firewood, told tales of the wild horses coming down to the camps at night, whinnying and neighing, exciting the horses and enticing them to break free. Many a farmer lost a horse or more in the old days. Now, the trips were usually made by truck. Farmers without trucks exchanged work for wood. The old man sighed, remembering the excitement of the cold trips, the campfires, the days spent chopping down trees and sawing them up. He remembered the time he had lassoed the wild colt, and before he left for home his conscience drove him to decide on turning it loose, but the horses did not come that night and he was reluctant to leave him alone. It took a long time to break the colt. The old man got Starry, a young mare his size, and the colt, Buck, worked with her peacefully. One rainy night when the horses were grazing on the open prairie, Starry slipped over a rocky cliff above the half dry creek and broke her neck. Chip was already dead of a stomachache, and Buck had to work with Dell. She was the large mare, and Buck never liked it. He went wild and stubborn again, shirking his share of the work. Dell put up with him patiently, long accustomed to her load. Sometimes in the spring he would tease her, and perhaps this frisky show of affection appeased the quiet mare for the trouble he gave her at work. They had been the old man's only companions in a lonely and impoverished life, and he cared for them and talked with them more freely than he ever had a friend. "You can always be trusted," he'd say to them, "and that's more than I can say for man." This thought

37

always gave him a twinge of conscience. He half-retracted it to himself. Deep in his mind was a lingering and eager belief in man as a human being. Some indefinite thing in himself that had been pressed back, unused, decided him. He was no different from any other man in this, his wordless hunger for dignity, to have faith in men, who seemed to him misshapen by the world they lived in, never reaching their fullest bloom. Living was a sorrowful business to the old man and all the people he knew, filled with hard work, worries of every kind, fear and doubt for the future. A man forgot his youth in securing his old age, and there was no certainty even in this. Had he himself not worked hard since he was a boy? Had he not done right, save for the years when he struck out savagely against things that were more than he could bear? And then only alone, drinking, to forget, to escape. Why had he not drunk for joy? At the little church in town where he sometimes went at first, he listened to the repetitious gloomy, preaching against human joyfulness, the stern pleading for men and women to endure their burdensome earthly lot. Happiness came after—a pure and indefinable happiness that did not sound very gratifying. The things that made men laugh and sing and know their blood and minds—these things were wrong. Knowledge was dangerous because it created doubt. Doubt and question belonged to the charlatans. Endurance, acceptance, the sad hard experience belonged to the good. Religion was for the poor; this much was clear. To him, the crust of bread, the sip of wine was not the flesh and blood of Christ but a symbol of life—the inadequate, betrayed life of people everywhere on the earth.

Was not Christ a man, with blood in his veins and a heart for people? He did not die that they might be saved; he was murdered, as good as lynched, for his ideas that woke the poor enduring people like the ones now in this little church in town, he was killed for his ideas that threatened the enthroned greed of the times. Why was the earth he loved—with its tender magnificent beauties, its treasures within and without, its order and change—not a fit place for a full and joyous life? Work, yes, because work itself is no hardship, if done in reason, a reason connected with life. Why should a man wish to leave his body and the earth to reach completion? Had he no respect for himself and for the world? What of the many lifetimes wasted in endurance? Could not these lives moving together change the world?

The old man years ago had done with his faith in religion. He had not made a sharp conclusion. He had grown away from it because it had nothing to do with life and more and more was no guide to living, but only a guide to death, a humiliating guide at that. He knew that many of his neighbors felt the same, although there were no declarations. There were at first doubts, then the fear of having doubted, then the long and patient recognition that religion had failed them in their greatest need, not once, but altogether. It betrayed them into a humility and a patience unnoticed by God but noticed and used by man. The old man was not one to hold on to bitterness and disappointment, and gradually, as he was freed of the other, his belief in men grew, and as it grew it took shape in simple questions for the things he could not answer. It seemed to him the whole of his experience and observation of others pointed straight and true to one thing: that man was capable of making a good life for himself, of guiding his existence, of finding a better answer to the longings of his spirit, once he learned a way to throw off the halter of power on earth that controlled the things men created in their work. Farmers around him would not be living the way they were if this were not true. The earth was generous and could give him his needs, and stir his heart and soul. Did he not many times stand and look at the far horizon, feeling the tug deep in his thoughts as if his being were stretching and drawing out beyond him? Did he not hunger for more than he knew and felt when he stood like this? If a man was free, he might find the answer.

The old man always thought of these things when he was doing some simple task, and now that the horses were dry and contented, and he had come to the usual conclusion in his "studying," he hung the currycomb on a nail near the harness rack and went out, closing the door securely against the wind. It was dark. The rain had ceased. A high clean wind was blowing fresh and sweet and a little cold off the fields. Clouds were

39

moving swiftly overhead, spent and broken, still dark, showing the sky and stars far above them. Off to the northwest, sheet lightning still trembled, showing the slanting dark blue curtain of rain falling many miles away. The old man stopped by the door to clean the mud from his shoes with a stick.

Seven

In the night they all came awake with the sound of sharp, hard, caught breathing and crying in the ears of their sleep, feeling it was a dream, stirring themselves a little to shake the clinging shreds of fear from their minds. The old man, sleeping lightly and easily as the old do, was the first to come clearly awake. He lighted the lamp.

"Julie, that you? What's wrong? What is it?" he asked in a low troubled voice. Julia was holding the covers over her mouth to quiet the groans. She did not answer except with an apologetic "Oh-h" and pulled the comfort tight over her mouth again as if this would stop the pain. The old man swung out of bed, making sure Myra was still covered, and quickly drew on his overalls over his long baggy underwear. Milt leapt up startled and dressed quickly, putting on his shoes first because the floor was cold. The old man began to build a fire to drive out the dampness that had settled on the room.

"Goddamn that old woman!" Milt shouted. "Goddamn her hide! If she hadn't been so scared she'd lose a meal, Julia could have waited for me to get her. Goddamn her!"

"That can't help matters now," the old man hushed him. "Tend to Julie."

Milt looked at Julia for a moment, angry that she groaned so, and he could do nothing. He would have thought he was dying with the same pain or less. He felt ashamed and frightened.

"I'd better ride to Brennermann's and get a hand to take me to town in a truck for the doctor," he said. "They're the closest, damn them."

"No, no, don't leave me alone. Something's happening. I feel so queer. You couldn't get back quick enough. Put on some water." The old man went to get a bucketful from the barrel. He was back in a moment and put it on the small stove. Then he began to stuff cowchips into the fire to make a high blaze. It roared up the tin chimney, and he turned the damper at an angle to preserve the heat and still keep a strong draft. The little girls were sitting up in bed looking scared.

"Lonnie, get in Dad's bed with Myra and cover up your heads and go back to sleep." The little girl flew across the room, her fine white hair mussed into a "mouse's nest" on top of her head. They were too much frightened even to whisper in the close warmth of the covers. They heard their mother get out of bed and walk about bumping into things in the crowded room, then she went outdoors.

"Maybe we could get Julie into town before . . . " the old man suggested cautiously.

"That's crazy!" Milt interrupted him. The old man said nothing. "It's prices or hail or wind, something all the time, and now it's this. I can't figure it out."

"Good thing we didn't have the wheat in or that wind would of taken 'er right out of the ground. When the sun's up I'll go out and see how much moisture we got. If it would rain before it blowed, the soil would hold." The old man was trying to get Milt's mind off the misfortune. He had been worried lately.

"Well, we'll start drilling tomorrow. It'll be dry enough by then. I'm getting so I dread the summer coming. If the dust storms get any worse next year we won't have a field. We'll be starved out. This land is going back to desert."

"They may stop," the old man said. "We have to be patient."

"Patient, hell! These farmers start starving next year, you going to say be patient?"

"Reckon I won't have any say. All I say now is the summer ain't here yet. No use crossing the river before you get to it."

"I've got to see about Julie." Milt went up the steps and opened the door. The sky was cold gray around the edges and the light was coming slowly. Julia was walking across the yard. Milt fastened the storm door back on the outside.

"Storm's over," he called to her. "You feel any better?"

"I feel like my insides are coming out. I've got awful pains."

"You'd better go back inside and lay down if you can and take no chances losing him after he's this far." He went ahead of her into the dugout and awkwardly turned back the heavy bedcovers for her. The old man had a hot iron in bed for her feet.

"You cold?" he asked.

"Yes," she said, feeling the iron. "Thanks. You want to make some hot coffee, Dad?"

"Yep," he laughed a little and got busy. "It's nigh time anyway. Almost sunup." He usually boiled the grounds several times to make the coffee go as far as possible but this time he made it fresh. He looked at Julia and the tears were running down her cheeks, and she was biting her lips. He nodded his head sidewise in a quick gesture of sympathy. Milt was sitting by the stove waiting. Now and then he looked at his wife. He thought she would be all right now. When the coffee was done, she drank a large cup and said it made her feel better. There was a sudden bright light through the windows, and the old man blew his breath above the lamp chimney.

"You kids can get up," Milt said. They reached for their clothes and pulled them into the bed to warm them. Just as they sat up and started to dress, Julia began to have long sharp pains, one quick after the other, and no matter how much she tried to hold back the cries, they came out naked and terrible.

"It's coming," she screamed. "I can't hold it, oh, I can't hold it!" The startled men began to do what they knew, swiftly.

"Stay in bed and cover your heads!" Milt yelled at the little girls. They went under like prairie dogs.

Between pains, Julia told them what to do. "And put the yellow comfort on the floor. I'll ruin the mattress." Milt tore a sheet in pieces and she looked at it, hating to see it go. Then the pains came again and again and then her screams filled the little room with a terrifying finality. The little girls stirred breathlessly under the covers, possessed by a fascinating terror.

Milt and the old man hardly knew how it happened, but when it was all over they felt dizzy and sick, and Milt was as pale as Julia. She was exhausted and felt very light and far away from the pain. She wanted to open her eyes but she had no strength left for it. She felt Milt taking care of her and lifting her back into the bed and then she went to sleep. He covered her well then opened the door. The bitter odor of blood was everywhere in

43

the room and under the covers in the bed with the children still awake. They heard their father making trips in and out.

The old man put the coffee on to heat and sat down a moment by the stove and leaned his chin in his hand.

I'll be danged, he thought to himself. *Poor Julie.*

Milt spoke to him and he started. "A boy, this time, all right." Milt had been thinking about one, and if they had to have a baby now, he wanted a boy. His voice was bitter but it was too soon after to feel much connection with what he said. He wrapped the piece of blanket loosely as if it were alive and needed to breathe. Then he folded the blanket back and looked again.

"Want to see him again?" he asked the old man.

"No."

"Poor little sprout, wonder what kind of a life he would've had?"

"No telling."

"Don't do any good, but you can't help wondering what he was cut out for."

"He's better off, like as not," the old man said. "You can't plan much of a life these days."

"It's so. Maybe he's better off. But he didn't have a chance. I suppose if we were in town we could have had him put in one of those incubators. He didn't last long because we didn't know what to do."

"No use blaming yourself," the old man said wearily. "It can't be helped." Milt picked up the little wad of blanket.

"Let the kids get up now." They poked their heads out, still frightened, and stared big-eyed at the blanket in his hand. "Get up and go outdoors so you won't bother your mother." He went out walking toward the dried cane patch carrying the spade. The dog was sniffing at the bundle. He shoved him away with his leg.

"Go back in the house. Get!" *The coyotes are liable to dig him up some night,* he thought. It made him feel sick. He walked quite a ways beyond the cane into a field that was lying fallow and dug a very deep hole. The earth was dry and hard beneath the moisture from the rain. He got on his knees and put the baby carefully in the hole. He could not resist looking once more. The little boy was curled up, wrinkled and queer-looking as if he had been alive a long time. Milt had not felt this before about the baby being dead, but only as if he had had no being at all. The puckered face looked unborn and helpless. His big head lay on the side, and he looked terribly still. Milt turned the blanket over him once more and scooped the dirt into the hole with his hands. At the last he beat the ground down hard with the back of the spade. Suddenly he began to cry. He did not lower his head but stood as he was, his shoulders jerking with hard cruel sobs. He did not know what to do. The broken sounds came out of his throat and his whole body shook. He could not stop because he felt a hard loneliness and despair breaking up in him, crashing against the walls of his being. It was the boy and it was everything unnoticed and unknown in him. "I ain't cried since I was a boy," he mumbled. He stooped down on his knees again and pulled loose dirt carelessly over the grave to make it look like the rest of the field. When he had finished he stood still looking at the pure circle of earth around him, the far, smooth, lonely plain. The earth was very clean and fresh after the rain. He could see the long straight fences miles away. They were frail and small so far beneath the great clear morning sky. The desperation of living came up in him again, in anger and humiliation; in anger he shook his fist, shook it hard and fierce at something in the world.

Eight

The kitchen was full of steam and the smell of soap and the rhythmic sound of clothes rubbing up and down a washboard. Water had splashed over the top of the board and wet Mrs. Starwood's apron across her fat belly so that the green-figured cloth stuck and made her front look like a ripe melon. She stopped now and then to poke the clothes boiling on the stove. Her husband, Ned, had given her the copper boiler for Christmas out of the last good crop three years ago, and it was still bright and undented. The tubs hung on the back of the house with the mop and alongside the watery mirror hung above the wash bench. Except in very cold weather the morning washing and hair combing was done outside. The copper boiler came outdoors only when it was emptied. All other times it was kept carefully behind a gingham curtain that hung from the clock shelf. The boiler was Mrs. Starwood's greatest pride. It was a symbol of the better things of life. It was real copper and it was pretty to look at even while she was sweating over the washtub. This morning, sweat ran down her face and dropped into the tub. Her hair was wet with it and kept falling into her eyes. She was washing Ned's and the two boys' overalls, the last heavy things, after the white and then the colored clothes.

Young Tessie Starwood was splitting a long-necked squash she was going to cook for the noon meal. Since the frost, the boys were digging the potatoes to put away for the winter. Tessie would much rather dig potatoes than cut up a tough squash although it did smell good inside. This was a good one, so she scooped the seeds out and put them in a pan to dry for next year's seed. She shot one into her mouth with her thumb and first finger and began to chew the large flat seed.

"I declare! Tessie, you'll do something like that before somebody yet. You don't know the name of manners."

"Oh, I do, Mama. Can't I do what I want at home?"

"I reckon. It's no use talking, you're just like me."

"Want one?" the girl asked shooting a seed at her mother.

"Land no! I've no time to be chewing." The seed went down the neck of her dress and she shook it out on the floor. "Being a girl, you should take after your papa. He's as easy as an old shoe, and he never says a word out of the way." She was quiet a minute to savor her admiration for him. "Just works, works like a horse." She was wringing the last overall. "I could of got many a worse man. Sometimes I wonder how I got him at all. Seems to me since we lost the farm and been renting this place, your papa is quieter 'n ever and his shoulders kind of droop."

"Felix can help him a lot next summer when he's twelve," Tessie said. She was thirteen and pretty, with her father's grave sad face, disputed by her manners. She laughed a lot without ever laughing aloud, turning her lips together and the laughter inside shaking her. Her brothers called it snickering but her mother said she had a dry wit. The other boy was Marsh who was eight. Felix was eleven, short and dark and very strong. He was serious and thorough about everything he did, and he could be open and merry like his mother. Marsh was quiet and hard-working like his father. He went his own way except when he wanted to tease Felix. He did not recognize his name if he heard it because his father always called him Pard. They all called him Pard, but sometimes his brother and sister called him Little Red Hen because he tried to do everything the others did not want to do. This was to please his father, whom he followed all the time. Once at a roadside gas station a well-dressed woman with a big car waiting for her told Mrs. Starwood that she had the best-looking brood of children she had ever seen, that they all had "so much character" in their faces. When she drove away, the children laughed in good-humored derision and thereafter they called themselves "The Characters." They made a hilarious game of it that ran on like a serial. They imitated and parodied everybody they saw, but their parents let them play the game only at home.

Mrs. Starwood had just started taking the clothes from the boiler, turning them around a stick and dropping them into a tub when they heard the mailman's honk at the gate.

"Tessie, go see." She picked up some ball blueing tied in a small cloth and gave it a swish and a squeeze in a tub of clear water. She went to the window and looked out. She saw the mailman wave Tessie back and call out, "Send your mother out." She raised up her skirt and wiped her face with it and hurried out to the gate. *What in the world?* she was thinking.

"Nothing for you today," he said, "but I had to pass to get this package from Monkey-Ward up 't Brennermann's." Mrs. Starwood peered into the backseat of the Ford. "Jes something for one o' the girls," he told her. "Say, I come by old man Dunne's and he told me his daughter-in-law was mighty sick last night."

"Well, I declare!" said Mrs. Starwood anxiously. "I wonder what can the trouble be, poor woman?"

"Well, it 'pears TB 'er some woman trouble, I reckon. The kids was with him and the oldest one said she couldn't tell but something 'bout a lot of blood. People shore ashamed of TB, so it may be, but I ain't telling nobody else yet. Thought maybe you'd be going over to lend a hand if need be."

"Well, it ain't TB, I can tell you that. It's the baby! Much obliged you telling me, I'll get right over. I swan, us poor people have their share!"

"Indeed they do, but we can't never give up," he said seriously. "I reckon being a farmer I'm right down lucky getting this route after leaving one leg across the water."

"Be glad you didn't leave all your bones there. My brother is lying buried in a foreign soil. God forbid my sons ever have to fight like wild beasts without good enough reason." She started off. "Bring me some mail tomorrow, old soldier."

"I ain't as old as you think," he called back.

Mrs. Starwood came into the house out of breath and found a clean apron.

"Tessie-hon, you'll have to rinse these clothes and hang 'em out for me. Leave the dinner be for a little, there's time. When your papa comes in from the field tell him I drove over to Dunne's. Julia's sick. She may be needing her neighbors. Get me a little dish of butter and a pail of milk. Their calf gets most of the milk." Tessie hurried out to a large box under the windmill where they kept the milk in a trough of running water. In a moment Mrs. Starwood had the things she needed. She climbed into the old truck and went rattling down the road. Tessie went back to the work, thinking how she would mop the kitchen with suds and surprise her mother who would be expecting to have to do that when she came back.

* * *

Mrs. Starwood came in on the Dunnes' like a whirlwind. The old man was sitting in the yard mending shoes. His mouth sprouted the tacks he was using for half-soling. He nodded and waved the hammer, motioning her to go in. Milt was making potato soup. He had stayed out of the field, not wanting to leave Julia. In no time, Mrs. Starwood had them all fed, sent Milt to the field, and began clearing and cleaning the house. She gathered up the soiled clothes to take home for washing and announced that she would take Lonnie home with her for a few days. Myra could stay and help her mother. She heated water and bathed Julia, and she said it might be better if the doctor looked her over. Before Julia could protest about the expense, she said it might save trouble in the long run, and anyway, before, they would have had to worry about paying for having a baby.

"Doc Thayer don't ever worry about the poor folks not paying their bills like he does them that can afford to pay and put him off. They do the best they can even if they have to take him stuff to eat." She looked about to see what remained to be done. "You want to be careful or you'll get rheumatism living in this place."

"If we ever have a few good crops we plan to build a little house," Julia said, "but I guess we started farming at the wrong time."

"Ain't no right time to farm. It's always hard work, but it's worse now, of course, with the dust storms and the depression. Ned keeps reading in the paper the depression is over, but for the life of me, I don't know when! This'n's lasted longer'n any others. I've lived through 'em about every seven years regular, and I heard my father tell about the panics and the booms. Seems the world's like an old horse that's had spells of colic ever so long and finally has such a bad one he can't get up and knows he's about quit kicking. If it was a horse, his master would shoot him and break in a new horse." Julia laughed.

"Did you always live on a farm?"

"Ever since I was born. My folks came west from Ohio. We come west from Missouri. We had a fine farm once, white house and fruit trees and a big garden. We got a lot of land and kept mortgaging it to buy machinery to farm it. You know how they do—they can sell you a wooden leg! We could of paid it all right but when the depression come we lost everything, and come west to rent. Renting's a bitter pill when they squeeze your insides out. But we got a happy home, trying to make the best of things. What else can you do?"

"Would you like to move to town?"

"Land, no! I wouldn't live cooped up in town for anything you'd give me. Town folks think they're better'n farmers, though God knows why, we all got the very same identical joys and troubles," replied Mrs. Starwood.

"Some of them don't."

"Oh, I reckon there's all kinds of good folks in towns and cities. I ain't got nothing against 'em. It's just they act kind of stuck up when they smell a horse or see the sun on us."

"It's the style now to look tanned," Julia said laughing.

"Well maybe they're changing. Lord almighty, they wouldn't have a crust of bread without us." She paused. "And I reckon, we couldn't get a yard of goods or machinery or our truck without them. I reckon the ones that makes these things ain't so stuck up anyway."

"You certainly think about a lot of things!" Julia said, who had been lonely for talk a long time.

"Just plain horse sense that farmers get from living," she said. "Now it's high time I got home, Julia. I'll be over soon with the ironing. And anything you want, you just holler. Don't worry about the men folks, they'll take care of themselves till you feel all right."

"The house smells so good and clean," Julia said. "I don't know how to thank you."

"No thanks coming for what's no more'n right." Mrs. Starwood called the little girls in from the yard. "Find your nightie," she told Lonnie. "You'll take good care of your mama, won't you Myra?" The little girl nodded. Lonnie was afraid to be away from home, but Myra said it was right until she could sleep in the big bed again. "All you kids will have more fun than a picnic," Mrs. Starwood told Lonnie when she saw her reluctance. Myra handed her sister her own "Mr. and Mrs."— two clothespins they used for dolls, who lived on a little farm fenced in with nails and twine. They got in the truck and drove away, Lonnie waving for a long time. Myra went behind the barn and cried a little. She watched Milt in the field planting wheat, waiting until he saw her. They waved, and she loitered along back to the house to see if her mother needed her.

Nine

The next day and the days that followed, farmers driving by brought their wives to see Julia. The men sat around in the yard with the old man who was doing one of the endless odd jobs, or they visited with Milt at the end of a row. Each wife brought some bit of food and spent the visiting time at work that Julia would have been doing. Even Old Sandy walked on over, an old settler who lived a mile and a half away in a little adobe hut alone on his unfenced claim. He had been known to go for months at a time never talking with anyone, and his visit was a surprise. They did not know how he found out the news but he sometimes stood on the main street in Flatlands listening to talk but never taking part in it, and it was possible he had learned it in this way.

When he came down the steps and into the room, his small face hidden in the grizzly curled beard looked as frightened as a timid animal's. He took off his large, sweat-stained Stetson and held the rolled brim tightly.

"You sick?" he asked quietly. "I heard you was sick."

"I'm getting fine now," Julia said. "Don't you want to sit down?"

"No, thankee, I got to be moving on. I jes stopped to see how you was. Me and your father-in-law there, we've knowed each other a heap of years. Me and him is old nesters. We proved up goviment claims side by side in the early days."

"It's nice of you to come see me," Julia said.

"Well, days is getting cool now and I was out on the prairie a-picking up cowchips, laying in a little fuel. I leave my land unfenced next to Terwilliger and he pastures his stock on it so I get a lot of fuel." He laughed. "I thought I'd come in." He wanted to get away now.

"When you go out, send Myra in," she said, giving him a chance to leave. He hurried up the steps, sighing his relief. *I wonder how he lives without farming,* she thought. *No one knows. No one bothers to ask. You don't put your nose in where it's not wanted.*

* * *

When Mrs. Brownell came, she cheered Julia more than any of the others with her quick laughing talk and her generous warm understanding. She brought a jar of watermelon preserves she had just put up, and a large white cake, which wholly secured her esteem in Myra's eyes. She wrapped a piece of cake and hid it away for Lonnie.

That Saturday Mrs. Long stayed with Julia while Milt, the old man, and Mr. Long went in to town. She brought the twins, bashful little girls of eight, and they played in the yard with Myra. The Longs were the poorest of all the farmers in the neighborhood. They had never recovered the losses of livestock suffered under the Agricultural Adjustment Act, which paid farmers to not produce. Due to the poor condition of their cattle, many were shot, and after paying the process tax on the ones they shipped, they had no return at all. The drought forced him to buy feed for what remained of his herd, until the bank took the cattle on a loan. So he was totally dependent on his crops in the dust years. Folks all knew that one winter they had to rip the floor out of their small house for fuel, leaving them to walk on the dirt. Mrs. Long was a shy, meticulous little woman whose cleanliness was fanatical. Almost anyone in the neighborhood could have lost a floor with less irony, although to the sweeping and scrubbing farmwomen, the summer dust was a nightmare in their homes. Sometimes in gatherings someone told the story of Jim Long chipping up the floor for firewood, and they all laughed uproariously, including Long himself.

Because she was a quiet woman, Mrs. Long hoped there would be plenty of undone work at the Dunnes' and because she could not find a speck of dirt, she found something else to do. The thought that she was unable to bring a present of food made her uncomfortable at first, but later when Julia suggested she bring in a watermelon that had been cooling in the water barrel, and sit down for a while and eat a slice with her, she felt better. Feeling more easy, she smiled more, and her hair pulled

53

tightly to the top of her head drew her eyes up at the corners in a kind of jolly sly look. Julia looked at her and thought how pretty she must have been as a girl. Finally, as Mrs. Long warmed to Julia's good-natured talking, she drew a letter from her deep apron pocket and wanted Julia to read it.

"It's from my sister Bess in California," she said. "I hadn't a letter in years and didn't know what had become of her but just supposed she was still in eastern Oklahoma. Never seemed to have time myself to sit down and write. Jim and I been thinking all year of a change, and when we got this, we set right down and talked it over. Of course, it ain't the best in the world, but beggars can't be choosers, and these last few years has made us as near beggars as I ever hope to be. Jim says we'll have one more try at the farm. He's almost through drilling wheat, and with the school opening this fall here, we might as well wait. I ordered the kids some shoes with my egg money this week, and we felt mighty proud we could buy 'em."

"California's a long way off," Julia said. "I always heard only the people with money live there."

"Well, they have to have somebody to do the work and there's lots of farmland with fruit and vegetables and cotton and all kinds of things we've never seen. Jim don't like to give up his own place and go out and work, but we might get a little place of our own there if times get good again."

"I hope you won't have to go," Julia said. "I hate moving. I lost my piano moving."

"Would you want to read Bess's letter?" Mrs. Long asked. "It's a regular story the hard times they had." Julia opened the long letter, written in pencil on school tablet paper.

"I'll take the kids some watermelon," Mrs. Long said, and she went out on tiptoe while Julia read.

Dear Sis:

I guess you'd think we was dead but I was waiten to write something cheerful in our new home. Ain't no use waiten for that in these times so I better tell you where we are and whats been happenen to us. I just got over a cold and been settin round thinkin a things and kinda want to talk to somebody who knows me. Its gettin cool here now and kinda damp, and this morning in

September still brings the remembrance of 1931. Then when the depreshin and the drouth first begin husband and I and our four children lived on our own farm. We was very happy up till that time. I never told you all this before but we had borrowed rite around $100 that spring to make our crop with, went ahead planted our crop, 35 acre corn 15 cotton 5 sargam cane. But we had to give security on this money we borrowed so we mortgaged our teams and our cow, calves and wagon, harness and most everythang we had. I remember the drouth was so bad all our crop dried up. It looked like it had scaldin water poured on it so in Sep 1931 when the time came to pay this money back we hadent raised enough to feed a cow and 6 or 7 hogs I don't remember just how many now and somewheres around 90 big Bar Rock hens. Anyhow this money had to be raised and we couldent get anythang for our teams. If we could of got a sale for either one of our teams we could of cleared the note at the bank but there wasent anythang raised to feed stock and there wasent no sale for them and these banks wont wait. When the note came due they came out and took our teams and wagon and harness cows calves everythang we had but my chickens for $100. Just left us sitting there no way to do anythang.

Finely husband got a job in the timber at a dollar a day 5 miles from where we lived. He had to walk to and from his work he would start mornins before day lite and get back home away after dark at nite so he worked at this till he got sick. And it wasent long till there wasent any bread or lard in our house and no nothing to fix to eat. I tell you now it was a thinking time. 4 hungry babies and a sick husband and there wasent a thang I could do. I had a new rug which I hadent used and I had a neighbor that lived a mile and 1/2 away so I got to her I knew they had a pretty plenty. I begged her to take the rug and give me some flour and lard for it and she did. I would make pancakes out of the flour which we would eat with the homemade syrup we had growen and made the year before.

But by this time husband got well again he dident have any job and couldent get any. He would get up early mornins go out and find somethin to do and anyone could see he was hungry but maybe he would get a job that he would make 75 or 50¢ a day at and maybe he wouldent. So we got my brothern law to move us over to Arkansas but it was still a hard problem. There wasent any work to do to amount to anythang there we worked at anythang we could get to do and there sometimes the wolf would howl at our door.

Then we decided we would leave here. We had nice furniture but we knew we couldent sell it and get anythang out of it to amount to anythang. We decided we would fix our old car and start to Calif. this year. So we sold our nice furniture fixed our car had barely enough money to get here with bad luck on the road. We thot there we was going to get hungry but we dident. We wired to my mother for money and got $6 and came or got to Bakersfield. We was brok not a dime or very many groceries there the wolf began to howl again we didn't have anythang to eat for 24 hours then but husband hunted a job rite away and found one lasted long enough to get us a tent and some groceries. In the winter no work and dont let anybody tell you its warm here in the winter. Finely when we was hungry again and almost to give up but we know we couldent we got help from the guvment FSA $27 a month and comodities ever two weeks beans and dried apricots and sometimes oranges and dried milk. A Workers Alliance got us some lard too. We was helped three months huntin work all the time but husband couldent stand not workin any longer so we moved on to another county and sometimes we get work and sometimes we dont but you can see we are here trying to get work to make alivin for our children. Husband never gives up wantin a farm of his own but farmin heres different and we got to just try to get farm work now and do the best we can. We like pickin apricots best but everybody does. You ought to see the fruit and grape vines big fields of them sure a pretty sight. Mountains too snow on top and things growen green in the valley. It seems funny sometimes seein so much to eat and not dare touch a thang. Well I expect I weary you but I just got hungry to talk to some of my kin. I hope you folks are making everythang allright. Husband and children say hello. We are well but its a wonder. Hope you are the same.

Your sister Bess.

P.S. Wish I could send you some oranges I picked myself. We will when we work steady.

* * *

To Julia this was from another world where the bitter struggle to live and the rich excitement of many things growing in a beautiful setting contradicted each other so sharply she could not decide what she thought of the Longs' desire to go there. *It is pitiful the way people have to fight nowadays to make a bare living, roaming around over the country like a pack of wolves hunting something to eat and begging people to hire them for any money. Which way is a poor man to turn if there isn't even work and honest pay?*

Mrs. Long interrupted Julia's thoughts as if she felt them meet her own bewildered questioning.

"We wouldn't think of leaving here if it wasn't for the drought and the depression. Ordinary times we like it well enough and it's healthy country. Drought'll come to an end, I reckon, always has before, but this time the depression don't end. Nearly ten years long now. My kids never lived in good times. I'm scared sometimes they won't have good health and won't get an education. I always wanted 'em to know something and be what they want." Mrs. Long ran her hand up over her tight hair and smiled shyly, almost guiltily. Just then the unmistakable sound of the Long Ford severed the country quiet and they heard the children yelling and laughing on their way to the gate.

"Did you bring anything good?" one of them yelled, and they all took it up like a chant and sang it over and over. Mrs. Long began to gather her things and put a last tidying touch to the house. Long came down the steps and looked around the door at Julia and Mrs. Long.

"You ready, Mother?" he asked, and his voice boomed the room full. He was tall with a long thin face and very blue eyes that seemed to be laughing at something even when the rest of his face was still. "I hear you run right square dab into trouble," he said to Julia. "But you don't look sick. Reckon you're just pretending, jes to get company cause you're lonesome." He laughed greatly making Julia laugh too.

"Don't pay no mind to him," Mrs. Long said. "He's always going on. Even when he was chopping up our floor for firewood, he got to talking crazy, and it was so terrible it was funny. Here we was, laughing like loons and feeling sad enough to cry."

"Shore hope you feel better!" he said, and Mrs. Long smiled and nodded at her as they both went out. Julia could hear Milt and the old man talking to them in the yard and the children saying goodbyes, and it all sounded so cheerful she lay back with her eyes closed and listened to them. Long was like a big friendly wind. His laughter rose above the laughter of the others in powerful gusts, blowing hard against their fears.

Ten

Sometimes Julia thought of the little boy who was so nearly born, saying in her mind it was better he was dead, but in spite of this reasonable comfort, she felt the monotonous ache of grief and of Milt's frustration. That peculiar ripening joy she had felt—with the child filling her and moving strongly with his secret life—had left her. The emptiness of her womb crept into her emotions, and she went through the days and nights feeling numb and alone. Milt was morose and easily angered, and although he spoke of the boy only once or twice, she felt coming from him some undetermined blame toward her.

After the wheat was in, and school began, the hurt receded, and she felt the change in Milt as in herself. He laughed with his father again, and played with the little girls at night, interrupting them while the old man helped them with their schoolwork. Often when the house was too quiet with their studying, Milt went out, taking the dog, and walked to a neighbor's, and when he came back, flushed with the cold and the fast walk, his face was warm and alive with the talking he had had. The years in town when he was able to walk out on the street after supper and talk with strangers or friends had made the first returning to the country lonely. He had made friends among the farmers, and he knew many people in the little town. But whatever other pleasures he had in town, nothing was quite like the satisfaction he felt after he planted or harvested a crop. *This kind of feeling is one of the things a man lives for,* he told himself on one of the long walks to a neighbor's farm, *the feeling that I made something, I made something with the soil, together we made a crop grow in order and loveliness.* The unused words startled him in his quiet thinking; they were words out of the past; he had heard his Welsh grandfather use them when he spoke of the corn. He remembered with pleasure the extravagant Irish brogue, the rolling and lilting Welsh, the strong and rhythmic Spanish of his people—

58

these grandparents who had come to America when they were young boys and girls. What drought and severity had caught their tongues in America that their children and their children's children were fearful of tender words? In his memory he could see the huge old man who lived to be ninety-nine and was never too feeble for a temper of wild and picturesque oaths or the fantastic poetic praise he had for his wife before or after a disagreement. She was a strong little Irish woman who outlived him and gave her husband as good as he sent in a quarrel, which pleased him mightily. Once when a friend had told her anxiously, "He'll be the death of you yet," Milt overheard her answer spiritedly, and she was a very old woman then, "We don't mean a word of it, and it keeps our blood running. Mark my words, you'll lie in the grave before me. He might be killing another woman, but not me!" Milt's own mother died when he was a child, and he lived with first one set of grandparents and then the other. The others were pale in his memory; they were pious and stern and detached, and he never really knew them. The grandfather was Irish and English and very proper and the grandmother was Spanish and very religious. It was said that she had been a gay young woman but as years went on she took on her husband's coldness. Concerned only with death as a gateway to a spirit utopia, they missed the simple, lusty joy of being alive on the earth. This was the only feeling he had about them, that their well-meaning goodness would pinch his youth back into him. His other grandmother had told him many times, "It will out sometime or other, if not, it will fester and work itself up in some bad way." He had taken her advice and got out for himself, not knowing very well what she meant but wanting to be free.

He drew his hat more firmly to his head, walking with his shoulders forward a little, leading his body. A light wind pulled gently but sharply at his clothes and he felt it smooth and cold against the warmth of his skin. Lights shone in the farmhouse windows far away, and the high stars gleamed and winked with startling brightness as they do only in windy places, or after a rain has washed the air. The late autumn sky looked clearer than at any other season, but it was cold and distantly blue. A deepening coolness sharpened odors dulled in the day by the sun. The dry and dusty smell of buffalo grass mingled with the freshness of the field, and now and then the disturbing smell of sagebrush blowing strongly made him turn from his thoughts to a pleasant awareness of the fragrant wind. This was a western wind, heavy with the pungent, lively smell of desert weeds and the dry earth filled with sun. He felt the night around him, the great endless dark, and an intimate friendly feeling sprang up in him for the road that his feet followed by touch and familiarity. Strange how a man longed for both freedom and security, and the one could not be had together with the other. He could walk home by this road, or he could walk to the highway and then into the world outside, which he had seen so little. Was it some planned contrariness of nature or some vast mistake in the framework of men's lives? What things were in the world that he would never know or see because the simple needs of staying alive captured his life from sun to sun and year to year? Why was one man with leisure to waste and another with no hour to spare? The papers were filled with pictures of people coming and going from coast to coast, to foreign lands, around the world. Well, he was a common man content with common things. Yet, why did he feel this hunger? Why did he hanker after the unknown? And he was no different from the rest. He saw it in every man he knew, in one way or another. What he had missed he hoped his children would know, and in some vague and clumsy way a poor man offered his hunger to them when he had no answer to give. Maybe that was why he wanted a son. He sensed Julia's fear of his bitterness, and yet the bitterness he felt was not toward her, and he did not know how to tell her. It was a mounting hulk of fear and doubt, ponderous with the question of the future uncertain and invincible against the strength he had to earn their way. This heavy dread lay in his mind, unstated and confused, against the relentless fact that each year was harder than the last and giving back less. This led his thoughts to the weather, and he looked at the edges of the sky, hoping for clouds or the steely haze that might mean early snow. Off to the northwest a bank of clouds lay just darker than the sky, still like a great animal waiting to spring, showing the sleepy fire of its eyes when the faint autumn lightning winked. It was far away and would spend its strength on other land. His wheat and that of every other prairie farm was waiting in the ground for rain.

Eleven

The long hard winter set in brutal and dull in its unfolding, sharp and wild with the high cutting winds blowing off the Rocky Mountains from the west in an unhindered giant sweep across the plains. The country wore a cruel magnificence, softened and made beautiful only by rare snows. The big frost had scarcely cracked the twigs of the cottonwoods along the creek and driven the green from the weeds when the night air lost its pungent autumn smell and turned bitter cold. The buffalo grass, that tough low-curled quilt of the dry lands, changed imperceptibly from drab green to gray. Russian thistles, tugged by the wind, broke their strong roots and bounded off over the prairie, jostling thick against the barbed wire fences. There drifted the dirt blown from the fields, making deep ridges, which in some places left only the top of the slender cedar posts showing. Late geese flew southward, honking high above the endless plains, sending down into the hearts below their strange cry that spoke of other places. The never-settled hearts of these pioneer-bred people, working hard to make a lifelong home in an unrelenting land, stirred uneasily and dreamed of newer lands.

Max and Pete Brownell were up before the last stars faded into a cold morning sky. It was like working in the night, while the deep blue banks of receding dark slept against the horizon, and they spoke of it as they did each beginning of winter. As the first quiet light rose from under the rim, the earth lay around them with no rise or fall to mar its splendid purity. Even the huge rising sun appeared cold, reluctant, but its sparse warmth would soon be felt on the wind-broken sides of the farm buildings. The boys' steps on the frost-bitten ground were the only sound in the early morning world. But no sooner had the light come fully than a meadowlark, ruffling its feathers from the cold, swung itself on a fence and sang its brief song, a song at once like the pure waking day and a signal to it. The bird uttered its phrase of round, crystal notes a second time, and a third, then flew away.

In the barn the animals were beginning to stir. The vigorous odor of their dung and the strong warmth of their bodies enveloped the boys with a swift homely pleasure, drawing them away from the unreality of the dawn they had each secretly appreciated in their walk from the house. As they went down between the rows of stalls, they called the stock by name. Bits of stray grain and hay had dropped on the stone floor of the clean barn and slid under their heavy shoes. An old cow moved one ear when she heard her name. She swung her heavy neck around and kept on peacefully chewing her cud. The horses cocked their ears and switched their tails and began nuzzling in the mangers for leftover hay.

"Hinting for something to eat, eh?" Max laughed. "The young ones can't wait. Why don't you learn from the old girls and boys; they know it's coming so they don't waste a fuss." While the boys were milking, they heard a commotion in the chicken house punctuated by crowing that soon rose into chorus.

"Those darn chickens, you can hear them clear in here, raising Cain at the first sign of life. Only a crow now and then before we get up, but one footstep in the yard and the crazy old hens start in." Pete went to let them out, and before he opened the door of the chicken house, he could hear them crowding against it, flying down from the roosts, clucking and cackling in a low excited way. He stood by the door a moment wanting to tease them, and when he finally opened it they flocked out, trying awkwardly to fly over the backs of others, trampling and knocking one another about. Feathers flew in the air. The roosters stood about crowing while the hens made for the barnyard and began at once to scratch and peck for food. In the afternoon they might sit on the nests and lay, scratch lazily, or shuffle their feathers in the ash heap, but in the morning they were shrill and excited and very busy. Pete usually let them out and he always stood a while watching them. They were so silly and important with their instinctive diligence, they made him laugh. A hen pecking at some manure on his shoe turned her head when he laughed and stared at him from her strange unfeeling eyes. He looked at her sleek head and the healthy crimson of the dainty little comb growing in the center of it. Then he went back to the barn to help Max finish the chores before breakfast. Already the sight of the smoke rising straight from the chimney into the still cold air made him hungry. The first thing Max said when he got back to the barn was, "I wish I could ride over to the schoolhouse and build a fire for Anna these cold mornings."

"I reckon you could if you could get in, but it would make the kids tease her so she'd turn against you. Why does she walk to school when she's got her own horse to ride?"

"Oh, she likes better to walk, and there's no windbreak for the horse when it storms. All the kids have to walk and she says she feels mean riding when even Lonnie Dunne and Pard Starwood and the Long twins walk. The twins are only eight, and the little Hull kid is seven. He walks a mile by himself and his toes were out till she got him some shoes."

"Seems like yesterday when we walked to school. Remember the sled we built for the snows? Say, you know, it used to snow a lot more than it does now. Winter was a lot of fun. It'd be funny some winter if it forgot to snow at all and the wheat didn't come up."

"Funny for me if it happens this winter because I'm going to get married on my wheat crop," Max said.

"Is that all you think about anymore?"

"No, but I think about it. Everything depends on the wheat."

"It's been looking like snow up north," Pete said. "I reckon we'd better get ready for the shivaree." Max smiled.

"Let's get on with the milk before Mom calls us for breakfast," he said, and they went toward the milk house by the windmill, carrying the shiny pails. The sun was lightly warm on their backs but their faces and ears tingled pleasantly with the cold.

Twelve

Early in November there was a blowing snow that lasted two days, falling sparsely, not very much of it lying, but the wheat that had already come up in patches showed more evenly afterward. Everywhere under the blasting cold lay the fine green spread of wheat, contradicting the dreary gray pastures. Men walked in the fields and compared their stands. In places where the wheat had blown out and had to be replanted, it was not up like the rest, but digging to the seeds showed them swollen and sprouted, pushing their little spear leaves through the drying crust. Through the hope and the uncertainty and the mounting hardships of the dry years, there appeared, like a pardon flung over the country, a gladness in the way people greeted one another and spoke of little things with pleasure. The got-to-put-up-with-what-comes silence lifted. Lesser misfortunes became a source of humor. Wheat prospects reflected from the farmers to the people of the little towns, and even the city news papers ran long stories on the wheat belt promise. It gave the farmers a sudden feeling of being a vital part of the whole of America, even the world, when they remembered the export of wheat, a warm good feeling of working together with people they would never see. Bankers and loan company officials were more friendly than they had been for years. They even drove into the country to look at the crops and took time to talk a little. Merchants saw a chance of getting their accounts paid when the farmers paid their grocery bills next harvest. Friendly talks with the merchants were natural and pleasant, but most farmers distrusted the new friendliness of the bankers and loan companies and showed it in their taciturn replies. Many farmers would spend every cent of their harvest money to repay crop loans and mortgages. The only hope for them was to look ahead for several years of good crops.

Everyone was laughing and repeating a story about old Mrs. Blankenbaker who had been farming alone for years with the help of hired hands. The second drought year she had to mortgage her animals and machinery, but she was fortunate enough to pay before she lost them. These years were exceedingly hard for her, but staying out of debt was her passion. She was determined to go through anything rather than get another loan. Her hired hands were fond of Old Granny Cyclone and were now working for board and room and tobacco. She had 320 acres of wheat up, and the hands told how she greeted two men from the bank when they stopped at her place for a little visit. As they were getting out of their car, she said, "What are you buzzards sailing around over my farm for? Got your greedy hawk eyes on my wheat, eh? And your manikerred claws ready. Well, you ain't gonna git none of it. Just put that in your craw. Why, I never even laid eyes on my wheat check from the elevator when I owed you. You didn't trust me to pay you back free will. Well, now I don't trust you neither since then, so you git off my place. Git, you buzzards!" They tried to talk to her, then, saying she did not understood, but she went back in the house and came out with the shotgun.

"This is what I use for hawks and buzzards," she said, and she stood in the yard watching them get back in the car and go out the gate and back down the road.

* * *

During this period of good humor and good times, there was a Friday night pie supper at the school, and the usual secret pre-arrangements to assure the boys' got their girls' pies, or some hoped-for matchmaking by others. Anna had already told Max the color of her box and the way it was wrapped, so he would be sure to know it from the others. Competition always ran high for the teacher's pie, but by this time rumor got round that Max and the teacher were going together and the neighbors were planning a joke. Frieda made a box identical to Anna's for Granny Cyclone. One of the good-looking Knox boys from the Hayward ranch was going to get Anna's pie just after Max bought Granny's. It all came out as planned. Anna sat on one side of the room with Layton Knox, and Max ate pie with Granny, who poked fun at him through all his politeness to her. There was no danger of hurting Granny's feelings, and the merriment got hilarious and wild for everyone except Anna and Max, who though shyly pleased blushed miserably most of the evening.

* * *

There was a dust storm in January, earlier than any had come before, and apprehension blew over the land with the brown wind. But little damage was done, and early in February the farmers woke to a white world, still and pure with snow.

The Dunnes got up in the cold dugout, seeing the windows blocked and white, and when Milt went up the steps and pushed hard against the storm door, it did not move. When he finally opened it a few inches he saw that the snow had drifted almost to the top of the door and it was some time before he could get out to shovel a trench to the barn. The old man and the little girls helped after they had waded through the deep snow to see about the horses and milk the cow. Ice had to be broken in the barrels, and Julia had to melt a block of ice in a pan on the stove before she could make coffee.

"No school for a day or two now," announced the old man.

After breakfast, when the trench was finished, the little girls played in it. The old man took care of the horses while Julia fed the chickens in the henhouse and kept them from flying through the partly opened door. They would be penned up till some of the snow melted. Milt dug the woodpile out of a drift and chopped enough wood for two days and piled it in the doghouse to dry. They would have to go carefully on the wood because there was none to spare and cowchips were now either sodden or frozen under the snow.

A wonderful stillness and beauty lived in the world. As they worked, they had the sense of being the only life in a snowbound universe, and there was something exciting and marvelous about it. The wind had gone down, and a still cold began freezing a crust on the soft abundant snow. They watched for the sun and the gentle warmth that often accompanies snow, but the day grew colder and by four o'clock Julia lighted a lamp in the quickening dark. The old man went out with the lantern four or five times to look at the horses. In the dim arc of light he could see his own breath and that of the horses in the barn, and he laid his hands on their warm bodies to feel the possible cold. He carried on a long conversation with them, speaking for the horses as well, all about repairing the barn next year if there was a crop. He gave the cow a friendly swat and a few words but his favorites were the horses. They had known him for much longer. The cow was all right but she did not show much interest in his affectionate grumbling. *You can't tell whether she has any sense or not, but I reckon she has. She knew enough to bawl for her calf when we had to sell it to Brennermann to get a little cash. Well, that's all over now.* He went back to the house. There was no moon, and no lights showed in the distance. A frozen silence, different from the radiant pristine stillness of the morning, clasped the sleeping world. When he went in it was almost eight o'clock. The fire was dying in the stove and they went to bed.

The snow stayed on, and large flocks of snowbirds settled on top of the barn and walked about thickly in the barnyard pecking at the horse manure for seeds. The yard was now all tracked up, and the frozen snow had a dirty look. Beyond the fence the world stretched white, broken only by the road and by rises here and there where the ground showed through the sinking snow. The weather was changing, the sun showed faintly through the gray waste of sky, the air was losing its sting. There had not been much to eat in the house before the storm but now there was nothing but flour and lard and molasses. The gunnysack of potatoes was empty, save for a few at the bottom that Julia wished to hold back somehow for a greater emergency. The old man felt a nettling hunger for meat, and he had struck upon an idea for getting it. After he built a small frame of old boards with heavy mesh wire on the top, he called Myra from the house to carry out his scheme. At first she was reluctant, but once she got started, she went about her task with the casual unfeelingness of children. She knew these little birds stole the grain from the heads standing in the field, and although they were not the same as the pack rats from the fields that carried off seed from the granary, nevertheless they were enemies of a sort. The whole thing revolted the old man, but he was hungry. He turned it all over to Myra and secluded himself in the barn to mend harness.

Myra sat in the barnyard on a low box holding the end of a long cord. The other end was fastened to a short peg. The peg rested under one tilted end of the frame. Under the frame she had scattered grain. The foolish hungry little birds flocked under the trap and were caught when she jerked the peg free. A few of the birds were killed by the edge of the trap, but the rest she stabbed with a sharp wire, very carefully, with an unconscious concern to end their lives quickly. She gathered the birds into a bucket and sprinkled more grain under the trap. This went on until she had enough for a good meal, and again a number of times on lean days throughout the remainder of the winter.

When Myra took the bucket of birds to the house, Julia looked at them a long time in surprise.

"Heavens! I'd about as soon eat an owl as fix these tedious little things," she said to Myra, and then seeing the disappointment in the child's face, she said, "I'll bet Grandpa thought this up." She put water on to boil and scalded the birds. A thick odor of wet feathers filled the room, and she began the long process of picking and cleaning them. When she had a large pan of feathers and a small dish of fowl, she began to clear the table. The old man stuck his head in the door and called out in a merry singsong, "Four and twenty snow birds baked in a pie."

Julia smiled. "I'm going to stew them and see what kind of soup we get," she said.

"Suits me. I could eat a jackrabbit if it wasn't for them dang blisters on 'em."

"You don't mean you're hungry, Grandpa?" Julia teased him.

"By golly, I didn't want to say anything before because we just have to make the best of things, but I'm right down hungry for something to stick to my ribs. A man can just live so long on wind-pudding and walkabout." He turned to the little girls. "Go see if you can find an egg or two. Dad-blast them old hens lately!" They put on their coats and went out. "Now, look here, Julie, I just want to say something to you alone. You ain't too strong this winter, and I noticed you giving most of your vittels to the children. I don't hold to that kind of thing, you may get sick. They're young and wiry and the milk keeps 'em going pretty well. I'm thinking of going into town Saturday if the weather's clear, and I'll see about getting some more stuff on time till harvest. We got a mighty big bill there now, but so have all the farmers, and Flanery knows he'll get his money. It's a good crop this year! He's a kind man to boot. Few more months we'll plant the garden, this snow'll help."

"We've used what potatoes we raised. If you could get a hundred pounds, and maybe a little canned stuff so we can have a change. And some dried beans. I'd get another side of bacon from the Brownells if we had any cash."

"It may be we can get that too," the old man said. "When I was a boy we used to have the smokehouse full of our own meat and the cellar full of canned fruit and winter apples. The apples would smell up the whole cellar."

"Stop, you make me hungry. I wish we had fruit like we had back home."

"It's healthier here, though," the old man said. Julia laughed.

Thirteen

"They *are* snowbirds," Lonnie held the little body up and looked at it. "They *are* snowbirds!" she cried. "To think I'd ever be eating a tiny bird!"

"Then shut up and eat it!" her father said.

"But it's so little and funny," she persisted in a lower voice. It seemed to Milt she was reproaching him, and he tried to push the absurd thought out of his mind. He picked the small strands of flesh away from the frail bones, and he thought he would go crazy trying to stifle his hunger with this daintiness. He bit into the whole body and the bones snapped and he spat them into his plate. They flew onto the oilcloth and Julia felt a fine spray of saliva on her face.

"Oh, Papa!" Myra said in disappointment. "Just play like you're the king with the blackbirds." Julia laughed aloud.

"Have patience," the old man said. "They're not so bad." A pile of bones almost filled his plate.

"Who did this, anyway?" Milt demanded. Myra's face was nervous and flushed. She sat looking down at her plate, not eating.

"I was hungry for some meat," the old man said.

"You," Milt said. The others ate quietly looking at their plates in a portent of silence. Milt left the table and was taking his coat and cap from the back of the door.

"Now, Milt," Julia begged. "What are you going to do? Why don't you eat the birds this time?" She wiped her apron across her mouth as if she were through.

"Hell, no meat on 'em. I'm going out and kill a steer, tough as it'll be from starving too. It'd cost money to sell 'em time they pay the freight." He buttoned his coat up tight about his throat. "But I ain't gonna eat no more *snowbirds*." He opened the door and turned half around. "And I ain't the only farmer spouting off." Tears were dropping into Myra's plate, and she got up, taking the plate with its two little birds, and sat down behind the stove.

"Myra was all day catching the birds," the old man said to Milt.

"I can't help that," Milt said and went out, banging the door.

"This is going to be a good year. No use getting so het up."

"He's as cross as a bear lately," Julia said to the old man, "but I guess he's had about all he can stand the last few years. Don't you kids pay any attention to his talk about stealing a steer." She felt worried and fearful.

"There's a lot of suffering going on everywhere," said the old man, "and it makes some people feel ornery and mean when they don't know which way to turn. He'll cool down out there in the cold. It's a wonder there ain't more stealing than there is. I ain't heard of none, have you?"

"No. I hope he won't."

"Better come back and finish your supper," the old man said to Myra. "Your dad's just riled up about something else. It wasn't the birds you caught. Sit down, now." Myra came back red-eyed and sheepish.

"They are a nuisance to eat, but they taste pretty good to me," he said.

"Be better if we had something to put in to take the game taste out. I don't like that."

"I figger everything'll be all right after harvest," the old man said. "This is a good country if common folks could just afford water. It'll likely rain in the spring, and we'll be on our feet again. I can't say as much for the troubles of the world. Seem to be getting worse. Danged if I understand much of it anymore."

"I got too many troubles of my own to be worrying about the world," Julia said.

"Well, now, I don't know about that. Since the depression it 'pears to me the same troubles bothering us are the ones bothering everybody else in the world. Everybody has to keep his nose so close to the grindstone he can't know his neighbor or anybody else. When you get right down to it, everybody has a lonesome life."

"I reckon, but I don't want to argue about it. I've got to wash the dishes and do some patching before the kids start to school again in the morning."

"No argument, no argument," the old man said quickly. "I reckon I talk too much. I'll go out in the barn awhile." His feelings were hurt, and Julia felt cross and did not care if they were.

"You don't need to," she said, "unless you're going anyway." He put on an old coat and a cap with earflaps and went out quietly.

"Oh, the deuce!" she said, and got up and poked the fire vigorously. "They can both go to blazes!"

"I'll tell Papa on you," Lonnie said.

"Tell him! Listen, you kids, here's some hot water. Wash your arms and neck and feet good. The mailman said Max will be over in the morning to take you to school on the sled. The snow will all be gone in a day or two, and you can walk then. It'll be fun to ride on the sled."

"I bet we'll all have a snowball fight tomorrow," Myra said.

"Well, go ahead, but don't get too wet. And don't let the boys put snow down your necks."

"Oh, I can whip most of the boys at school," Myra said casually.

"My goodness, is that a nice way to act?"

"No, but I can if I have to."

"You get that from your dad. What would Konkie think of you fighting?"

This seemed to call for serious consideration. Myra scrubbed hard on her elbows and finally said in a low voice, "He wouldn't like me. Don't blab, Lonnie. I'd better watch out."

"I don't tell everything I know," said Lonnie crossly. She pinched Myra on her bare arm, holding a little fold of flesh and twisting it. Myra yelled and hit her with the washcloth. Julia separated them, and when they were finished washing she made them go to bed.

The old man came in on tiptoe. He hung his coat and cap on the door and sat down on his davenport near Julia, putting his feet on the bottom of the stove and holding his long thin hand over the top.

"It's snappy out!" he said making a low whistle through his teeth. He rubbed the warmth into his hands. "Milt's in the barn. When I went out he was filing the hoe by lantern. Says I, 'You getting ready to garden this early?' Says he, 'I got to do something   73 or I might bite the horses.' He kind of laughed. He didn't even look for the steer. You don't need to worry about him ever stealing 'les there's nothing else to do."

"I guess we all get mad," Julia said.

"He's talking of selling the land in the spring and trying to buy the Brennermann half-section that joins mine. He wants to build you and the kids a house of your own."

"Most others have decent houses. Seems with all our hard work we could have one. I don't take much stock in that land of his. There's plenty of land here, I doubt if he can sell it."

"Not unless he wants to give it away," the old man said. They heard Milt's steps on the hard ground and stopped talking. The old man began to unlace his shoes.

Fourteen

Julia was standing in the yard shading her eyes with her hand, looking at the northern sky. The April sun was delicately warm through her dress. It was midafternoon. Milt and the old man were working in the field. They had borrowed one of Starwood's teams for a few days to get on with the work.

Each time they turned at the row ends she saw them stand and look at the sky. They talked a moment and started on another row. Once Milt saw her in the yard and waved. He pointed to the sky and shouted, but she could not distinguish the words.

Along the north the sky was a pale yellow, the strange dead color of a lamp flame through a window in daylight. This dull inert mass had been lingering on the horizon for the last hour, but now she saw it take the shape of a curved wall rising slowly in the air. As it rose the color changed to faint brown, and she realized with dread that it was moving in a great cloud but still a long way off. Her concern was distracted by the sound of a car. Brownell's truck was coming down the road from town. She waited in the yard, and Max leaned out and waved as he turned in the gate. He pulled up and took off his large hat, leaning over the wheel, looking at the sky and back to Julia.

"It's coming," he said.

"It still looks 'way off," she said hopefully.

"Well, it might not get here, maybe blow itself out before that. Strange things, aren't they? Several years of 'em now but none as mean-looking as this one."

"Gee, it's been so pretty and nice, I thought sure there wouldn't be any this year," Julia said. "It makes me feel queer to see that thing hovering around. I thought it just came up, but I remember now when I let the chickens out this morning I said to myself it looked hazy up north. I thought it might be a snow somewhere, then it began to look yellow."

"They're not the same as our regular old dust blowing. That's not so bad and we're kind of used to it. Some place else it's mosquitoes." He laughed but she looked worried. They both looked at the young wheat. A small peaceful wind was making lively ripples in its tender green leafiness. *When it is ripe,* he thought, *it will bow deep to the wind in long waves like a gold sea, and nothing's prettier.* They looked at the wheat a long time and did not speak. Finally he seemed to rouse himself from his thoughts.

"Maybe I'd better go round to the school and pretend to be a school bus. It's about recess, and it might be better if the kids get home. I suspect you'd feel easier if I bring yours home, wouldn't you, Mrs. Dunne?"

"I'd certainly thank you to."

"Did you hear the school is closing after this year? They can't get enough taxes in this dust to keep going, but they may be able to send one of the school buses out from Flatlands. They'd get a better school in town."

"I'd like that better, but it's too bad Anna will lose her school."

"She was going to give it up anyway. I hope we have a little place of our own by next winter, Mrs. Dunne." She felt the quiet compliment of his words.

"I hope you do," she said. "Anna is a nice girl."

"We can't say anything yet because of her folks. They may like me better after harvest," he said laughing. Julia looked at the sky again as if he had reminded her.

"Oh, that'll blow over, Mrs. Dunne. Don't worry about the wheat. It'll stand a little wind and dust. I'd better be off now. I'll bring your girls. Goodbye." The cloud was still rising with an ominous slowness, but it was far away. Perhaps she was too anxious. She went back to her interrupted work, peering out the window now and then. Tomorrow was wash day. If the dust flew she would have to put it off and that always upset the whole week. She began to think about Anna.

The heavy even thud of the horses' feet and the sound of the harness and the unhitched double trees dragging behind them startled her into new anxiety. From the window she could see Milt and the old man walking behind the teams and holding the lines tiredly. The old man watered his team, threw the tugs across their backs, secured the lines, and hoisted himself onto the back of one of the bays. He slapped the horse on the rump and they started toward the gate, the mate staying close alongside. *Why in the world does he have to start off to Starwoods now? They aren't finished with the team. Maybe they are, or maybe he wants to get them back in the barn?* Their own was large enough only for the horses and Bossy. She ran up the steps and shouted to the old man. He pulled to a stop.

"Better watch for Max along the road and get a ride back. He's bringing the kids home." He raised his hand in acknowledgment and went on. "That cloud gives me the creeps," she said half-aloud, and she went back down the steps. Then she thought, *Maybe we better milk early tonight,* and she put water on the stove for scalding the milk pails. She was getting ready to pour boiling water in a pail when she heard Milt running to the house, not fast but running. His shoes sounded out on the bare hard ground.

"Julie! Julie!" he called from the door in a quick voice. "Come out!" She put the teakettle on the stove and hurried up the steps. He was standing with his hands in the hip pockets of his overalls looking at the rapidly changing sky.

"She's coming!" he said. She stood beside him and they watched the high moving wall of dust spread from east to west in a semicircle that rose into the sky and bent over at its crest like a terrible mountainous wave about to plunge down upon them. The cool spring air held a sudden faint smell of dust.

"Where are the kids? I hope Dad caught Max!" Julia was excited.

"They're coming down the road aways. They'll get here. Look, did you ever see such a sight?" The dirt had dropped over the Brennermann farm like a curtain. He looked at his wheat and his face tightened. The smell of dust was strong in their noses now, slapping their senses like a thick fat hand.

"Look!" he said again, and they stood together not saying anything, awed by this new attack of nature. It was an evil monster coming on in mysterious, footless silence. It was magnificent and horrible like a nightmare of destiny towering over their slight world that had every day before this impressed upon them its vast unconquerable might. Grains of dust sounded against their shoes in a low flurry. The open land beyond was blotted out as the brown mass struck the edge of his field

"She's on the wheat now. It's a gonner. It'll cover it up. Funny though, it's so quiet and not as thick as it looked. Maybe it'll stay in the air and blow past."

"No wind," Julia said in surprise. The truck turned into the gate. Milt watched the dust sift slowly over the wheat and creep toward them. "Good heavens! The chickens!" Julia said, and she began shooing them into the henhouse with her apron.

The old man helped the little girls from the truck.

"Better come in, Max," Milt called to him above the sounds of the motor.

"Thanks. I'd better get home. The folks might think I'm under that thing. Looks like the end of the world," he said, trying to be cheerful.

"Think it'll get us?" Milt asked

"We'll know as soon as it's over. I don't think it's as bad as it looks. Well, good luck to you."

"Same to you, boy. We'll all need plenty if this keeps up."

"S'long," Max called to all of them.

The air was getting thick now. Some of the green field showed, fluttering before the low wind. Lonnie ran to Milt and held onto his trouser leg.

"What is it, Papa?" she asked. "A still cyclone?" He looked at her and laughed.

"No, pardner, it looks like Canada raised up and flew this way."

"Oh, I've got to gather the eggs!" Myra took off her stocking cap and ran into the henhouse with the chickens. She came out holding the cap carefully. The old man was helping Julia.

"These blamed hens haven't got sense enough to come in out of the rain," Julia said.

"That's the truth," the old man said. The hens were running up to the door, then turning off around the house, excited by the hurried urging, uncertain about going to roost before sundown. Finally the last hen was shooed in, and Julia fastened the door. Milt watched the dust until the last of the wheat was covered.

"We'd better go in or we'll choke," he said bitterly. The dust rolled over them in thin clouds, stealthy, quiet, moving as if by an obscure power. There was no sound. They retreated into the dugout. Milt was last. He shielded his eyes and nose and looked up. The top was far above him, taller than a tree. Then it passed over the house and he could see nothing but dust before his eyes. The barn was a mere shadow. He noticed in surprise that the dust was fine and soft, unlike the harsh grains that cut against his skin on windy days. He felt it in his throat like fur and had to cough. He went in and shut the door securely, kicking a sack against the crack. As he went down into the room, he saw the dust like a mist.

"Look how it's sifting in around the windows," Julia said. "How will we sleep in this!"

"We'll sleep," the old man said wearily. "When you're tired you sleep."

"We slept last summer and the one before," Milt said.

"Well, we'll have to milk. We'll wait awhile. Maybe it will slacken. I can scald the pails and put cloths over them." They watched the windows for a sign of clearing, but the dust kept on in a monotonous soundless deluge.

Finally, Julia and the old man tied handkerchiefs about their mouths and noses and went out to milk. Milt sat on the bed waiting to look at the wheat. When they came back he had not moved. They shook the dust from their clothes onto the steps and pulled the kerchiefs off. The upper parts of their faces were dark.

"Whew!" they said together, spitting the powdery film off their tongues.

"Let up any yet?" Milt asked.

"No," the old man said. "This is a real siege. Worse than any so far. I wager it won't stop all night."

"How can you tell?"

"Can't for sure. Somethin' steady about the way it's coming. Like the way a steady rain falls different from a shower."

"Wish to hell it was rain! Next year we won't be able to plant if it don't stop. If the top soil's not gone, it'll be covered up. If all of us farmers wasn't so stubborn we wouldn't have planted this year!"

"Well, we have to take the bitter with the sweet," the old man said laconically.

"Where in hell is the sweet?"

The old man nodded his head sidewise in a sharp movement and made the clucking sound with his tongue and teeth. He had said the wrong thing.

"I'll go out and look around," Milt said.

"Wait till we eat," Julia said impatiently. "Dust or no dust, we have to eat." She drew her finger along the oilcloth table cover and it left a trail in the dust. She wiped it off carefully and sat down on the lard can with a pan of potatoes in her lap. The peelings fell away paper-thin with no waste. When she dipped into the lard can where she kept the flour, she noticed how low it was and scooped the cup cautiously so as not to strike the bottom and call Milt's attention to it. In the silence, they heard the dog scratching and whining at the door.

"Let him in," Milt said to Myra. "It's even too much for Rusty!"

Fifteen

The early morning light had the unreal look of being pasted on the windows over the film of dust curved thick in the corners. But it was good to see the day. They dressed and washed quickly and hurried outdoors. The dog was curled up asleep outside the inner door. He followed them up the steps wagging his tail and ran out into the yard shaking himself violently, raising a cloud of dust. Against the buildings, the woodpile, the fence, the fine dark loam was drifted like snow. The air was clear but the smell of dust was everywhere. The rising sun drove some of the desolation from the scene and from their spirits. Milt and the old man, tagged by the little girls, walked off toward the wheat and Julia went in to get breakfast. The bright green leaves could still be seen, and the men began to feel better. As they came into the fields they saw that the dust had settled lightly and caught in tiny drifts against the young stems, but the wheat was standing bravely. They went back to the house, relieved of the fears that had fled through their dreams. The clothesline was sagging with blankets and quilts, pillows and coats. Smoke came from the chimney, and the odor of coffee and of eggs frying in bacon grease was already in the air.

"We'd better get on with the chores," the old man said, sniffing hungrily. Julia came to the door.

"You can eat first this morning," she said. "I want to get break-fast over and get to cleaning out this mess of dirt." She took a deep breath. "I didn't know how good the fresh air smells! How's the wheat?"

"Not so bad. I reckon most of the dirt kept going." She felt a vague stir of relief, but disappointments had come with such frequency that she wondered if the greatest of all, the loss of this year's crop, if it had happened, would have aroused any feeling but helpless resignation in her. As soon as breakfast was over, she tied a towel around her hair and began a thorough cleaning.

The old man hauled a barrel of water, and when the dust was carried out in buckets, she scrubbed the floors and washed the windows. The day was fine for washing, but there was no choice but to clean. Since there was but one change of underwear for all, she providently rubbed out the five suits and hung them on the line while there was still sun.

In the afternoon, Milt decided he could wait no longer to pay Flanery a visit in town to see about another bill of groceries. He shoved the lard can under the table last night with his foot and felt how near empty it was. They had to have flour and lard and potatoes. He had never taken advantage of his credit at the store to buy more than necessities because there was always the risk of crop failure. After a good harvest when there was money in his hand, they enjoyed a feast or two, and in the summer there was always something fresh from the small garden. In the last few years they had learned how to do without things they always considered necessities in other days. *Maybe you wouldn't call it hunger,* he thought, *but it's a kind of left-handed starvation in more ways than one.*

Flanery was in the back of the store arguing with a town woman over the price of boiled ham. Milt walked through the maze of counters, cases, wire racks, a conglomeration of displays. Dry goods occupied one side of the store, meat was in a back corner, and groceries everywhere else. A fat-bellied stove was in a small clearing in the center of the store. Old chairs surrounded it, and a flat box of ashes served for a spittoon. There was an odor of apples, potatoes, coal heat, and new overalls, mingled with last night's dust. Milt stood by the stove and listened to the woman's sharp tongue. When she was gone, Flanery came up behind the canned goods counter and smiled at Milt.

"Howdy, Dunne," he said. "Hear that old heifer trying to beat me out of a few pennies? They jes bought a new car and a bunch of furniture, and I figger the few cents'll do me more good than her. She haggles over every dime she spends. I'll argue all day to get the best of her." He laughed loudly. "Thought you fellers was sunk last night, but guess they ain't too much damage done, eh?"

"No, we're going to make it all right, I guess. Close shave."

"What can I do you for?" Flanery said and winked. He said this to everyone.

"After harvest you can do me for all I got. Right now I need a fifty-pound sack of flour and a ten-pound can of lard."

"What's the matter with a hundred pounds of potatoes for dessert?"

"We got a few left. I don't like to buy till we need 'em."

"Well you might as well take 'em along today. Last time you got 'em all at once so reckon yer about out now."

"All right," Milt said.

"You in a hurry?"

"Well, I had to make this special trip middle of the week, so I reckon I better get back to work." Flanery came out from behind the counter and stood with his back to the stove as if he were getting ready for a talk.

"All right," he said. "I'll get the stuff. Just thought if you wasn't in a rush we'd chew the rag awhile. I'm feeling kinda sore at the world last week or two. Goddamned if I don't think ever'thing's going to hell ever'where. Nobody got any money anymore, and I hear on the radio they're trying to stir up another war over there in Europe now. We'd get in it soon enough. You recall, I lost my son in the last one."

"Yes, I knew that." Old man Flanery went on, not giving Milt a chance to continue.

"What I say is somebody ought to blow hell out of them militarists—that what you call 'em? And wipe Britain off the map. Most treacherous nation on earth, mark my words!"

"I reckon there's people there just like us," Milt said, "who don't like it anymore than we do. You have to get at the rotten spot."

"Man, you read the papers, you think the whole world's rotten. When you get old like me you want a little peace, but I never had so many worries in all my life. I used to have a little fun. Why, I ain't even got any grandchildren to play with since they killed my boy. Say, how's them little shavers o' yours?"

"Fine." Milt felt depressed by what the old man said. Flanery looked at him and began to laugh loudly.

"Say, I best get going," he said. "I get lonesome and I jes feel like a crab apple. Maybe I'd feel better if I'd take some sulphur'n

83

molasses and thin my winter blood out." He laughed loud again. "Better get your groceries or yer missus'll wonder what's become of you." Milt put the sack of flour over his shoulder and carried it to the wagon. He made another trip with the potatoes, and when he came back for the lard, Flanery had put a few things in a box and left them on top of the can.

"What's this?" Milt asked. "Not mine." There was a gallon can of peaches, a box of cookies, and a large bag of candy with two fat sticks showing out the top.

"A little present for the missus and the kids. Hold on, I'll send your old dad a cut of chew tobacco."

"We don't need any charity yet," Milt said. "Give me a bill."

"Now, jes hold yer horses and don't get huffy, young man, or I'll box yer ears. T'ain't no charity about it. I reckon I can still make a present of my own stuff."

"I'd rather pay for it," Milt said without anger. "Give me the bill, Flanery. You can't afford to give this stuff away."

"Take yer goddern bill," he said, writing and tearing it out. "Womenfolks like something dainty now and then."

"I know that, but Julie knows I can't afford it now."

"Well, take 'em along. Give 'em my regards."

"I'll tell 'em you sent it because you thought of it," Milt said. Flanery smiled.

"In my day," he said, "I always knew how to treat the women-folks. Take a tip from an old man. They'll work and save with you, but you bring 'em a little something nice once in awhile and they like you better for it. They're kind of peculiar, you know, ain't never satisfied with their lot. Reckon it ain't quite right yet. Once they find out, won't be no stopping 'em. Ah, I know 'em," he said, nodding his head wisely. "If the world wasn't going to hell I'd like to come back to earth a hunderd years from now and see the women. But a hunderd years from now won't be nothing left with these newfangled wars." He sighed deeply.

"I hope you're wrong," Milt said.

"Well, so long, young feller. Mark my words, and don't believe nothin' I say." He laughed and his whole body shook.

"So long," Milt said. "See you Saturday." Flanery stood in the door and waved his hand once and disappeared in the darkness of the store. Milt drove home feeling strangely moved by the old man's bitterness, wondering if old age held no more than Flanery found. He thought how queer it was he had given him the fruit. But he did not like the discomfort put in his thoughts by another and he tried to shake it off, feeling irritated with the old man. The irritation spread to his body. He tied the lines slackly to the seat spring and got out to walk beside the horses on the road shoulder. The spring air was sharp and sweet. Great clouds lay in the eastern sky, beautifully white against the deep clear blue. *This is the way the sky will look all summer,* he thought, *over the dry lands, except in a storm.*

Sixteen

The next day was Wednesday, clear and bright. Milt was in the field, listening, making the ground ready for any possible moisture. About ten o'clock in the morning, dust began to show up around the edges of the sky and by noon the air was filled with it. The sky was obliterated. Julia hurriedly took the damp clothes from the line. As darkness came, the surprised chickens went to their roosts. Old man Dunne nailed gunnysacks over the windows outside. The children were sent home from school at the first sign of the rising dust and knew not to come back until the day showed clear. At noon, they ate a dusty meal by lamp-light and then sat about afterward, saying very little, waiting for the storm to pass. The old man got restless and went to the barn. "I've got a little tinkering to do," he said. "This sitting gets my goat." They did whatever had to be done about the farm and went back to the house feeling irritable with the discomfort and fearful for the wheat. Milt said nothing, but his silence was as ominous as that of the storm, broken only by the small pecking sound of the dust against the house. He was nervous, worried, but not yet quite hopeless. Julia tried to iron the clothes, but the dust, sifting in from places that had kept out even the wind, gave them a dirty grayness. She put the clothes away quietly, trying to make as little fuss as possible, knowing they were all on edge. She felt the dust in her clothes and on her skin, in her mouth and nose, on everything she touched. They were glad when the evening chores were done and they could go to bed. She awoke many times in the night feeling Milt turn and sigh in his sleep. Now and then the children coughed, and once Lonnie cried out fretfully for a drink. Only the old man slept soundly noting his oblivion with snores.

* * *

The next day was the same. All night the dust blew and by morning the yard wore that melancholy look of a place revisited after years of desertion and ruin. The machinery was almost buried in drifts. When the quietly insidious wind subsided several times during the day, the dust could be seen lying in gentle waves, like pictures of desert sand they saw on calendars. Again everyone did their necessary chores, the old man spent the day in the barn with the animals, busy at odd jobs he invented to keep down his growing irritation with the dust. During one clear interval, Milt walked through the field, finding the young wheat smothered out of sight except in a few places where the wind had swept leaving a clean oasis. He picked up handfuls of dirt and let it fall smoothly through his fingers, feeling the alien texture. It was fine and silky, with an oily feel. He knew it was not his own loose field soil that was often picked up by the regular winds. This was a rich, organic loam, torn from its bed because it was without root and moisture to hold it. If no rain came and the wind kept on, this same precious layer of his own field would rise and follow the great dark clouds to other land. There were so few trees to draw the moisture, so much land broken and free to blow, he wondered when this new disaster would end. If it ceased tomorrow and rained, the wheat would be lost, but he could plant a row crop. As he walked back to the house, his feet sinking each step deep into fine dust, he abandoned his wheat with a great weary patience. He heard his thoughts, as if removed, wishing for rain, urgently, planning the cultivation of forage. Even if no rain came till later, he could still plant maize. Before he reached the yard, the air grew more dense with dirt. He pulled his hat down over his eyes and walked with his head down, knowing the way back by the familiar feel of the ground. A small winter bitterness left over into the spring pinched his flesh as his coat flapped open. He went into the house and sat down on the davenport by the warm stove. He took out his pocket knife and began carefully to trim his fingernails, guarding his silence with this small preoccupation. Julia looked at him and wanted to speak, but she put the questions to the back of her thoughts and went on with her work.

* * *

At nightfall the old man came out of the barn, carrying something under one arm and shielding his face with the other. He felt the sharp sweetness of spring even through the air so hard to breathe, and his hope stirred carefully, checked by an old lurking belief, doubted but undying, that if he expected nothing, something would come, and the other way round. He knew that it came from a childish belief in magic and an old religious severity and fear, both of which made him shove the superstition away with scorn. But he tried secretly, nevertheless, to believe that no rain would come. "This is a bitter spring," he said, talking to himself, "when a man needs patience." In the sound of his words his impulsive believing might be lost.

When he went inside, they looked at him and waited for him to tell what he had made. He set the tin tray down on the table and spun a tin-bladed fan slowly.

"Well," he said. "I made a little something to moisten the air in the house so we can breathe. Put some water in the pan and it ought to work. With power it would run like a top, but I had to fix up this contraption with a weight and string to make it turn for a spell. Now just hang a wet rag on this wire frame like this," and he took a dish towel for an example. They all stood around to see how it would work. "There's plenty of string with weights ever' so often so the fan will keep turning even when one weight reaches the floor." The cloth fluttered faintly in front of the fan. "It'll help some."

"It's fine!" Julia said. The old man smiled.

"I wish you could invent a cloud," Milt said.

"Well, I got my own ideas on making the dry lands a garden, but I never thought of it till this dust. Just locking the barn after the horses are stole now."

"Let's do the chores before it gets worse," Milt said. After removing the cloth, the old man carefully set the pan on a shelf and filled it with water.

"I'll just put a clean cloth on it," Julia said.

"If it keeps up," he said, "tomorrow, I'll have to board up the windows."

"Good land!" Julia said. "We'll feel like moles."

"Can't be helped," the old man said resignedly, and he went

out.

Julia took five pieces of thin white cotton from a drawer and called Myra.

"Look here," she said, "do you want to help me a little?"

"Yes, Mama."

"Then sew these strings on where I've cut a V and put them in the drawer to keep clean."

"What are they, Mama?" Both Myra and Lonnie were curious.

"They are masks we're going to wear to breathe through when we sleep, and when you go outdoors."

"Can we wear them outdoors tonight just once?" they asked.

"You'll get to before you go to bed."

"Gee, this'll be fun!" Myra told Lonnie.

"I'm glad you think so," Julia said and laughed, feeling the fuzzy dryness on her tongue. "I'm so sick of this dirt I feel like I'd go crazy with another day of it."

Seventeen

"Dad boarded up the windows this morning as the dust was still blowing, looking like it would never stop." Julia brushed the dust from the rough school tablet paper and looked back at what she had written. She had decided to keep a record of the strange phenomenon of dust. The old man kept a record for years of the great storms, droughts, deep rains. He named the day and the year of natural disturbances the way another man names the events of his life.

She read her description of the first storm and felt frightened again, and pleased with herself. She closed the tablet and placed it on a shelf and went about her work.

April 4. A fierce dirty day. Just able to get here and there for things we have to do. It is awful to live in a dark house with the windows boarded up and no air coming in anywhere. Everything is covered and filled with dust.

April 5. Today is a terror.

April 6. Let up a little. We can see the fence but can't see any of the neighbors' houses yet. No trip to town today. Funny how you learn to get along even in this dust.

April 7. A beautiful morning. Everyone spoiling the happiness of a clear day by digging dust. Sunday afternoon we walked for miles to see other places. It was a sight. It looks like the desert you read about in books, desolation itself. The day began and ended as a real sunshiny western day.

April 8. Morning bright and skies clear. Ten o'clock. Dirt began to show up around the edges. By noon the sky and air full. We try to do our work as usual, thinking rain may fall and end our troubles for a while. We don't speak much of the wheat anymore. Going to bed. Dirt still blowing.

April 9. Sometime in the night about ten we think it started raining. We heard it and got up to put our heads out and get a fresh breath. Dad scared us. He heard it first and began to wake us up. He was excited and kept saying over and over. "It's raining! Hear it, it's raining!" We were so glad, we could hardly believe our ears. It rained on and off till morning. We all slept like dead.

This morning we all felt so happy over a smell of rain and the sight of it, but by nine o'clock dirt began to show up high in the heavens and got thicker and thicker. Mailman came by with another man along in case anything should happen. Had flit gun filled with water to shoot in car when dust got too thick. Also chain fastened to car and dragging, to ground electricity. He told us the town school buses go out with two drivers, mechanical air conditioners, water, everything needed for service in case they have to stay overnight. No school on worst days. The district school still closed. He told us he heard of some youngsters strayed off in wrong direction with dirt blinding them. Word was sent out over radio and men tied themselves together with rope to keep from getting lost in duster. The children were found out by the Cimarron River. At one town he said he heard on the radio it was blowing dirt and started raining and plastered the town with mud. Good to talk to somebody again.

April 10. Blowing all night again and all day today. Got up at 5:30, very dark and dirty. At nine o'clock a car stopped and people wanted a drink. Looked like bandits with noses and mouths tied up, faces and hair dirty, and clothes covered. They told us people in town were asked over radio to keep porch lights on overnight to aid someone who might have to get out. Said hospitals refuse to operate on anyone unless it's life or death. Some people getting dust pneumonia. 10 a.m. Just lighted lamp, fierce dark at times. Hope those people get where they are going safely.

Noon. Ate on a dirty dusty table. Took up 15 or 20 pounds of dust to make room for more. The dirt is in waves. Think someone's farm is in our house, maybe our own. Max brought over his little radio for us to use for a while. They have a big one. I washed my dishes and sat down in the dust to sew and listen to reports coming over radio. It took a big passenger bus from 7:30 a.m. till 3 p.m. to go 25 miles between towns. 3:30. Pitch dark, has been by spells all day, but the blackness is scary and makes me feel creepy. Dad made a water spray for the house and one for barn. We needed something stronger than the fan. He stays in the barn most of the time spraying air for the cow and horses. The cow is sick with the dust. It's a wonder we all aren't. 4:30. Had to tend to the chickens. Some have died. It is terrible out. Monster gusts of dirt sweep across the yard like great clouds of black smoke from a fire. The kids hate to stay in the house so much. I wish it would clear up for even a day.

April 11. Everything covered from last night, and still blowing. But we have at least a peep of daylight through the dirt. 9:30. Still dirty. 10:00. Little lighter. 11:00. Still too dirty to start cleaning. We ate some potato soup standing up, too dirty to sit. Looks favorable to dust to keep up. 7:00. Cleaned up at last. We will sleep better tonight.

April 12. What a day! Sun out bright. No one could ever believe it was such a week. Must start in moving furniture and cleaning out. Milt shovels dirt up, takes it out in buckets. He's going to wash clothes while I clean. We can't lose a good day.

April 13. Dirty again and blowing. Sifting in all over my clean house. The last few years of dust are about more than people can stand but this year is just awful.

April 14. Dad found Bossy dying this morning. We all did everything we could think of but she was wheezing hard and choking and finally died. We had to tie the horses out till we got her out and skinned. The horses sniffed and rolled their eyes. They are frightened by death same as we are, poor things. Dad says he is going to sleep in the barn and spray the air at night. If we had a better barn it might help, but nothing would keep this dust out. The kids cried about Bossy, then we all did. The animals are like persons to us. I feel worried that the kids won't have milk now.

April 15. A real spring day. When it wants to be nice here it seems nicer than any place in the world. Looks desolate everywhere you look, but the sky is clear and you can see across the prairies to the end of nowhere. Cleaned again and put out a pretty wash. Myra and Lonnie played out all day. Milt and Dad walked all over the field, anxious to get to plowing for row crop, but we can't take chance on losing the seed if it doesn't rain enough and stop blowing. Maybe it will clear off now and be right. I feel like I could stand anything if the dust would stop. Mailman told me today that one of the little Long twins has a dust infection on her mouth, pretty bad. This blame dust has brought us all new worries. We sat in the yard tonight till bedtime.

April 16. Another spring day. If this keeps on we will try to get the ground in shape for planting. We need a good rain. School tomorrow. It's like coming back from another world.

April 17. Kids just left for school. It's so clear I can see the others walking from their homes. 9:30. Kinda hazy. 10:30. Teacher sent the kids home before it gets bad. They got here just in time but the dust is thin this time.

April 18. Blew all night but clear this morning. School today.

April 19. Rained a little last night and showered this morning Myra came home from school saying the little Long girl died. Poor Mrs. Long.

April 20. Well, today is one of the worst we ever had. A black duster. Just when we thought it was better. I don't know where this dirt is coming from but not here. We listen to the radio and know we are not the only ones to suffer. It is just terrible for everyone. The drought years are bad enough but this is almost more than people can stand on top of being so poor from the depression and all.

April 21. Lovely morning. Cleaned and had everything fresh. We all took baths and changed our clothes and dressed up so nice and thought of driving over to Longs', and 1:30 came a fierce cloud sweeping on us, this time from the south. We hadn't finished our dinner and had to cover things as we ate. I was so discouraged I cried. If the land is ruined we can't just sit here and starve, and that's what we'll be doing if we can't grow our crops this year. This was about the last year most of us could stand the drought and keep from losing the farms. Seems queer that just at the time the world is hardest to make a living in, nature turns on us too. Well, as Mrs. Starwood is always saying, the meek shall inherit the *dearth.*

April 22. Cold but nice. I washed and ironed.

April 23. Dust. I am sick of writing about it.

April 24. A black one. Started at 7 a.m. and got worse and worse. We had to nail a cover over the door when we were inside. Everybody's house has canvas and boards on the windows and smells of this infernal dust. Blew all day. I notice Dad has a cough.

April 25. Blew all night and still blowing almost black. It is a terrible feeling to be in this blackness. You don't know what is going on outside and you imagine all kinds of things. It is so still, just blows and blows but as if there is no wind, just rolling clouds of dust. We haven't seen light for two days. I am worried about my chickens, some of them are acting droopy. Dad is sleeping in the barn again, worried about the horses.

April 26. A little lighter but still blowing. The sun looks sick and yellow above the dust. Mrs. Long stopped in on way home this morning. Had to stay in town all night. Yesterday the other twin was sick and she got scared and drove to town to doctor. She said she guessed she could stand the dust because she was so desperate, but the little girl began choking. She had to spit in her mouth. It was the only thing she could do to keep her from choking till she got to the doctor. He says she will be all right in a few days but kept her there out of the dust as nearly as possible. She said Gaylord's ceiling fell in with the weight of the dust in attic. Just heard on radio of 24 deaths this month so far. Might be worse if we had a flood but I'd like to see a little water. Some people get lost in the dust and choke. A lot of dust pneumonia. Suppose the effects of the dust will be showing up on a lot of people later.

April 27. Black as night nearly all day. This is one of the hardest weeks. Many nights we can hear the cattle bawling for water. They sound so pitiful and helpless, and there's nothing any of us can do. I hear them in my sleep. We need groceries today but don't dare venture out. With our wheat gone our credit won't be worth anything.

April 28. A beautiful morning, but everything is buried. Spent all morning cleaning house and getting ourselves cleaned up. Brownells came by in the afternoon and we drove all around. Nearly all the yuccas we saw had roots showing, even the thin ones that grow so long out around them. Maybe in a few years the country will be all right again but now it looks like a desert.

94

It is sad every direction you look. No feed, water, cattle dying. People imprisoned in their own homes behind covered windows and doors. Myra and Lonnie wanted to visit Bossy, so we drove to the draw where her bones are. The wolves had dragged some of them away. I knew they would cry but they wanted to see her. Even Brownells have to mortgage something this year, but they can hold out several years maybe and the drought ought to be over by then. Max says the land may be ruined for years. Mrs. Brownell brought us some milk and butter. When it clears up, I'll make her a nice cake.

April 29. Dust came up in the night and still blowing. Something terrible happened. Poor Mr. Starwood got caught in it last night and when it got black he ran his truck into a ditch and couldn't get out. He turned the lights on and stayed in the truck afraid he'd get lost if he walked home. Nobody found him till this afternoon. He wrote his will on a paper sack, leaving what little he had to Mrs. Starwood. That wasn't much but the truck and luckily it's clear. He was revived but there isn't much chance for him. He is such a fine man, quiet and kind and hardworking. Hope the dust clears a little so I can go over and help Mrs. Starwood. Mailman told me that out where he used to live there was six square miles where not a soul lives and was thickly settled once. He says about every other place is vacant and he asked the papers to publish it and they said "No sir never."

April 30. Mr. Starwood died. Mailman just told me. We all feel bad. Mailman said he had carried life insurance for years and had to let it drop last few years when things got so bad. What a world! Dust is still blowing, sometimes light, sometimes dark. No use to keep on writing dust, dust, dust. Seems it will outlast us.

Eighteen

Rain fell half mist and cold the day of Starwood's funeral. Neighbors drove for miles to the small schoolhouse and stood about in the yard waiting for the preacher to give them a sign. *Blessed are the dead the rain falls on* shuttled their thoughts in gentle cadence. Mrs. Starwood and the children were sitting inside, their faces swollen and red from weeping. The bare coffin rested on two low benches in front of the teacher's desk. The smell of dust was not even driven out by the rain. The preacher sat in Anna's chair with a worn air of professional patience. His greenish black coat shone with age and special care. His dark eyes at once lonely and fierce looked out from a sallow wasting face at the empty seats. His long fingers pecked hard on the desk partitioning his thoughts from the scene. Like his suit, he looked as if he too had been taken out of a trunk for the occasional participation in death. Mrs. Starwood watched him and wondered absently how he could look so much like the cartoons she had seen of his profession. A warm pity rose up through her own sorrow and loneliness for this miserable-looking man. She went up to the desk, and after making an effort to control her voice, she spoke to him quietly. He roused himself and listened.

"You won't say all them fancy things, will you? Just say the truth about him. He was a good man. I was always able to say that when he was . . . alive."

"Of course, I'm glad you feel that way." He sighed.

"Not too long, either," she asked. "I can hardly stand it." He looked at her impersonally and nodded. She saw that his forehead was damp, and he took out a handkerchief and wiped it back toward his dark thinning hair.

"I understand," he said and stood up. "Perhaps we can begin." She went back and sat down with her children. *No preacher airs about him, thank goodness,* she thought. *If anybody said a kind word to me now I'd not be able to hold up.*

* * *

The rain had turned to mist and the men stood about hunched with the cold, waiting for the others. Several of them went between the cars and sat on the running boards and they all followed. The women crowded into the car talking. The children were quietly playing in the woodshed. Anna was with them, seeing they did not tear their clothes or get dirty from the coal. Conversation among the men about Starwood's death led them into the usual discussion of dryland farming. Max and Pete had been telling their new ideas on the depression, farming, the prevention of tragedy, and since everything they said was logical, the farmers listened respectfully, interrupting with comments, even questions.

"It's only horse sense," Long said, "but it needs us and the government working together. Some things is just too dern big for us to do alone."

"This may be rich farmland well enough," Pete said, "but first it's grassland, and if we don't keep enough grazing country the soil will blow. We've been here for years and the dust wasn't so bad before the land was mostly all broken. The wind is bad enough anyway without blowing our wheat out."

"Yow," Gaylord said. "And we need trees. My wife always said we ought to plant trees because the place was unnatural." They laughed. "She was lonesome for the woods and streams."

"We need dams, too," Max said, "but we need big ones, not just private ones with high-priced water the way it is here now."

"That's where the govamint comes in, I suppose," old man Barr said sourly. "I aim to take keer o' my bizness, and let the govamint take keer of its."

"If you had any sense, old man," said Gaylord's old father, "you'd think awhile before you separate the milk from the cream. That's the way I look at it after hearing these young men here. The best should go to the top to help and advise us. I ain't saying things is run that way now, but people change the world all the time, and who knows?"

Max smiled with pleasure. He liked to have the old men on his side. "There's lots of things we don't even know yet, of course, but one thing sure, farmers have got to realize that they belong   97 with others who work. We've got to wake up and find out about things and stick together more, the way the workers do in the cities." Old man Gaylord was still thinking about what he had said.

"Things been plum bad now for many a year," he said, "and 'pears to me they git worse. I figger farmers been too easy going, maybe all the people been thata way. 'Pears to me we ain't taking enough part in the govamint. Ol' Honest Abe said something about govamint for the people, by the people, of the people. I reckon we been taking it for granted that it was for the people without their recollecting that part about by the people. They's always some people you got to keep a weather-eye on and we been too trusting." He stopped and puffed his pipe and shook his head. "We got a fine country, big and rich as you can find anywhere in the world, I reckon, and if things was right we'd all be getting along fine. Powerful lot of money tied up somewheres, and old Moon was telling me Saturday he heard on the radio the president told how a third of all the people is poor like us, some worse—not enough of things. He says the rich has got it. You don't reckon a man can git a million dollars honest, do you?"

"Must be some skull-druggery somewheres."

"Reckon we ought to git together when we want something. A herd of hungry cattle bawling shore can be heard plainer'n one here and one there." They all laughed and wagged their heads in agreement.

"I ain't wanting to do anything that ain't right," Hull said.

"What's anybody said wrong?" Pete asked. His calm, small face suddenly looked worried.

"Hear, hear," old Gaylord said, "a young feller talking without spunk."

"He's got enough spunk," Long said.

"Then let him know the place for it. All of us want to do the right thing."

"None of us done anything yet but suffer it out and talk."

"None o' you know what hard luck is," old Gaylord said. "Why when I was a farming back in Missouri afore I come on west, a summer I was trying to hurry along with my heading, my mule team dropped deader'n doornails right in the field!"

Everyone was silent, aghast, not knowing what to say. One of them ventured, "You don't say!"

"The heat, maybe?"

"Yep, it got so hot the corn started popping. The mules thought it was a snowstorm in the middle o' summer, and they jes naturly froze to death!"

"You old devil! You had us scared there for a minit. A man ought to know better'n believe a word you utter." They all laughed and began to rummage in their memories for tall tales.

"Well sir," said old man Dunne, "I've seen things in my time, and I'm living to see strange things take place. I've seen the country boom, and the whole world bust. It sets me thinking. A man just sitting and thinking by himself is like a dog chasing his tail. Now I read a paper year in year out, but of late the truth is stranger than fiction, as the old saying goes. A man needs to know what's back of things or he'll dang near give up the ghost."

"You're too serious, old man. Poor Starwood in there has got you brooding over things."

"Not that," old man Dunne persisted, his black eyes burning like hot coals in dark pits of wrinkled flesh. "We all must come and go. I'm getting up in years so it's not about myself so much. I've got a son, Milt here, and two little grandchildren. I can't even die in peace for wondering what kind of world they'll grow up into, or maybe they won't get a chance to grow up and live. Goddang it, the world is loco."

"You need a yardstick, granddad, to measure the world by, and things happening in it," Max said.

"If you know what it is, lad, I want to find out. We ought to sow it in the four winds when we know it."

"Well, we know things are as black as you say, all right, and maybe worse than we know, but there's more to it than that. It's like nature, maybe it's human nature, that when something dies and rots something new and healthy grows up to take its place. Not everybody in the world is rotten, there'll be a few won't decay. They're the clean seeds that fell off the old tree. Right now the tree still stands and it's hard for people to see the little one, but it grows while the rotting one dies. The little one has to be strong enough to be laughed at, but that's easy, because it knows where it's going. I believe there must be some people like that who are working hard to grow up clean, people who believe in 'liberty and justice for all' (as the kids say every morning in school in flag salute) and really work for that. People who know where they're going. I'll find out who they are and help. I want to do something with my life." Max sat silent for a moment, rummaging in his thoughts for what he felt. "You know, it'd be fine if we could go fishing or learn things or do everything we wanted to, and have a lot of fun like Dad did, but unless you're a donkey you can see we can't do that even if we wanted to. We got born into a time when we'll have to fight harder than the other young men before us." Max paused to get his breath and Pete eyed his brother with admiration.

"Every man ought to do his duty, but consarn it!" old Gaylord said, "I'm blamed if I think duty is going off and fighting and killing other people in a war. Seems to me it ought to have something to do with making the best kind of life for ever'body."

"That's exactly what I mean," Max said. "I don't get a chance to talk much, I can't say it straight, I guess."

"It's plain as a hog's nose it won't happen helter-skelter," old Dunne said. "Max was right a while ago when he said big things ought to be planned as well as little ones. How would it be if I up and planted my fodder in December, or only fed my horses when I made plenty of money? If men don't run the world with reason, they're no wiser'n a bunch of four-legged animals."

"What you gonna do about all this, old dad?" one of the men asked with a smile at the others.

"I'm not saying. I'm asking you younger men with your life before you. When I was a young feller, there was work to do for anybody with a mind to it. That's not saying everybody was well off, and that some didn't make mistakes. But if there was no need for a man one place he could go another. New land to claim—why, I had two horses and a spring wagon and I rode like Blitzen into the Cherokee Strip and didn't get any land, but I just went someplace else. Lots of men were running on foot. In those days we just went somewhere and started building a town. I proved up this land, I was going to settle down so I wouldn't have to worry 'bout getting old. Well, I got one foot in the grave and I got nothing to show for my work, and I ain't the only one." He hesitated, seeming on the verge of a confidence. He looked down at the ground and his voice came lower. "I may lose my farm and then there's no place to go. No more new land, no more free gold out west, besides I'm too old to be tramping around hunting day work. Nobody wants an old man." He seemed ashamed that he had spoken of himself alone. He looked at the men again and went on. "And all of a sudden in the cities, from what I can figger out, the big ones that have been eating up the little ones have got profit indigestion and belched up millions of men. They don't need 'em anymore. Should some men be God that they don't need 'em anymore? It's time everybody found out his place in the world to keep everything from running in the ground. I'm an old man fretting about these things. Seems you men with wives and children and years of living to make better be studying how to take part and save yourselves."

"Granddad," Long said, "you sure make it sound bad, but there's something in what you say. Only a mule could think things is good right now. It may be though we'll come around the corner and things'll be dandy."

Brownell, who had sat listening without a word looked at him and spoke quietly, "I think we just about turned all the corners that go uphill; going downhill now. Farmers go up or down with the rest of the world."

"Them farmers back east always been having milk strikes, getting together for relief, and kind of sticking together for things. Must be something powerful wrong or farmers wouldn't get together. Having to take relief too—that's the last straw. I reckon they got right on their side." This was Long.

"I reckon they got right and starvation—they's old cronies," Gaylord said. He smiled slowly.

"We can't strike against dust," Hull said, "and us farmers in western Kansas, Oklahoma, eastern Colorado, New Mexico are a different lot. Must be thousands of us but we all live farther apart than the farmers over east. Even the prairie dogs got sense enough to git together but us farmers ain't got sense for 101 anything but to work hard. It takes a strong back and a weak mind to be a farmer, I reckon."

"I've got more respect for a farmer than that," Max said. They all uhmmed their agreement. "Besides it takes more than a strong back. We're getting more and more scientific. We want improved farming, and we want improved conditions to lessen the gamble."

"Danged right," Gaylord said. "A money-farmer can afford to hold off and sell when the price is high. But let a good crop come in and we all got to sell when the price is lowest to pay off the harvest, the grocery store, and every dang thing a man needs the year through."

"Someday these things'll be in the past," Pete said. "What we're all saying now may sound like a lot of meandering, but it shows we're kind of putting out feelers."

"Yes," Max said. "We have to fight the past; that is, we must fight against the past overtaking us again. If we don't watch out, the big ones will plow us under, and we'll just be farmhands for them, maybe worse."

"Not me!" said Hull.

"You may not be so high and mighty when you're starving."

"That's exactly what they think," Max said. "And if you're starving by yourself, they can buy you for a song."

"Lot of people going west now to try to git work," Long said. "Did you see the big ads in the papers for farm workers in California? Reckon some of us'll come to that, but the ads sound pretty good, may not be so bad till we git on our feet again and come back."

"Danged if I know what we'll do when we 'Mericans run out of west to move on to," old Dunne said. "Guess we'll go to sea." They all laughed a little but they were thinking of leaving.

"If it wasn't such a long depression," Max said, "most of us could have weathered the drought years. Droughts come and go, but if the bank takes your farm, you can't pick a new one up in a day."

"My old lady don't want to move," Hull said.

"Mine neither," said another.

Milt was listening to the men, and they all wondered without asking why he was silent. He was Starwood's closest neighbor.

They put it down to that. Flying about in his head like angry wasps were all the things the men had spoken. They wanted to avoid speaking of death, so they spoke openly of themselves. Their thoughts were formless and disordered, but every word seemed to him a raw index of the torment they had suffered silently in the years of hardship conquering the dry land, an almost unconscious torment revealed now only by the stark savagery of nature. Not one of them was safe, secure. All their lives were bent to that one end, and the lives of their wives, and their children. He saw it all clearly. It felt good to be a part of the talk, but his mind was aching with confusion and question and the answer was nowhere. Max talked in his clear strong voice about the farmers' Grange and farm cooperatives. When Milt looked up he saw the preacher come from the misty dusk of the schoolroom and stand in the doorway. Milt stood up and nodded at the men. Their words died away as they walked toward the schoolhouse. When they got inside they saw Frieda Brennermann sitting in a back seat, and they saw the red geraniums on the coffin. There were only a few, but all she could get from her dusty potted plants; she had woven the leaves into a circle and secured the flowers between them to make a respectable wreath. Mrs. Starwood was sitting stiffly looking straight ahead at the flag draped across the front wall above the blackboard.

Nineteen

Anna was sitting at the desk grading papers when Max came in. He moved a rock along the floor with his foot to hold the door open. She smiled happily watching him.

"How did you come? I didn't hear you."

"Walked. It's a fine evening, like old times. Smell it?"

"Uhmmmm." She lifted her head and sniffed toward the open door. He watched her, showing pleasure that she was flushed.

"You're as sweet as a colt when you do that!"

"Only then?"

"Only then! Now what can I do to help you get out of here?"

"Oh, you can erase the boards, burn the wastepaper, sweep the floor, and if you finish before I do, you can help me grade these." She touched a stack of neatly folded papers, each marked with the name, the grade, and the subject.

"We'll rush them out together," he said.

"No, we won't. These papers are as serious as life and death to the pupils. We'll grade them carefully."

"Yes, Teacher," he said and began to erase the board. She went on with the grading, not talking.

Max finished quickly and sat down at one end of the desk looking through the papers.

"Take the arithmetic, Max. I know you haven't forgotten that. And the spelling. I'll do the rest."

"All right, but first . . . " He got up and began taking the pins from her hair. The long fat braids fell down and he unwound them, shaking her hair loose all about her. It was yellow and thick and showed lights where the braid had curved it. He put his face against the back of her head and smelled her hair. Then he sat down with the papers and looked at her.

"Oh, Max," she laughed, "I feel silly."

"Why? You look wonderful. We'll work and I'll look at you now and then."

"Aren't we silly though?" she asked.

"Oh, that's because when we see each other we feel so free of everything and everybody."

"That's so, because we aren't really thoughtless."

"I am right now. I can't remember exactly how to get the volume of a cylinder."

"Supposing it were your silo, you'd find out."

He poked about in a desk for an arithmetic book and looked up the rules.

"These poor kids. I'll bet you use that old German discipline on them." She laughed.

"I don't either. I suppose you'd use your old English muddling."

"Nope. I'd do the old American Way."

"You've been reading signboards again."

"Anyway, I'm half Irish too, and all American. Funny how we talk about our roots when our people have been here for generations."

"Interesting too," Anna said, "how we're not really divided according to our nationalities, but by how much or how little money we have. Most of the differences are acquired, they depend on what money can buy you. I suppose they influence in some way the differences that aren't acquired." She paused and looked out the window over the forlorn and ravaged plain. "These poor kids didn't get much schooling this year. If they hadn't tried to keep up at home during the dust, they couldn't pass these exams." Max picked up a box and shook it.

"What's this?"

"New toothbrushes, parting gifts. You should have seen the morning tooth inspection they initiated. Gee! I've had the finest kind of time with them. You know, Max, it amazes me how they can be such real children; they know many of the serious problems of living already. I don't know how often I've heard them say, 'No, I can't get something-or-other because we can't afford it this year.' Said with no bitterness and all the understanding of a grown-up. Children shouldn't have to worry about these things!"

"Our grandchildren won't have to, maybe our children. Who knows?"

"You really believe that, Max?" She looked at him seriously, wanting to be assured.

"If I didn't I wouldn't want any. Some of us fellows used to talk about these things at school. No answer in what we learned, so we read and talked a lot. I've got to find out some more then we'll talk about it. One of the fellows took a magazine I wanted to read. I mean to write him but this dust has got me so I just do what I have to."

"I'd like to believe in something with you, Max, something close to our lives and big enough for everybody."

"That's it, that's the way it will have to be now; anything else is a chew of locoweed." He looked at her serious eyebrows, almost the color of her delicate skin.

"Frieda used to think the world was her own little eggshell, and now she's so miserable she'll do anything to get out of it. I thought she just wanted a husband, and it is partly that, but she says now that isn't enough. She says her life is useless and she thinks about it all the time. I feel sorry for her, because I know how she feels, but I've got you to help some." Max took her hand and pressed it, and the pencil fell to the floor. Her blue eyes were thoughtful but her mouth was soft with tenderness.

"And now what have you got?" he asked. "My wheat ruined so I've lost my start. We can't get married on nothing, and things are even shaky with the folks. Yours are still safe; I'd be taking you away from something sure, and I can't do that. This year meant we'd start building on our own house. Your folks would never forgive you if you married me now, and you don't want to live here in the same neighborhood at outs with them."

"They're stubborn but they'd get over it. I have to live my life, Max. If we just had a place to live, I wouldn't worry about losing what I've got at home." She began gathering the ungraded papers and putting rubber bands on them. "I'll take these home. We don't have much chance to talk."

"We could rent a place, but what's the use renting a field of dust? We can't raise anything next year. I can't even borrow money with no security. Dad would probably do it for me, but it would mean mortgaging something of theirs."

"We mustn't do that."

"Every time I have an idea it runs into snags like these. We won't know a thing till next season, and another year seems a long time."

"Terribly long," she said. "But what can we do? I'll keep on making things for my hopeless chest."

"Oh, Anna, don't say things like that."

"I don't mean it, goose." She laughed at his solemn face and kissed him lightly. "You know, Max, maybe it won't be so awfully bad. I intend to keep on seeing you regardless of wind and high water and Papa and Mama, and if the dust stops blowing, there's a few things we can do. Maybe you can get that magazine you mentioned, and we might scare up a few books, and on good days we could go down by the dried-up creek and read aloud. There are a few cottonwoods trying to bud now. I think I've got spring fever! I wish I could just be in nothing but love for awhile without feeling guilty."

"Guilty?"

"Well, you know—everyone is so miserable here, mortgages, no crops, dust, that I feel as if I haven't any right to feel so happy sometimes."

"The very ones you're thinking about would be glad for you."

"I know it," she said thoughtfully.

"I told the Dunnes we're going to get married. They certainly approve!" She smiled at him and stood up.

"Let's go, Max. It's getting dark." She suddenly became aware of her hair hanging down and braided it quickly, winding it around her head, sticking the pins in deftly. She held a small mirror close to her face. "I can't see. Am I all right?"

"Of course."

"Of course," she mimicked him. "Let's close the windows." Max felt such a surge of pure friendship for her, he put his arm around her shoulders in a warm unintimate way and looked at her in the dusk. Her honesty was like a swift cool stream running through his thoughts. He felt the liking they had for each other holding their love like an earthen crock. He wanted her to be with him like this in their own house every day. He wanted to know her and be known to her. They went out, crossing the schoolyard, and the road to the pasture, walking with their hands in a warm embrace that trembled imperceptibly between impersonal and intimate. They walked a long time in this wordless full communication. When they came to the Brennermann pasture, he stepped on a low wire and held up a higher one, and Anna stepped through the opening with one easy movement. As she bent softly forward and rose quickly, Max sensed the fullness of her young body. She was like a ripe fruit he wanted to touch and taste again and again. He swung himself over the fence and stood a moment looking at her. They smiled at each other in the growing dark and turned toward the walk across the open pasture. The little bunches of tough grass under their feet made walking difficult. Ahead of them a light came on at a farm, then the lamplight low against the earth showed from the Dunne dugout. These lights were small and far away and only accented their aloneness as the night rose up around them like a darkening mist. Anna could see the lean outline of Max's face and felt a sudden desire move through her body like a tender sword of fire, plunging her mind sweetly, fiercely, into chaos that sent tiny lights whirling around the desolate line of earth and sky. She stood still, drowning in her own emotion, and then she swayed a little against him, lost in a blinding dark that swept over her like a flood. It seemed to Max in an instant of joy that everything he felt now was identical in her, there was no need for question and answer as once there had been in their shy hesitation. They knew each other and in this knowledge they were released. He held her strongly. Through the gentle gloom he watched the tense urging beauty of her face lifted for him to see. He took off his coat and spread it on the unyielding grass, and they lay down, holding each other and kissing, sometimes laughing low and joyfully.

"It's been a long time," he said.

"A very long time."

They felt suddenly sure of their whole lives together, surer than they had ever been, and interrupting their delight a strange solemn reverence overcame them. It demanded and permeated their closeness, and in it Anna found herself. She was eloquent of all her nameless inarticulate feelings, and Max was joyous in her response. Afterward, she clung to him, mystified and happy, aware of the wonder of wholeness and harmony she had touched for a moment. In this beautiful strange joy there was a faint yet overpowering sense of old sorrow, not of herself yet of love. She wanted to cry out this unknown sorrow, but seeing his wondering face when he felt her tears, she lay quiet, and touched his hair and his face wanting the knowledge of it in her hand. They lay a long while with their faces toward the high dark sky, watching the stars come out, sensing the great body of the earth beneath them. Lying small on the prairie, watching the sky, lent their feelings an unexpected grandeur. Their wonder and their yearning and their love seemed as infinite as the space above them. They were reluctant to give up the moment, and yet by the sky they knew how late it was in the evening and Anna should be home. They stayed on as if inseparable, and afterward Anna was in a state of exaltation. She sat up beside Max holding his face and kissing him until he held her away.

"I am glorified," he said to her, whispering low because the words were strange ones he could never speak aloud.

"Oh, darling! I want to laugh and run and *oh* I don't know what, but I feel so happy! Come on, darling, put on your coat, let's run a ways."

"Anna!" Max was smiling at her. He kissed her quickly and took her hand and they ran together until they were breathless. They leaned together resting and caressing each other with their laughter.

"Isn't it wonderful!" she said. "We never felt like this before."

"We know each other," he said seriously.

"Maybe we've just really fallen in love."

"No, but maybe into another degree." He was holding her shoulders tightly wanting to say something to her. She stopped laughing and waited.

"We're married, Anna. You're my wife. We've been married since the first time."

"Yes. And you're my husband, Max." Her voice was calm and very low.

"We'll finish it up as soon as we have a place of our own to live." She began walking and he came up beside her.

"You don't need to say that, Max. I know it."

109

"I know, but I want to say it. I wish we could get married in the morning."

"We can't though, darling, and let's don't be unhappy about it tonight. I feel so happy."

"I feel happy too—that's just it." He held her hand in his pocket and they walked fast. "I feel like working hard!"

"But you always work hard, darling." They were nearing the fence back of the corral, and she turned and kissed him good-night. "You'd better go back now," she said. He waited while she walked through the long yard and he saw her mother pull the curtain aside and peer out. When she saw Anna she opened the door. Her voice came out into the quiet night.

"My land, child, you had us worried."

"Don't worry about me, Mom," Anna called to her. "I'm growed up and big and strong."

Max heard her laughing away the old woman's grumbling and watched her come out of the yard into the lighted doorway and up the steps. He turned with her laughter still in his ears and walked into the darkness toward home.

Twenty

The Starwood truck rattled to a stop near the bank and waited. The bank's letter to Mrs. Starwood lay on the seat beside her. It was dirty with the fingermarks of the children who had read and handled it as they talked of a solution to the problem it raised. Mrs. Starwood had alone come to a conclusion and was carrying it out with no further discussion. She had been up and working for almost five hours before the bank opened, but this morning, sitting in the stiff uncomfortable seat of the truck, absorbing the delicate spring sunlight through the bright windshield, she felt peculiarly patient. When at last the door was unlocked, Mrs. Starwood got her heavy body gingerly out of the truck. Several people were already going into the bank and for a moment she hesitated. Then after getting a bundle from the back of the truck, she walked as quickly as she could, entered the bank, and stood looking for the manager's fenced-in office.

The bank was clean and quiet with only the small private sound of money clinking and the polite low voices of the clerks. Mrs. Starwood walked firmly over to the manager's railing and letting the newspaper wrapping fall to the floor, she lifted something by a long fluffy tail and laid it on his desk. It was a skunk, and suddenly everyone in the bank knew it was a skunk. The manager looked up startled and then jumped from his chair. His small white face grew red with embarrassment and outrage.

"What's . . . what in the name of . . . !" he sputtered. Mrs. Starwood stood unmoved. She laid the letter on the desk beside the odoriferous corpse, not yet stiffened with death.

"Here's the answer to your letter, Mr. Wighton. This is all we raised this year above the interest." She turned and walked toward the door. The distraught manager came to his senses and swung through the gate after her.

"Take it out!" he ordered.

"It's yours," said Mrs. Starwood. He saw that she did not intend to remove the skunk, whose penetrating smell was defiling the formality of the bank. He turned to look for a clerk.

"Take it out!" he ordered again, and the young man he addressed hesitated with a slight expression of mutiny in his blue eyes before he thought better of it, picked the animal up by the tail, and carried it out a side door. He did not come back at once and was probably finding someone to bury it.

"We could have you arrested," the manager said controlling his voice.

"Pray, what for?" asked Mrs. Starwood. "I done nothing against the law."

"You've disturbed the peace!" he shouted, forgetting himself again. "And God . . . and damn . . . oh, blast it all, you've upset the whole bank, business too. Right enough, you've disturbed the peace!"

"You've disturbed my peace for years," she said, gathering calm as he grew more excited.

"You don't understand," he said, aware of the patrons once more and speaking in his modulated public voice. "We meant no harm. It's simply business."

"I know that all right. You're a good enough man yourself, I suppose. You can't help it because you work in a bank no more'n I can help farming. You got to live like the rest of us. It's the bank holding all the mortgages and goading us to death. That letter's inhuman, telling me if I don't pay by the first you'll take the little bit of machinery, the stock, my chickens. Is it business to take all that I have to make a living with? Mister, my husband is dead now, and I got a houseful of children to raise. I can work in the field like a man, and when there's a crop, I'll pay my debts, the same as we always have. But . . . " she gulped for breath, her eyes stern and straight in her pale face, "but, godalmighty, I can't make it rain or stop blowing dust, and I can't make the world right when it's busted. All I know how to do is work and if I can't pay back that little mortgage on our things you'll stop me working. I'll see you in the hot place first. I brought the skunk as a present. If the building wasn't rock, I'd of nailed it over the door for a trademark. First National Skunk!" Someone snickered and smothered the sound quickly. An old man hurried out chuckling to himself. Mr. Wighton stood in front of Mrs. Starwood's furious torrent, proud and cold.

"Well, this hardly settles the business we asked you to come in for," he said icily, settling himself upward in his careful coat, seeming to rise above this unpleasant but occasionally necessary encounter with the common. He felt suspiciously like a martyr, and indeed, he must appear one to the others in the bank. This gave him new courage and patience, and he cleared his throat politely as if waiting for her decision.

"Well, you can have what crop is left after two years feeding and dust. That's all I got. That's everything I got. If I owned the land, you could have it too. You got everybody else's. What will you do with the land when we can't pay no more? I hope you blow up and bust with your gluttony. You eat up our land like a filthy hog, you banks do. You and your flunky loan companies. I hope all the banks in America eat themselves to death. We poor people will then have to eat the corpse. We'll be good and hungry by then. Understand? Good and hungry." She moved toward him, shaking her finger. "You tell the rest of 'em that—all the banks in the big places, all your bosses. You tell 'em for a farmer's wife who's worked hard and honest." Her weathered brown hand shook nearer his face. He flattened against the swinging gate and backed in. She stopped suddenly and laughed. She turned and walked out, still laughing, a great strong laugh that shook her body and echoed through the bank. She walked into the street and climbed into the old truck and drove off. Her hearty laughter trailed down the street above the sound of the motor. A few people on the sidewalks watched her in surprise. She looked back, and the manager had run out of the bank, remembering his unfinished business. She slapped her hand against the steering wheel and got her breath.

"Whew!" she laughed to herself. "I ain't felt so good in years." As she drove through the main street toward the country, she passed Flanery's store and saw farmers standing in front, one of them shaking the door. The group on the edge nearest the street was laughing, and suddenly one of them stepped toward the truck and raised his arm.

"Hi, there," he called out. She pulled up and shouted above the engine.

"What's up? Flanery gone fishing in the sand?"

"Don't know yet." The others laughed louder when they saw her stop. The old man who had passed her in the bank was talking. She turned off the motor.

"—and say, she's the beatenest old heifer I ever heered. Dogged if she don't laugh louder'n a braying Jennie Jack."

"You old codger, you ain't laughed in twenty years. It'd crack your face open," she called out.

"I'd laugh well enough but I've ne'er seen nothing funny in twenty years."

"Look in the crick next time you ford it," she said, and the men laughed. One of them poked the old man in the ribs.

"I'll be deviled, you're all locoed," the old man said, and they roared again.

"Don't lose your temper, granddaddy. She's liable to take you for a banker." The old man began to repeat all he had told them, and some of them listened again as if they had not heard the story the first time.

"All fooling aside," said Mrs. Starwood, "where's Flanery? It ain't him to stay locked up till this hour." One of the men turned away from the door, his face serious.

"I can't make out," he said. "Drive around the corner and ask the sheriff to come round. We been here quite a spell and can't raise nobody."

"Maybe the old man's sick and in there by hisself," she said and drove away. She was back in a few minutes with the sheriff. He tried the door solemnly, as if he had some power the others had not. He peered inside and stood back and shook his head.

"Something funny here, boys. Better push 'er in. He might be sick in there. I always tell my wife a man ain't got no business living alone." Together the farmers broke the door in and trooped to the back, the sheriff going ahead. Past the tall cookie rack there was a peculiar smell they all noticed. Back of the stove, Flanery was sitting in his curved-arm chair, with his head blown off. A double-barreled shotgun was resting between his knees. His arms dangled stiff. Shreds of his face hung down over his neck. Stuck hard against the cans on the shelves were pieces of the old man's head and his splashed brains. A few teeth and something that looked like a piece of eye were lying in the blood on the floor. His shoulders were drenched with sticky blood. The men backed away, removing their hats. Mrs. Starwood came up from behind them, and when she saw Flanery she could not look away until she had seen everything. She tried to move backward but her body refused. With a great effort she groaned, and two of the men led her outside, where she sat on the curb leaning against a post, breathing hard to get the clean air in her lungs. The men went back inside, and with their immobility broken they roused the others out of their helpless staring.

"We better do something, fellas."

"Yes, we had," the sheriff said. "One of you men get the undertaker Ragsdale. We'll be looking about for a note if he left one." It was clear that Flanery had been burning his books in the heater. The battered cardboard files were lying empty on the floor, and the pigeonhole file where he kept the individual charge books was leaning against the pile of boxes. The sheriff went behind the little cage where Flanery had kept these things.

"Everything's bare." He opened the cash register and saw the money as it was taken in the day before.

"He did every man that owed him a good turn before he shoved off," the sheriff said. One of the men looked at the sheriff in an unbelieving startled way.

"He burned all us farmers' bills?"

"He burned 'em all and never even left a letter explainin'."

"That don't want explaining," the farmer said slowly in a voice shaken with gratitude and unburdened relief. He stood without speaking and the others deepened his private thanks with their own fumbling silence. One of them stepped carefully near Flanery and placed his sweat-stained hat onto the old man's neck.

"I can't stand to see him like that," he apologized.

"I wonder why he did it?" the sheriff said musingly.

"None of us can know the whole reason a man takes his life in his hands, but part of it is clear as day. I'm mighty sorry, but I reckon Flanery knowed his own mind."

"I reckon."

"I tell you, many's the time I figgered life ain't hardly worth living in these times, but I can't never give it up till I have to," another farmer said.

"I reckon not," the sheriff said, interested in his own thoughts.

"We best see about Mrs. Starwood. Just losing her husband, this may affect her." Several of the men went through the quiet aisle of the store to the outside. Mrs. Starwood was still leaning against the post.

"You all right?"

"I'm alright now. I'll be going home in a little."

"Poor old man Flanery burned all us farmers' bills," one of the men said to her. She looked at him. He repeated it. Mrs. Starwood put her hands up to her face and cried. She wiped her tears on a corner of her coat, but the sobbing shook her big shoulders so she could not stop. The men went back into the store and brought her a cup of water. She drank it and got up, and walked toward the truck.

Twenty-one

Almost halfway home, where she turned off on the fork, Mrs. Starwood saw Milt Dunne coming in the wagon. She stopped the truck and waited for him. *He must be going to town for groceries.* He came alongside and whoaed the horses, and they crooked their hind legs for resting and began to doze.

"Hello, Mrs. Starwood," he smiled, raising his hat.

"Hi, Milt. Say, man, why don't you get yourself a car with some of that money you been making off the crops? Look at them horses—gone plum to sleep as soon as you slack the lines."

"Maybe it's the sun today. More likely they don't get enough to eat and drink though we give 'em every bit we can. I'd rather go hungry myself than the horses, they can't say much."

"How's your feed— pretty low, huh?"

"Pretty low, but we figure we'll plant this spring. It's clearing up."

"It's high time. I sure hope you're right."

"You know," he said, "you hit the nail right on the head. I'm going in town to see a fellow about trading my land for a second-hand car. I want to get some good out of that land while I've still got a clear title. I hope it will stay nice weather like this or he might change his mind."

"Must be something powerful wrong with that car, Milt." Mrs. Starwood leaned forward in concern.

"Maybe so. We looked at the land yesterday though and it's pretty clean and the grass is as good as any right now. He wants it for grazing, and maybe put a well in on it. That's about all it's good for."

"Well," she said, "I hope you don't get stung, but I would like to see you folks have a car."

"I guess I'll move on," he said. "I want to get a few groceries from Flanery before he decides to close up and sun himself."

"How's Julie and the kids?" Mrs. Starwood asked suddenly.

"Fine. How's yours?"

"Dandy." She leaned on the wheel thinking a moment.

"Well, so long," he called out and raised his hand.

"Say, Milt! I hope you're not too low on groceries. Flanery's dead, last night, shot hisself." Milt looked at her unbelieving. "He burned all our bills before he done it."

"He did! Poor old devil!" *This isn't real. This is something you read about in the paper that happens to people you don't know!* He forgot about the groceries.

"Come to think of it," Mrs. Starwood said, "all them farmers there trying to get in the store this morning must have been needing groceries. What'll they do now?"

"What'll you do?" he asked.

"I don't hardly know. Have to get my thinking cap on."

"Our credit's no good with anybody else these times. Everyone of us paid him something every time we had it but all the same we ruined him, poor old man."

"It wasn't just us, Milt. Don't let that prey on your mind. It's the times and the drought. Flanery and us are all in the same boat. Well, I must get along."

"Don't let your kids go without as long as we have some spuds at our house," Milt said. She smiled and her face looked tired and dry.

"So long," he said.

"Don't waste your money in town," she called out, trying to make him laugh. *I bet they ain't got one potato*, she thought.

"She's got a lot of spunk," he said to himself as he drove on, wondering what they would do for groceries.

Twenty-two

The quiet of Sunday pervaded the farmyard and the comfortable Brownell house with the afternoon sun streaming in across the long kitchen table. The blue oilcloth cover shone brightly around a large white frosted cake and tall glasses of milk. Mrs. Brownell was cutting the cake into fat pieces and putting them on a plate. Two pitchers of milk stood on a corner of the table. She placed five pieces of cake on the plate and she handed it to Lonnie. She handed one pitcher of milk to Myra.

"Now, you take these and I'll bring the glasses," she said, and they went out into the warm yard.

"Look what's coming!" Pete yelled from where the men were sitting around talking lazily.

"Well, you said you were too full at dinner for dessert, so here it is now," Mrs. Brownell said gaily. Lonnie passed the cake shyly to the men and each took a piece in his hand and waited for the milk Mrs. Brownell was pouring. Myra brought the milk. When she gave the glass to her grandfather, she bent near his ear and whispered.

"It's the fullest." The old man winked at her and smiled.

When the little girls finished their milk and cake, Julia told them they might go play in the sun.

"I can't believe this weather," Mrs. Brownell said. "I guess we'll all start planting right away. A lot of people will have to get seed loans again, but they won't have any trouble if these clear days keep on, and maybe a little shower." She laughed at herself.

"Since we haven't any wheat, we'll plant corn and maize," Julia said. "My, it will be fine to work hard in a harvest again, won't it? I never thought I'd look forward to that!" She had brought two shirts to be patched and mended and started to get them. "You don't mind my sewing a devil's seam or two, do you?"

"Land, no. Sunday is just about like any other day."

"You know the Hulls are leaving?" Julia asked.

"No, where?"

"Arizona, to pick cotton. He heard he can get work there and they can't stay here any longer even if it clears now."

"Well, that's too bad," Mrs. Brownell's gay eyes looked serious. "We ought to go over and see if they need anything to take along. My goodness, my heart aches to see the cars going along the highway all the time now. There used to be only one now and then, but this spring it's terrible." Sometimes they would stop for a drink, but mostly they drove past, the cars piled high with household goods and children. Few of the men and women waved or shouted as they passed the house the way they used to that first year. Their thoughts were too close to the homes they were leaving. They were going out of the country, to the *outside* with a hostile hope in their hearts. They went out together and alone, like animals moving with their backs to the storm, moving to shelter they knew was nowhere, yet they could no longer stand still in their stricken lives.

"Longs have already gone to California. I wonder who'll be next?"

"Well," Mrs. Brownell said after a long sigh as if she had come out of sleep, "it won't ever be us. We're getting on in years, and we've put our best into this farm. We can't leave. It seemed a few years ago we were settled comfortably for the rest of our lives, and now, Julia, we've had to mortgage part of our land after fighting not to. We don't want to tell the boys yet awhile. Max wants to get married and we'd always planned to give him that section for a start, and help him build, and do the same for Pete. They've taken such an interest in the place and worked hard so they've earned that." Julia looked up from her sewing.

"You mean they can't get married now?"

"Of course they can, Julia, but knowing Max, he won't if he can't offer his wife at least a place to live. Even if we can pay off the land, we still can't build a chicken coop this year. I'll ask them to stay here, but when a young man can't count on his future, it's harder to start on nothing."

"It's hard to do anything with no future to look to," Julia said. "It makes Milt cross when he thinks about it, and it seems there's always something to quarrel about before the kids. It's hard to get married, and hard to stay married in such a world."

"I know, dear." The understanding caress in her words touched Julia's heart.

"I hope they can get married," Julia said. "Maybe it will be a good year after all." She sewed awhile thinking, and then aloud she said, "I wish Frieda could get married too. I know her better than Anna. She's so lonely. Anything would be better than living at home."

"I've seen her sometimes working at the bank. When her father gets her on steady there maybe she'll meet someone."

"Maybe."

Twenty-three

The children were in bed, and Mrs. Starwood was still moving about the naked room unable to make herself go to bed for thinking it was the last night in this old house she had cursed so many times. She snorted at herself, but tears ran down her nose over her dry lips. She tasted them along with the grit on her teeth and the powdery dryness on her tongue. There was a scratchy feeling in her throat, and she remembered her husband—remembered him as she imagined him in the ditch with the thick black dust blowing over him, remembered him afterward as she watched him die, his lungs rattling and blowing his chest up hard and full in that determined ever-quickening instinct to keep alive. How could fine soft dust and flesh together make that queer hard rattle that came at the last? *Godalmighty!* she thought, *what's the matter with me, picking at death like an old hen pecking apart something too big to swallow?*

She thought she heard someone running on the hard bare yard, but it was only her wits end and the wind. She shuffled her heelless slippers along the gritty floor and found something else to do. This time the steps were real and someone came up against the door with the strong wind. *Good God, somebody else lost in this dusty hell?* She opened the door, pressing her weight against it to keep the dirt and the gale from tearing through the house and waking the kids. Frieda came in and dropped at once onto the chair by the door. She began untying the cloth around her mouth and nose, breathing too hard to speak. Her face was brown and streaked with dust. She looked fat and distorted with the several coats she was wearing and a flat suitcase tied across her back. She began to laugh, but she still could not speak.

"What're you doing out in this?" Mrs. Starwood demanded. Frieda waved her to silence. Mrs. Starwood began undoing the suitcase.

"I knew I'd never get through the wind if I didn't have every-thing tied to me," the girl said. "Usually the dust just comes quietly but it *would* blow hard tonight."

"What on earth you bringing me that you had to come out, you crazy kid?"

"I'm not bringing you anything I couldn't get on my back and sneak into this case. I'm going with you. I made up my mind because there's no reason to stay here in the dirt. Anna will be gone soon enough. I can't stand to stay at home any longer, let alone by myself." She stood up, slipping the coats onto the back of the chair. Mrs. Starwood looked thunderstruck.

"God knows, I ain't blaming you wanting to get away from that corral, but—girl, you ain't going with me! I got my hands full with these kids and caring for 'em. I don't want that old devil dad of yours after me. You don't need to go out in the storm again tonight, but you go home in the morning. We're leaving at sunup soon's we have a bite to eat."

"Leave before sunup," the girl begged. "I'm going." She looked at the older woman filled with such a lonely stubbornness and took off the sweater she had on under the coats and hung it on a peg on the back of the door.

"It's you doing it," Mrs. Starwood said. She turned the wick lower in the lamp until the room was almost dark. This sudden visit had destroyed her last chance to poke around and say good-bye to the house. *You old fool,* she called herself in her thoughts. "Let's get to bed. You'll be dog tired in the morning," she told the girl. Frieda was already undressed. She was rolling her underclothes inside a coat to keep them free of dust. Mrs. Star-wood watched her.

"You Germans sure are cleaner'n anybody," she said, and the girl laughed. "And stubborn too."

Ignoring the last remark, Frieda said, "I see you've got on clean sheets."

"I washed and ironed yesterday. I want to start out halfway clean, but this dirt's got me so I don't care if I'm dirty or not. What's the use?"

"You know that's not true," Frieda said. "Look here."

"What is it?"

"Come and see." Mrs. Starwood carried the lamp and bent over the chair. She turned the wick up a little and held her hand on one side of the chimney to shade the children's bed.

"See," the girl whispered. There was a little pad sewed into the top of her vest. "This is what I saved from my share of the eggs and cream. I saved it for a long time."

"How much?" asked Mrs. Starwood wonderingly.

"Ninety-seven dollars. It'll help us get there." She folded the coat back over the clean clothes.

"Where?" Mrs. Starwood did not know she said this.

"Wherever we're going," Frieda said willingly. She got into bed.

"As far west as we can go," the older woman said bitterly, then almost dreamily. "Maybe someday I'll have a little farm in California. We got to pick a lot of fruit though." Frieda lay in the place hollowed out for years by Starwood. It did not fit her body and she moved a little hoping the shucks in the mattress would move with her weight. They made a small scratchy sound but the shape of the man's body remained like a knotty groove. Mrs. Starwood blew out the light and got heavily into bed. They said goodnight and waited quietly for sleep. The house creaked and strained, and the dust beat a soft tattoo along the wall, one tone on the wood, a higher one on the boarded windows.

Twenty-four

The dust was blowing thinly off the field and over the yard like a worn and dingy curtain flapping disconsolately at the window of the world. Through it the old man saw the faded landscape, gray and colorless except for the line of half-dead trees along the creek. *It will be another year*, he thought, *before the high wide plains are green.* He turned away. Standing a short distance from the Ford car he looked at it critically. The little girls, wearing dust masks, were playing at taking a trip.

"Come on, get in, Konkie," Myra called out the window. The old man got in the backseat, his sharp knees sticking up high as he sat down.

"Why won't you come to California with us?" Lonnie asked.

"Now let's don't go into that again," he said crossly. "I can't, and I don't feel like talking about it."

"But Myra won't come if you don't," the little girl persisted.

"Well, let's pretend we're off to Flatlands," he said. "That'll do, I reckon." They all began to play the game called Going to Flatlands.

Julia came out of the house with two traveling cases. He got out quickly and took them.

"I want to get these out of my road," she said. "I'm trying to figure out what I can put in the car this morning." He shoved the bags across the floor. Julia looked at his back, which seemed old and tired as it had not been when they first came to live with him. He closed the door and turned. His whole face was sad, and she knew by the tightness of his mouth that he did not want to speak.

"Anything I can help you with?"

"Not now," she said and started to go in, but it seemed too cruel to ignore his grief as he evidently wished she would. "Dad, what makes you so stubborn about staying here? It worries me. Maybe there's *something* out there. It's a cinch it can't be worse." 125

"Might be. You can't ever tell. I'm too old to be gallivanting around working out." He opened the car door and got into the backseat again.

Maybe he's right, she thought, walking back to the house, *but no telling what will happen to him here alone.*

Milt came out of the barn and on his way to the house, he stopped by the car and looked in.

"I cleaned out the barn for you. Don't let it go too long. How do you like her?" He looked at the car proudly.

"All right, I guess," the old man said, and when Milt was gone he said half under his breath, "Telling me how to run the farm. . . . "

* * *

Before dawn there was the sound of a motor at the road, turning in the gate, stopping. A staccato honking began outside the window. Julia was packing the last of the dishes and pans into a small box. She threw a coat around her shoulders and hurried out. The darkness was heavy and the air dry and cool. There was something eerie and lonely about being up at this hour, something unbelievable in their going away. The panting truck was like a big animal in the yard, which suddenly closed its eyes and stopped breathing. Mrs. Starwood and Frieda got out and came toward her in the night.

"It's me and Frieda," she said. "You kids get out and move around. You got a long ride ahead of you."

"Frieda?" Julia stood still in her surprise. "Gee! I'm so glad! Come in, we're just about ready."

"We're early," Mrs. Starwood said. "We want to get on the way before sunup."

"All right," Julia said. "We can make it." They went down the steps into the house. "Dad and Milt are in the barn. I hate to leave Dad."

"That poor old critter will starve to death trying to farm here," Mrs. Starwood announced.

"Well, he doesn't think so—says he's too old to work out, and I don't blame him for that."

"Believe me!" said Mrs. Starwood. "Getting old is scary business. Seems to me when a body has worked hard all his life and never earned nothing extra to put away, there ought to be some way to make his last days peaceful. I'll tell you, I don't want to live off my kids, and I sure don't want to live in some old folks home on charity. Best way, I reckon, is not to think about it, but that ain't my way of doing things."

"You'd better be careful," Frieda said quietly. "Grandpa Dunne might come in and hear you talking about him."

"I'm talking about ever' old man and woman. Well, Julie, we can help carry the rest of this stuff out and put it in the car. Frieda, help me with these bedclothes. Where's the mattress, Julie, and the bedstead and springs?"

"Already tied on top of the car. There's not much to take, just enough to get along with."

"I got enough for all of us," Mrs. Starwood said. "I brought ever' last thing I could pile on the truck. The kids even got the dog. I'm all ready to tell fortunes on the way." She laughed and went out with an armload of quilts.

When the two came back, the older woman was carrying something wrapped in a cloth. She set it down on the table and raised the cloth for Julia to see.

"We'll leave the old man one of my pies, so he'll have a little touch of home for a few days."

"That'll tickle him," Julia said. "I'm leaving all the food we've got, and it won't last long. We can get some on the way."

"Where in the world did you folks get any money?" Mrs. Starwood asked. Frieda laughed at her bluntness.

"Milt finally talked the rancher out of a little cash instead of an even trade of our land for the car. We can just barely make it if we can get work right away."

"Same with us. If we stick together we can eat cheaper."

* * *

The old man and Milt came in, both sober and quiet. They greeted the women and then looked with astonishment at Frieda.

"You're not going too?" Milt asked.

"Yes, I am."

"Well, you're among friends," he said accepting the idea with no more surprise.

"Let's drink this coffee," Julia said, filling the cups. "It'll make us all feel better."

They stood about drinking the coffee, blowing on it to cool it more quickly because there was no time to waste if they were to leave before sunup. The room that had been overcrowded and stuffed with two beds and clothes hanging on the door was once more in order with a little space to spare under the thin coating of dust. The mended curtains were stiff with recent washing, the floor was scrubbed, the old man's ragged books and magazines were on the stand. Once more the sugar bowl, the syrup pitcher, the glass of spoons and knives and forks, the old man's granite dishes were placed in the center of the oilcloth-covered table under a clean flour-sack towel.

The old man drank his coffee and set the cup on the table and went out. They could hear him rummaging about among his things in the doghouse. When he came back the cups and saucers were washed and dried, and Julia shook the little girls who had eaten their breakfasts early, dressed, and gone back to sleep on the old man's bed. They got up, stretching and yawning, and the women helped them into their coats.

"I guess we'd better start, Dad," Milt said, picking up his hat. Mrs. Starwood and Frieda shook hands with the old man and went out. They could hear them rounding up the children and slamming the truck door, then the engine sputtered and started and the lumbering sound of the truck moved toward the gate. Julia and Milt gave the little house a last look and went out. The old man followed with the little girls. Outside they put their arms around his neck when he stooped to kiss them, not quite realizing the finality of their goodbyes. Myra began to cry and the old man could not console her. She clung to him, sobbing. She refused to get in the car. Tears ran down his brown weathered face as he loosed her arms and lifted her into the backseat where Lonnie was already squeezed among the quilts. He closed the door and pecked on the glass with his long bony fingers trying to make them smile. Then he stood back away from the car watching Julia and Milt tighten and check their belongings. A faint gray was coming up over the sky. In this ethereal light the prairie became vast, more immense, the whole plain seemed unpeopled and deserted. The old man had come to bear the noise and the living together, and now he stood about waiting for his life to fall back into a peace he would not find again. His hand was in his pocket and he kept rubbing his warm coins, holding them back until the last. Milt came around the car and stood looking at him, anxiety stinging his throat.

"You're a damn fool to stay here and starve," he said.

"I'm going to get where there's some people." The old man laughed dryly. "Maybe they're in the same boat."

"Well, you could die and rot out here and nobody'd know it."

"What difference does it make who knows it after you're dead?" the old man said, trying to make a joke.

"Well, goodbye," Milt said, putting out his hand, "We'll drop you a card along the way and as soon as we're someplace for awhile, you write. If you get hungry, kill the chickens, but try to keep a few to lay."

"Any more advice?" the old man asked, winking at Julia.

"I'm just telling you," Milt said and got in the car. Julia kissed the old man on the cheek and they shook hands. He opened the door for her and she got in the car, biting her lips to keep from crying. Milt leaned out the window and shook the old man's hand again. "Take care of yourself, you old codger, and don't let the coyotes get your bones."

"I reckon you'll own one of the big valleys next thing I know."

"Can't ever tell. I sure hope I get me a little orchard someday. Right now—anything to make a living."

The old man opened the back door and handed the little girls each a quarter. The coins had turned black from lying alone in a purse.

"Don't spend them till you have good reason," he cautioned. Before they could reply, he closed the door and stood back away from the starting car, looking at the little girls with the tears on their faces. Their lips moved, but the sputtering motor covered their voices. He stood alone in the yard with his stiff old arm raised, and the stern, proud sorrow falling down his long dark face as the car drove out the gate and onto the highway. The dog ran after it barking, returning at the fence. Myra and Lonnie waved as long as they could see him and he waved back.

"Well, Rusty," he said to the dog, "if I was a young sprout. . . . " Rusty's tail drooped and his eyes were sad with the loss of the others.

The old man went into the house, poked the fire, and sat down. He felt the empty room like a final grief. He stood up, lowered the damper, and went out. In the east the sun was showing big and red. A rooster crowed. The morning smelled of dust. He walked slowly to the chicken house and unlatched the door. The rooster flew out over the crowding noisy hens, and he watched them absently. Feeling utterly desolate, he tramped off toward the dry creek with the dog trotting ahead.

Part II

California

Twenty-five

The shadow of the car slid along the east side of the highway, growing taller, blotting the sagebrush and the cracked dry earth for one swift moment. Out of Arizona into California, the dark shadow fled like a black wing toward the Imperial Valley. Now and then it fell darkly on patches of yellow and purple flowers blooming close to the surface like moss. Jagging crazily through the great desert, the yawning, parched mouths of narrow gullies showed their sandy tongues. Chaparral barbed and scragged waste as far as they could see. Lonnie and Myra watched the fleeing shadow with a hazy fascination. Julia leaned wearily against the back of the seat, moving her feet from the floor to the front and back to the floor again. Her head was tied with a cotton bandana to keep the dust from her hair. Milt hunched over the wheel watching the long straight road ahead. The imprint of the cotton strap marked his shirt. Julia moved.

"You tired?" he asked.

"Kind of. You?"

"No, but my back aches. Damn cotton picking'll break your back," he muttered.

"I wish I'd picked now; we'd have more money," she said.

"It's too hard for you," he replied.

"Other women were picking." He said nothing. "Well I'm going to pick the peas," she said.

"All right."

"I almost go crazy sitting in the tent patching, cooking on that camp stove, trying to keep clean in the dirt."

"I guess you'll have to pick peas anyway," he said. "The kids need shoes and clothes or they can't go to school."

"It's warm," Myra said. "We can go barefoot." They were glad the hours of silence had been broken.

"It's getting warmer right along, but you've got to have dresses and underwear. Seems funny that it's winter at home now."

"You better write Dad when we get to Calipatria."

"Why are we moving again?" asked Lonnie.

"The cotton's all picked, why do you s'pose?" Myra said.

"Where are we going now?"

"Imperial Valley."

"Then, will we move again, Papa?" asked the little girl.

"Uh huh. They say we can't stay in that furnace after May," he said to Julia.

"Are we going to be like the wheat tramps?" Myra asked.

"Not if we can help it," Milt said.

"It sounds awful when you hear yourself called that," Julia said. "People who are hunting for work aren't tramps, Myra."

"Well, that's what they called us."

"Don't pay any attention," Julia said.

"When will we get there?" Lonnie asked.

"Soon," Milt said.

"I'm hungry," Lonnie complained.

"We'll eat supper pretty soon."

"I'm hungry now."

"Peel a potato and give it to them," Milt told Julia. She leaned over the backseat and got one from the burlap sack on the floor. Milt handed her his pocketknife. She peeled the potato thinly and cut it in two.

"Here."

"Let's play like it's an apple," Myra said.

"I don't want to. I like a potato."

"I'll play like mine is, then." They all fell into another silence. The shadow of the car blended into the dusk. The cooling air smelled pure and fragrant with sage. Through the quick dark, the desert sky became brilliant with great white fiery stars. The headlights of the Starwood truck came on behind them.

* * *

That morning they looked at Calipatria, an uninteresting prospect. The gray stone buildings squatted along the dusty streets like tough beetles. Under the shady colonnades of the desert town peeked dismal windows of shops and diners with placard signs for Coca Cola, beer, cigarettes. Lurking behind the colorless fronts of cheap drinking joints, Milt had heard, gambling houses plied their drab penny-ante trade. Once they all saw inside the windows of a clean bright restaurant, with shining tabletops and a long low counter, sprinkled with men drinking their morning coffee. The door was open and as they passed, the mingled odors of food clustered in the warm air, tempted their faintly excited thoughts.

"So this is California!" Mrs. Starwood said to Frieda, with a grim look on her wind-tanned face. "It looks about as bad as home after a dust storm. Holy Moses! This is a lonesome-looking place. I always thought I could smell the flowers and see things growing everywhere I looked the minute I set foot on the state line. Suppose we been hearing things again?"

"This is the desert," Frieda said. "But, they say, things grow here like a garden when they're watered. We'll see the irrigated fields as soon as we're out of town. We came in the dark, you know."

"Glad you come?"

"Yes."

"Even if you spent the tail end of your money on a tent?"

"Yes. It looks lonesome, but I keep expecting something to happen. I feel it."

"Don't go falling in love with some poor pea picker. You got enough troubles."

"It's not just that. It's everything. Going to strange places."

"Well, you got a right to your thoughts," said Mrs. Starwood. "A young person ain't got much else these days." The truck rambled through the edge of the monotonous little town onto the road between fields of cabbage and alfalfa. Ahead they saw the familiar gray tops of tents around a small water tower. They passed great pens of fattening cattle and pasturing sheep, shipped from the dry Southwest and the snow-covered mountain ranges. Growing peas and carrots and sugar beets and fields of melons stretched far away on all sides. Where the green of watered acres ended, the wasted desert abruptly went its way. Greasewood, rank and strong, grew in ragged abandon and littered the valley floor to the edge and purity of the Yuma dunes.

Ahead the Dunne Ford swung round a curve and stopped. The Starwood truck pulled up alongside. In front of them was a row of tents, marking one side of a large open square, hemmed in by three other neat rows. The two families looked at each other in astonishment. This was a squatter camp all right but it was something more. They read the small signboard nailed to a post, saying *Federal Emergency Migratory Camp.* There was no gate and they drove in. Milt leaned forward, looking at a smaller sign on the nearest tent. *Office.* Along the lower edge of the board it said *Department of Agriculture, Farm Security Administration.* He turned off the engine and got out. A small, thin man, deeply tanned, came out of the office tent. He raised his hand in greeting as he walked toward the cars.

"Looking for work?" he asked, smiling as if it were a stale joke among them. They relaxed.

"That's it," Milt said. "How is it here?"

"Not so bad, not too good."

"What's that mean?" asked Mrs. Starwood.

"People who came for the fall peas are still here waiting for the spring crop. Fall peas froze and they had nothing to move on, nothing to stay on. Starving, so we set up this government camp to tide them through. Some of them are working now. Peas won't all be ready for a week."

"What's the chance of moving in?" Milt asked.

"Fine. Do you want to rent a floor—three dollars a month. We ask you to keep the sanitary rules of the camp."

"We'll have to live on the ground for awhile."

"Got tents?"

"Yes."

"Good. Lot of folks haven't even got tents. See that family sitting out there in the car?" He pointed to a clearing beyond the camp. "Been sitting there for four days, but they'll get a grant for a tent this week."

"This is something new?" Julia asked.

"Had to do it," the man said. "These people would be dying of starvation and exposure. As it is, there's enough of them hungry. We can't do a lot, but what we can. There's such a need we can only help if there's no other way."

"We don't want no relief," Milt said.

136   "No, we don't," said Mrs. Starwood.

"Well, I hope you folks won't ever have to have any," he said kindly. "FSA isn't exactly relief, more like farm grants."

"No disgrace to be poor," Mrs. Starwood said, "but cussed unhandy. None of us people wants relief if we could get work. God knows, a man could earn more with working and be a lot happier. We've seen hundreds of people in the last few months and ain't a one of 'em wouldn't rather work his way, and trying hard to do it."

"Where can we go?" Milt asked.

"Drive around to the right and straight ahead." He hopped onto the running board and showed them the way. Back of the southern row of tents was another long aisle and a last row. "Second street," the man said. "Go on to the end. There's an open place." They drove back of the spaces and got out, beginning at once to set up the two tents and unload their meager belongings. Myra and Tessie took brooms and swept the dry hard ground. No matter how much they swept, a thin powder of dust remained. The man watched them for a little while, telling them the rules for keeping the camp clean.

Finally he said, "How about your food?"

"We'll get by for awhile," Milt said proudly. "Till we get work."

"That's fine." He turned to walk away and then hesitated. "The bulletin board's by the office. Growers list the work there." He walked through the row of bordering tents and across the open square. In the center of the square stood a tall pole with the American flag beating in the wind.

"Queer, ain't it?" said Mrs. Starwood as soon as he was out of hearing. "He's real friendly. I got so I never expected to run into a friendly face again."

"Somebody hold the stove pipe while I put it through the roof," Milt called out. Mrs. Starwood interrupted her thoughts and held the pipe of the low camp stove placed on the ground, near the flap entrance. Frieda was setting the lard can, baking powder, coffee, flour, and potatoes on a box near a small homemade table. The bedstead was put up and Julia spread the covers on the bed. They were worn and dirty.

"There's a water tower here, I see. I'm certainly going to wash these covers the first thing." There was a single spring covered with a heavy pad, piled with a few quilts in another corner of the tent. This was the children's bed. "You kids go out and see if you can find some boards to put under your bed," she said, and they all went out, glad for the excuse to explore around the camp.

Twenty-six

Food ran out before the week was up and still the pea harvest had not begun. Milt was driving around the county trying to find any kind of work, and always there were others doing the same thing and no jobs. The gas gave out. They sat around in the tent all one day without eating and were getting ready for bed at eight o'clock when Tessie knocked on the tent pole and darted her head inside looking secretly excited.

"What's the matter?" Julia asked her. Tessie came in and talked in a whisper.

"Don't tell Mama, will you? But I thought of something. The kids are so hungry, and Pard don't understand and he's been crying. You know that alfalfa field about a half mile away?"

"Yes."

"Well, I thought maybe you'd let Myra come with me, and we'd sneak over there and pull enough alfalfa for greens. We could eat them up tonight and nobody would know it. It's not stealing when you're so hungry, is it?"

"To them it's stealing, hungry or no. We'd all get in trouble, and maybe get all the rest of these poor people into it. They'd find out some way. They got eyes in the backs of their heads for people like us."

"Shucks," Tessie said. "I could pull a little here and there so it wouldn't show."

"No, we can't take a chance," Milt said. "In the morning I'll talk to the government man."

"Well, I'll come along and ask about us too."

"You go to bed and try to forget about it," Milt said. Tessie turned to go and as she went out, she stopped by the door and bent over a lard bucket. The lamp was on the table and the doorway was dark. She felt into the bucket and brought out a handful of potato peelings.

"Gee!" she said. "We cooked ours. You throwing these away?" Julia looked suddenly guilty for having forgotten them. Before she could answer, Tessie went on, "Let's cook them now. We could have soup before we go to bed."

"You can take them home," Myra said to her friend. "We're going to sleep and then we won't be hungry."

"Mean it?" Tessie looked incredulous.

"Yes," said Julia. "Take them." Tessie held her skirts up and put the peelings in her lap. She turned at the door and smiled and made a face.

"Gee, thanks!"

The next morning early Milt went to the office tent and knocked. There was no answer and he walked away looking around the camp. He saw one of the camp guards and inquired. The young man pointed to a low tent, pitched soft on the ground without sideboards.

"He's in there. Just go over and knock on the tent pole if you're in a hurry." Milt hesitated and thought of waiting, then he walked over. As he neared the tent, he heard queer smothered sounds within, stifled breath coming quick and hard. He stood there listening, wanting to go away, but he thought of Lonnie who stayed in bed because she was too weak to get up. He heard a man's voice, low, and another man in answer. He knocked on the pole. A man about thirty-five, with a scared tense face pushed back the flap. He said nothing, just looked.

"Is Mr. Woody here?" Milt asked.

"He's here," the man said. "Come in." As Milt stepped in, the man looked as if he had not meant to say what he had and spoke nervously. "You mind to see him later?" Mr. Woody turned and looked at Milt.

"Good morning," he said, and seeing Milt going out, he added, "Wait. You can give us a hand." Confused by the muffled sounds from the corner, and the conflicting words, Milt came back into the tent, feeling uncomfortable. The air was close. Under his feet the dirt was powdered deep. As his eyes accustomed themselves to the half-light, he looked toward the corner Mr. Woody and the man were watching and saw a woman lying on the floor, with only a battered mattress between her and the dirt. Her face was tight with strain and her breath came hard. Now and then she groaned and whimpered a little. The ragged quilt swelled over her body. On the stove a bucket of water steamed. He looked at the woman again.

"Maybe they'd take me in the hospital now—maybe, if we could go now while I'm like this," she pleaded. "It's so dirty here, I'm afraid." The sweat ran down her face, making it shine in the dusky room.

"They won't take you, honey," her husband said. "Mr. Woody here's sent out trying to get one of the state nurses. Don't worry, now, just quiet yourself." The woman looked at him, and for a few minutes she was quieter, trying not to show her pain.

"Dunne," Mr. Woody said, "could one of the women come over and help? Ask one of them to bring some clean rags and if she hasn't any, have her ask in the other tents. See if you can find some newspapers. We haven't much time." Milt was glad to escape the heated tent, glad to have something to do. He forgot his hunger and his hungry children, seeing the woman lying in the dark corner, under the sloping oily wall of the tent. He hurried to his tent and told Julia, then Mrs. Starwood, and after showing them where to go, he went in search of newspapers. In a little while the whole street had come alive, and women were rushing about, speaking to neighbors they had not met before, finding rags, asking for baby clothes. Milt came back with an armful of old newspapers and handed them through the flap to Woody. He could hear them spreading the papers on the bed. Mrs. Starwood handed out a small pail.

"Get me some water. I'm going to sprinkle down this floor." The woman was quiet for a long time, then her groans came loud and strong. A knot of people stood in front of the tent ready to run for needs. Tortured cries ripped through the air and stopped, leaving an awful silence, to be rent again and again.

"Oh God, get me a doctor!" she screamed. Then her voice rose, cold, screaming louder. "I have to suffer like this because we're poor, that's why, only poor! They don't have babies without doctors, starved babies they don't want. Where is God's wrath? It only falls on us. Even God is on their side! Do you hear— *even God!*"

141

"Sh-h-h, Virgie, sh-h-h," they could hear her husband pleading.

"I'm not afraid!" she cried in anguish. *"Even God! You* can keep on praying but I'll die *hating—hating something out there* that keeps us from earning our bread! Keeps me from having a doctor. I don't want to live no more like this! I want to die! God let me—" A shrill scream of pain cut her breath and when it was over she groaned with weariness and was quiet.

The agonized hours dragged on, her weak voice whimpered faintly, then not at all. They stood outside until it was all over, looking at one another, shaking their heads when there was a tormented sound of life.

"That poor Woody's had to deliver a lot of farm workers' babies when they can't get a doctor. County hospitals won't take our women 'less we been in the state a year. Sometimes someone gets in."

"Not long ago a girl who'd never had a baby before got so scared she just up and went there whilst she was having labor and said she'd have it on the steps. They had to take her in, but they sent her out on the fourth day, and her husband had to take care of her till some of the women helped him out." The talk began and sagged but it seemed to help them in their own distress.

"By golly, it's fierce, you know," an old man said.

"What we need is one of them nurses to come out and tell us about birth control," a tall middle-aged woman said. She smiled and winked at the others.

"It's no laughing matter," a young woman said, looking hard at the other. "But I s'pose that's something we can't afford either."

"What's got into you womenfolks," the old man said. "Ain't you got no shame?"

"Shame, your foot, daddy. We been learning a few things since the government's trying to help us out," the young woman said. There were busy sounds from the tent.

"I see most of you carrying pumpkins under your aprons just the same," the old man said. They heard a baby cry, weak and thin, and they all stood quiet, waiting. Mrs. Starwood came out of the tent for a moment fanning herself.

142   "How is she?" several asked at once.

"That poor critter's too weak to move," Mrs. Starwood said, wiping the sweat off her face with her apron. "When a woman don't eat, it's a time again as hard for her. Her knees got up and they wouldn't come down. It was terrible!"

"Is the baby—?" a woman asked timidly, and Mrs. Starwood interrupted her, her face reddening with anger and her voice trembling.

"That baby looks like a little old man, and not a pound of good solid flesh on him. It ain't his fault he comes into the world and then he comes in starved. It's shameful." She turned abruptly and went into the tent. The people muttered quietly and waited. Mrs. Starwood came out again in a flurry.

"The poor soul's got no milk for the baby," she said. "Reckon any women in the camp nursing babies could nurse him a little and keep him alive till we can get hold of some milk? He's all dried up; even his tongue is dry." One of the women came up carrying some clean, worn baby clothes and handed them to Mrs. Starwood.

"I'm Mrs. King," she said. "I'm on the camp women's committee. We can see about it, and try to get some fresh milk tomorrow."

"Fresh milk?" a woman asked. "That costs money. None of the kids have fresh milk."

"Well, we have to find some way," Mrs. King said. She and three other women spoke together a few minutes, separated, and went their ways. One of them got in a car and drove off toward Calipatria.

"There she goes," said a woman, shading her eyes from the sun with her hand, as she watched after the noisy car. "They been saving that gas to drive to the field with the first day of work."

"Anybody in camp got any meat, I wonder?" one of the men said.

"He's having a little pipe dream," someone said, and they laughed quietly.

"Well, now, I was just wondering. Thought if we could find some we could make a little broth for the woman in there, give her some strength."

143

"I got no meat, but I'll fix her something hot after a bit," the woman said. "She ain't thinking about eating now."

The tent flap was pushed open and Julia came out, pale and tired. Her hair was damp and sticking to her forehead.

"She's asleep," she said, smiling weakly, and walked toward their tent. Woody came out next, carrying a hammock of stained rags. One of the men went forward to help him.

"We'll go out in the clearing and burn these," Woody said.

"We'll take 'em," the man said. "You better rest." Woody looked worn out and sick.

"One of these days, I'll get arrested for practicing without a license," he said, smiling at them, as he walked off toward the office.

"Nobody else to do it," a woman said, and after he was out of hearing, she added, "None these other 'fficial men *would* do it either." She poked her head in the tent. "I'll sit with her awhile now. You get some rest." After a while Mrs. Starwood came out.

"Where's he?" a man asked.

"He's sitting on a box sound asleep," she said. "I never saw a husband stay around like that. He felt sick and I told him to come out in the air, but he was afraid something would happen to her." She lowered her voice to a whisper. "It may too. We've got to take care. She was brave, all right, but sometimes it takes more'n courage."

"Don't they get an FSA check for a month or two?" a woman whispered.

"Yes, but they're a small family. It's only $22.50 a month for everything, and they been here broke since the peas froze."

"Lordy, Lordy!" said Mrs. Starwood, sighing heavily. "I got to see about my kids." The other woman went in, and before Mrs. Starwood had got far, she came out, looking glum, her mouth in a tight angry line.

"That baby don't need no milk. He's dead." One of the women sighed.

"He's better off," she said. "It starved to death before it ever saw the light of day."

* * *

Milt was standing in the group talking to a sharecropper from Arkansas and a wheat farmer from Kansas. When he saw Julia leave and then Mrs. Starwood, he began thinking again about the food and made up his mind to see Woody. He hated to disturb him now but he had to do something quickly. The men had told him about surplus commodities. He would ask Woody for a card, but he would not ask him for anything else—yet.

Woody's tent had a screen door. Milt knocked and the man answered at once. Inside the tent was nice. There was a cot, a washstand, a crude table covered with papers, a portable typewriter, and a briefcase. Several boxes served as chairs. The appearance similar to his own tent made him feel at home. Woody was resting on the cot, but he got up when Milt came in. Milt could see he was exhausted and thought he had better get to the point at once. Yet, it was not as easy as he had rehearsed it in his mind for the last hour, behind his talk.

"Some of the men were telling me about commodities," he began. "I haven't found work yet and we're clear out of anything to eat." It was out, and he watched the man's face. Woody sat down at the table and looked up at him. His eyes seemed to be afire in his bony face. His hair stood straight up, dry and thick, and his hand trembled ever so slightly as he picked up a pencil and marked on an envelope.

"How long you been in California?" he asked.

"We just came in from Arizona last week."

"Farmer before?"

"I farmed in the Oklahoma Panhandle."

"Why'd you leave—dust or depression?"

"Both."

"The other family dependent on you?"

"No, but I think they'll be in too."

"Here," Woody said, "you can fill this out. Sit down." He shoved a double sheet of paper toward him, and Milt sat down and filled in the spaces. "Put the first names of your wife and children, and the ages," he said. "Put your address." Milt looked up.

"We haven't got one anymore. Calipatria all right?"

"Good as any. You'll be here for peas."

Milt finished the sheet and handed over his history. Woody was filling out a red card.

"The only trouble is," he said, "you can get surplus commodities only on Mondays and Fridays, and this is Wednesday. You can get them once every two weeks. They'll keep this card, and you give your full name as it is here when you go again. Here's the address. Got any gas?"

"A little. We can manage."

"Try to save enough to drive to work when you get a job."

"A fellow named Kent here in the camp told me he was weeding carrots and I might get a few days of work where he is. He gets forty cents a quarter-mile row, hoeing and stooping, and says it won't pay much more than for his gas back and forth. That's awful, but I got to try it, anyway."

"I know. If you do that, you better ride out with him."

"I'm going out in the morning." He slipped the card into his coat pocket. "I sure appreciate this." He felt the warmth creep into his face. Woody looked at him and nodded.

When Milt went out, he noticed that he felt dizzy. He stood still for a moment, watching the tents swimming in a gray blur, then they slowed, and settled back into their places. The noon sun was warm. The camp was quiet, and he wondered how many more of the hundreds of families were secreting their hunger behind the tent walls. Near him a woman was washing clothes. The soapsuds on her moving hands showed iridescent in the sunshine. On the west side of the camp, back of the tent row, was a pile of new government plywood for platform floors. Beside the lumber were several newly built toilets. Farther away men were digging a deep hole. If he had a little something to eat, he would help. His muscles ached for exercise.

Suddenly he heard the small picks and tings of an orchestra tuning up, then a burst of gay music. Unbelieving, he looked toward the tent the sound came from, and through the wide flaps pinned back he saw a boy of about eleven standing by a huge bass fiddle, seeming to pound the strings with his small right hand, bringing forth grave and wonderful tones. Below him on the bed sat another boy, about nine, strumming a mandolin. A young girl with her back to the door was playing a violin. Deep in the dusk of the tent a man played a banjo. Over and through it all the heavy, somber strings throbbed like a great heart. They

146

finished the piece and played another, and toward the last they sang, faint childish voices blending in delicate harmony. They played on, not resting, and Milt watched the small boy's pliant hand rising and falling on the responsive strings. He felt the dizziness again, swinging across his eyes and through his ears in time with the music. He walked across the square, hearing the flag on the tall pole flapping in the wind. He thought of the woman lying on the ground with her tense face looking up at him through the dimness. He thought of Lonnie, sleeping all day to forget her hunger. He thought of Julia and Mrs. Starwood forgetting theirs. He thought of the carrots tomorrow, the weeds in the carrots. He thought of Friday and surplus commodities. His mind was clear and light like air. Music wafted through it like a feather. He felt very tall. His broken shoes whispered in the soft dirt far below. *Lonnie sleeping Friday   weeds   carrots three feet wide   a woman screaming   quarter of a mile tomorrow surplus commodities   walking   music   water running   forgetting forty cents a day   sleeping   forgetting   forty cents   floating like air clear water running sparkling through the brain   surplus brain commodities sleeping   a feather of music tickling   this is my tent   sitting down like a cloud floating   music   faces   fluffy sound in my ears flying away.*

Twenty-seven

When Mrs. Starwood came into the tent Tessie had put everything in order, and the two boys were asleep on the neatly made bed. Pard was lying crosswise with his feet off the edge. His once black leather shoes were now worn gray, and the tip of one was curled back, showing his toes. Felix was smiling in his dream.

"Lord almighty!" Mrs. Starwood said low, washing her hands and face at the washstand. "Lord almighty!"

"What was all that terrible moaning?" Tessie asked, big-eyed. "Somebody die?"

"Not yet. A poor woman having a baby. I wish to heck we had some coffee, I'm shaky. Is this all the soap?"

"One bar left for the clothes."

"Well, that's good. If we could eat tomorrow I'd do the washing."

Tessie said: "Don't you think you ought to take a nap, Mama?"

"I will in a minute. My stomach feels funny, I want to rest a little."

"Frieda is going to help the women's committee. Somebody sent some old clothes from Hollywood and they're going to wash and sort 'em and give 'em to kids who haven't got anything to wear to school. Mama, a lot of the kids here don't go to school, 'cause they haven't got shoes. I heard 'em say only some baby shoes came."

"Well, I'm thankful you kids still got a few shreds hanging together on your feet." She let her heavy body down on the other bed and pulled a quilt over herself. Almost at once she fell asleep, snoring fitfully.

* * *

She woke up a half hour later because she smelled food. She threw the quilt back and sat up sniffing, brushing her hair away from her blurred and sleepy vision. Tessie was bending over the stove swishing something around in a lard bucket. The tent was getting hot.

"What's that?"

Tessie turned looking into her mother's face with gentle defiance. "Greens."

"Is that where you went last night all hours—in no telling whose field?" She put her feet on the floor and felt for her slippers, working them on quickly.

"Well, we can't starve!" Tessie said. "I'm not afraid."

"I've a mind to tan your hide, young lady. Haven't I told you kids time and again never to touch anything where we're working? It'll go hard with us, harder than being hungry!"

"How can it?"

"Stop your sass," said Mrs. Starwood. She walked over to the girl and slapped her across the face, leaving a red mark, which soon lost itself in the mounting color of Tessie's cheeks. She looked down for a shamed moment, then straight at her mother without fear.

"Hit me!" she said. "If it makes you feel better, hit me! We've got something to eat just the same."

"See you don't do it again. I won't have my kids stealing! What would your father think?"

"I won't do it again," Tessie said, "but I'm glad I did it this time." Mrs. Starwood looked at her hard.

"Pray, what are you cooking in that bucket for, when we got kettles?"

"It's our last lard bucket and I thought some fat would melt out of the cracks." Mrs. Starwood laughed in spite of herself. She shook the boys, and when they smelled warm food, they sat up looking excited, full of questions, and scrambled off the bed. Tessie wiped the dust off the oilcloth and set the plates around the table. Part of the greens she put into a bowl in the middle of the table. They all helped themselves to large servings and ate ravenously at first, then sighed when their stomachs warned them, and began again more slowly.

"Gee! If only we had some butter."

"Put some more salt and pepper on."

"Gee, Mom," Pard said, "can't we buy a cow soon? I'm dying for some milk."

"A cow couldn't follow a truck, you crazy?" Felix said.

"Mama," said Tessie coming out of her silence, "sometimes they give dried milk on the surplus commodities. Can't we ask for some tomorrow?"

"I reckon I'll have to, but that dried milk ain't fit to drink, a woman just told me. It's only fit for cooking."

"Shucks!" Pard said. "I reckon I could drink canned milk even."

"I reckon you could if you could get it," Tessie said. "It's high."

"I'm going to play ball Sunday with the boys," Felix announced.

"I better get something in your stomach then," Mrs. Starwood said. Pard had slipped under the table and she leaned over in her chair and looked. "Well, for land's sake!" Pard was feeding the dog some of his greens and the hungry dog was gulping them down fast. Pard laughed.

"He thinks it's scraps and gravy," he said.

"Mama, will they hire me to pick peas? I want to too," Tessie said.

"No, and besides you got to get the kids off to school and look after 'em while Frieda and me pick. Quick as we know we can eat, you can all start. You're not very late for the second part."

"Well." Tessie shoved her plate forward and stood up. "I'm going to take some greens to the Dunnes."

"Mercy, yes." said Mrs. Starwood. Tessie dished them, covered them with a cloth, and went out.

When she knocked on the tent pole Julia called out wearily. They were all lying down, but they were awake. The smell of the food startled them, and when Julia saw the alfalfa, she said nothing. They washed their hands and ate. When Lonnie had eaten her share, she sat running her tongue over her lips reminiscently, and watched her father seriously.

"Papa almost fell down," she told Tessie. "Didn't you, Papa?"

"I just stumbled," he said, keeping his eyes down eating.

"Oh, no, you didn't," she teased. He smiled at her. The color was already coming back into her cheeks. When they had finished eating, Milt walked out with Tessie. He put his hand on her shoulder.

"You're a good girl, Tessie, and you kept us from all getting sick. But you mustn't do it again. Remember?"

"I won't," she said. As she walked back to their own tent and sat down outside, she tried to feel guilty so that her promise would be for real, but she felt only a vague sense of having protected them. Maybe she did wrong. She had never wanted to steal anything, and this did not seem like stealing. Who were They? There weren't any big houses around where They lived. The fields were just there by themselves as if they were growing for everybody. She knew nothing like that ever happened, but where were They, those mysterious people whom everyone was afraid of? *She* was not afraid. But she would have to find out who They were before she could defy Them. She began to imagine ways of helping these poor people she knew. In her thoughts she walked strongly through tale after tale, finding out what they needed, giving them back their farms, giving them houses instead of tents, giving them herds of cows and gallons of milk, giving them happiness. She saw them without their worried looks, working in the fields, in the houses they had built; she saw them singing and dancing and laughing; she saw them the way they were now, and it seemed they were waiting for her because she was not afraid. Her mother poked her head out of the flap just above where the girl was sitting.

"Tessie, what you mooning around out here for? You pouting cause I boxed your ears? I never knew you to pout before." Tessie looked up, her eyes shining with her thoughts.

"Come on, now. I'm going to wash out some things and iron in the morning. I need you to help me." Tessie got up and went into the tent.

Twenty-eight

On Saturday night, the end of the first week of pea picking, many of the farm workers, unable to wait for payday, drew money and went into town for food supplies. Some of them walked in the streets under the dim lights, suppressing the excitement of looking into strange faces, glancing into shopwindows, standing on curbs talking. A few young boys and girls thought a long time over their coins and then gave in to their hunger for pleasure and spent twenty cents to see a Western movie.

At the end of a side street, Pop's Store was filling up with farmers and their wives. Milt and Julia were there, and Mrs. Starwood with Frieda and Tessie. The kids had stayed in camp to play "Run Sheep Run," because it was dark-of-the-moon. Everybody was tired, but everybody was happier because work had opened. And there was something about Saturday night. The store buzzed with low voices. People moved through the wayward aisles between the stands and racks, wishing extravagantly, buying providently. Tessie was fascinated by the careless display of fresh vegetables, their colors intensified by a tiny spray of water sprinkling over them. The rest of the room was jammed with food and household goods. To one side was a cooler of soft drinks, and beside it a little boy, drinking pop through a straw, with a man and a woman better dressed than the others. They were waiting for the little boy to finish his drink but they did not hurry him. He drew the red pop into the straw and blew it back into the bottle, making bubbles. Finally the woman decided on something and her husband removed a round lid, reached into the cooler, and handed her an ice cream bar. Then he waited for the both of them. Tessie secretly watched all this, and the sight of the creamy white-and-chocolate bar started the saliva under her tongue. A man she knew was standing near her.

152   "Who are they?" she asked, nudging him.

"That's Mr. and Mrs. Patton. He's a grower, one of the kind that lives on his place. Some of our folks have worked for him and say he's right nice."

"Are they rich?"

"No, I reckon not, but I'd say, got pretty plenty."

"Where are the other owners?" Tessie asked.

"Say, you're full of questions tonight," he said. "Why, some around here in town, but mostly it's a big concern called Hayes and Berkeley; it ain't nowhere and it's ever'where at once."

"Oh," she said, feeling confused.

"Satisfied now?"

"Yes, thank you." He walked away. She wandered over to the butcher's counter and leaned against the cold glass, studying the array of meats within. She saw a tray of fat wieners. *How much is one?* she thought.

"Something?" a voice asked. She shook her head. Her mother and the Dunnes were still busy at the grocery counter. She saw a woman and two large men come in. The woman was middle-aged and wore too much powder. A smear of lipstick marked her thin, youthless mouth. The men were wearing high-laced boots. One had on a good leather jacket, the other a bulging suit coat. They stood aside for a moment looking over the people. Tessie glanced out the screen door at the men and women talking in front of the store. She looked at the men again. They were big and well fed. One of them had small ferret eyes. The other had a flat face and his pale blue eyes seemed to be stuck on from the outside. She almost giggled. The woman who had come in with the men walked through the people toward a rack. Mrs. Patton was just finishing her ice cream bar. Suddenly there was a commotion in the store. The powdered woman was saying something in a high voice. The two men rushed among the people and grabbed a farm worker, dragging him clear of the people. The man with the bulging coat began to beat him over the head with a short supple club. The worker put his arms over his head and bent forward trying to escape. The other big man shoved him back and with a hard blow on the head sent him sprawling on the floor. The man who had shoved him began to kick him with his heavy boots. Women began to scream. Tessie felt herself

153

yanked out of the way to her mother's side. The sickening fat sounds of the club smacked the tense air. The men moved toward the door, jerking the worker with them. Farmers drew together in front of the entrance.

"Get out of the way, okies, or we'll give you some." The men did not move. "Git outa the way, you white niggers!" Suddenly the grower Patton broke through the women.

"What's wrong? What's the matter here?"

"This goddamned okie got fresh with my wife, that's what's the matter." He gave the worker, who was held tightly by the other, a blow across the face. Patton moved forward.

"I know this man—Martin, isn't it?" He leaned, looking at the worker, whose head and face were bloody. "He's worked for me—I know him—he wouldn't do a thing like that."

"Oh he wouldn't eh? Well, he damn well did, and he'll pinch his own bitch's ass after this, or we'll kill the sonofabitch." There was a sudden stillness, filled with eyes full of hate and scarcely held-back anger.

"Watch your talk!" Patton said. "Let him go!" The big man swung on Patton and knocked him down. He fell back among the people and did not get up. Patton's wife came through the crowd, screaming and crying and threw herself on the big man, scratching his face and pounding him with her fists. A diamond ring cut into his cheek before he could push her off.

"We all know what you're up to," someone called from the outside, and the door flew open. Martin's wife rushed in, crying and tried to pull her husband free. In a moment, the women in the store surged at the two men tearing at them and beating them, and the men struck at the women with their clubs, cursing and kicking. The powdered woman fled. On her way out, one of the women took time to look her up and down.

"Wife!" she sneered, and spat on the woman's silk dress. "You'd earn cleaner money doing the worst!" One of the woman's tilted eyebrows had got rubbed off in the scuffle and she had a peculiar questioning look.

The women were dragging the two men through the door and out in front. The farmers were angry, but they were trying to
154   hold off their wives, but the women were wild and furious. Mrs.

Patton left them at the door and returned to her husband, who was sitting up rubbing the back of his head. Her hair was mussed and her clothes were torn.

"We'll have those men arrested," she said. "I could kill them myself. This is an outrage!"

"Let's go out the back door, dear," he said, and she helped him to his feet.

The fighting went on outside until the men succeeded in pulling their wives off the two men whose clothes were torn and faces scratched and bleeding. As they were let go, they looked about for their clubs, picked them up and walked away.

"You can't even hurt the brutes!" a woman said. "It's a wonder they didn't shoot us, only we was holding their arms while the others gave 'em a little sample of what the devils give poor Martin."

"Great guns! Where's Martin?" someone asked. They went back into the store. Martin was in the store; his wife was bathing his face. The women began picking up things that had been knocked over and helping to put the place in order again. The Pattons had gone. The farmers got their orders and left for camp. Milt and Julia, Frieda, and Tessie had managed to keep out of the fighting, but Mrs. Starwood had struck one or two blows at the last, and her dress was torn down the front. When they were all in the Dunnes' car going home, and out on the country road safe from ears, she said, "Well I've heard a lot about them vigilantes ever since we came, but this is the first time I saw one in the flesh. A sight for sore eyes, I'd say. They even busted Mr. Patton, *a grower!*"

"Everybody was surprised about that," Frieda said. "But I heard them saying either the bullies didn't know him, or else he isn't big enough to matter."

"Who are these vigilantes?" asked Tessie, trying the word on her tongue.

"Hired by a big company," Milt said, "a railroad company."

"How do railroads farm?" Tessie asked in surprise. They laughed.

"Tessie, my girl, you just as well get over your ideas 'cause you'll never see a farmer and his farm together out here. It's different than at home where every man has his own farm. Here it's bigger than a factory, with the boss way off someplace sitting in a fancy office or maybe taking a vacation on a boat. The farmers do the hard work for as little pay as they can make 'em take, and the companies hire brutes to beat up men like Martin—beat 'em up and maybe worse. Remember how that big oil company in Arizona had their vigilantes tar and feather that poor devil?"

"Well, but what did Martin do wrong?" Tessie asked.

"Martin," Milt said quietly, "is a farm worker like the rest of us, except he's been here longer, and he's trying to organize us, make us stick together, so we can get better wages and live decent and work without being afraid."

"He don't even get paid by the CIO union, 'cause it seems they can't afford to help the farmers right now, but he goes right ahead anyway, working in the field, getting fired and beat up and put in jail. His wife says he's a good man and won't ever stop trying to make us farm workers see how we can better our lot and stand on our own dignity again." Mrs. Starwood sighed, then she looked hard at Tessie through the dark. "Mind, you don't go talking these things."

"I won't!" said Tessie.

When they got home, the camp was an ant hill of activity. Others had already arrived, and men and women were standing with Woody outside his tent. Woody looked worried. Finally the workers drifted away and Woody went into his tent. The light showed through the tent and they could see him in silhouette, standing still, running his hand up and down the side of his face, feeling his whiskers as he did when he was preoccupied. The tents were soon dark and quiet, only here and there the deep, scarcely distinguishable words of quarreling mumbled into the night stillness.

Milt and Julia were awakened out of the sound sleep of their physical weariness by loud angry voices coming from the direction of the camp entrance. Milt got out of bed quietly and looked out the flap. There was a light in Woody's tent, but no shadow of him. Moving his eyes away from the light to get them used to the darkness, he made out the dim outline of a car and several men standing a little beyond the water tank. He heard Woody's firm voice, and following the sound he saw him standing just inside the campground, close to the men. Threatening swearing came from the men, lowered now to a growling undertone. Milt breathed carefully so as to hear every word. Woody's voice rose in what seemed to be a final statement.

"Gentlemen, this is government property. I'm sorry, you can't come in here for the reasons you want."

"But, we're deputies," one of the men thundered.

"You haven't got a warrant, and I'm in charge here. I'm responsible for these people."

Milt turned his head and whispered to Julia, "They've come after the people in the fight. Woody's trying to put 'em off."

"Come back in the daylight and show your credentials," Woody was saying. Again there was a low rumble of talk Milt could not make out.

"You're with these scum. We ought to run you all out."

"That's fine," he heard Woody say, "but who'd pick the peas?"

"Say, you sound like a Red, don't he, men?"

"Yeah."

"You fellas want to wait out here till morning, ok. I'm going to bed." Milt saw Woody turn and walk toward his tent. The men got in the car and drove away. The light went out in Woody's tent.

"I reckon hell'll be popping in the morning," Milt whispered and crawled into bed.

Sunday passed quietly, everyone taking baths in washtubs and coming out in the sun in clean clothes. Boys and girls played ball. A young man played a guitar. Men loitered in groups and talked. Women sat in the sun visiting. A little dust blew.

Monday night when they came from work, nothing had happened. The men from town had not returned, and rumors were flying about the camp. The most logical one was that the grower Patton had filed charges and had petitioned for the removal of the chief of police, charging him with being in the hire of the big company.

After supper, to quiet the worried talk and relieve their minds, Woody called the people of the camp together in the square. He spoke to them briefly, explaining what had taken place. At the last he said in a strong quiet tone, "Don't let them provoke you into trouble. Remember that. This is the toughest valley in the

157

state. If you get through here, you'll be ready for anything you're likely to meet elsewhere. I'm not speaking to you officially, I'm speaking to you man to man. Don't let them provoke you."

"That's easy to say," someone shouted from the crowd. "What we ought to've done was to let 'em come in and beat the god-damn hell out of 'em. It ain't too late yet." There was a silence as everyone looked for the man who spoke.

Woody said, "Well, folks, remember what I told you," and walked away. The crowd began to break up. The voice came again and the people stood still for a moment more.

"See how they beat up a man for trying to organize us into the CIO union? Where do you think you'll get with these big growers going round like a bunch of goddamn zombies? We ought to get 'em where we want 'em now and strike the peas. That'd show 'em how to beat us up. Nick the sonsabitches' profits." Voices rose and fell.

"Maybe something to what he says."

"May *be*, but we ain't wanting any more trouble right now."

The man said nothing more and was lost among the others as they turned toward their tents or stood in small groups talking. Mrs. Starwood had been watching him, and now, as she lost sight of him, she prodded Tessie between the shoulder blades, making her turn round sharply.

"Be careful now, Tessie-girl, but kind of keep your eye on that loud-mouthed fella, and find out which tent is his, and. . . . "

"I already know which one is—his name's Williams. Him and his wife's only ones here without kids."

"I guess kids'd be kinda unhandy."

"What?"

"Never mind. Martin's wife was telling me in the field we better look out for that man. She's kind of leery of him. Now, you and some of the kids maybe walk around over there, or if you're playing just glance in their slop bucket and see what they throw out. If you can't see good enough tonight look tomorrow."

"I can see good enough now," said Tessie. She went after Myra and Lonnie and they played awhile near the Williams' tent. The garbage pail was to the side and light enough came from the next tent for Tessie to see in. Mrs. Starwood went into the

Dunne tent. Tessie left Lonnie and Myra for a moment and went in.

"Well, what'd you see?" asked her mother, in a low voice.

"Potato peelins, orange peelins, eggshells, and—"

"You see? Not many of us got oranges, but eggs! Well, that settles it as far as I'm concerned. Ain't none of us in camp can afford eggs, nobody buys 'em and we don't get 'em on surplus commodities. We been noticing somebody throws out egg shells and now we know who's got money enough for eggs, and to let his wife stay at home and listen to the womenfolks that don't go out." She heaved a long sigh and whispered again, "That Williams is a stool pigeon, a dirty rotten spy!"

"That's how Martin come to get beat up," Milt said.

"Funny they got him in the store. Wonder they didn't take him out alone."

"Well," Milt said, "I reckon they want us to turn against him. Then too, he never goes off the camp except to go to the field."

"Well, we're sure learning things," Mrs. Starwood said smiling. "Beats all, don't it?"

"We haven't learned enough yet," Milt said, "and there's plenty right here in camp don't want to know this much."

"Give 'em time," Mrs. Starwood said as she went out. "Give 'em time."

Twenty-nine

They picked the peas and after that all the work left was stoop labor in the vegetables, for which the companies preferred fast-working, and nimble-fingered Filipinos, the resident hardworking Japanese and Mexicans. The terrible summer desert heat drove the white men out of the valley, but these men could endure it, partly because they were conditioned to stand it, partly because they must if they were to earn a living. The need that forced the Filipinos into the scorching fields was the same that sent them to the loneliness and alien cold of Alaska, into the stinking, sweating fish canneries to work days and nights without sleep when the fish were running. But the CIO was in Alaska now and things were better than they had been. Through the fields, unionization still moved slowly, without funds, wrestling with the complex design of a vast and shifting population: great ragged armies of hunger-driven people, fighting a phantom enemy for the security of one day at a time. A man with too little in his stomach cannot afford to think beyond it. This was a useful private theory for the practice of paying fifty cents a day while there were no active humanitarians looking. But in truth, a man with too little in his stomach can ill afford not to think beyond that: he has nothing to lose. This was a nettling theory, unrecognized but fearfully suspected.

Two hundred fifty thousand people moved—moved north, moved south—with more people coming in. Through harvests, through heat and cold and hunger, sunshine and floods, sickness, birth and death, violence and fear, struggle and hope—ebbing low, fluttering upward.

The Dunnes and the Starwoods moved on. They moved on through the desert, heating up like a cauldron of static fire, and over San Gorgonio Pass, through the Coachella Valley. They looked at the Orocopia and the Chocolate Mountains, the Martinez and the Indio Mountains, and one high crest was white with snow. They gazed in awe at the dead Salton Sea, stretching for miles out of sight, its leaden surface showing blue in the twilight. They moved on, past the date-palm ranches in the desert— then going higher into the green country again, through almond groves, apricot lanes, orange and lemon trees, they took long breaths of the high air heavy, intoxicating, fragrant with blossoms. Here were the tall trees, the Spanish names on signs, the tenderness and gentleness of spring.

A few miles on were the cherry trees, ripe and waiting.

Thirty

J uly was coming, and the long drive north to find the fruit, Yolo County, and apricots. Thousands were coming in. The squatter camps were filling up.

The summer heat was warm and soft in the nostrils, sweet with the almost imperceptible odor of fruit hanging ripe on the trees. The green earth was rolling and beautiful, and far off they saw the mountains rising to their cool summits. Here, in the pleasantest of all crops, the migratory workers toiled to make their winter stakes. Orchards lay on the undulating slopes to east and west and north and south. Between the trees, along the thousand fragrant aisles, people moved with baskets and pails, up the ladders, into the dark leaves, working, speaking across the heavy branches.

Outside and beyond the trees, waiting, were the people who did not find work, who looked every day for odd jobs, who asked every day to pick fruit, who lived with the fear of winter, and slept every night with this fear tramping up and down in their dreams.

Thirty-one

They moved on again, into August and September, into Butte County and peaches.

Some of the camps spread their ragtowns along the banks of Feather River, among the cottonwoods, poplars, and live oaks. Here was the chance to make some money, to be sure of winter. No matter how much they pinched and saved, there was not much money left, perhaps none, when the apricots were picked and they had to move on. But here somehow it seemed a little better. The people who could not find work moved into an abandoned apple orchard along the river, and they cooked green apples. They suffered from dysentery from the green apples, but this was better than hunger. And something good happened: for one reason or another, none of the women got with child. They thought it was the dysentery. They were all glad, but some of the men, even in their relief, became suspicious of green apples. They made poles and fished in Feather River, and sometimes they caught a catfish or a carp or a perch, and afterward the air was appetizing with the smell of frying fish and boiled-over coffee and apples being stewed. Someone got brave and cooked a frog, and then everyone was eating frogs. One of the men who had been to France in the world war began asking *Parley-voo Fran-say?* and in a little while it was all over camp, and everybody was greeting everybody else with *Parley-voo Fran-say?* They laughed a lot about eating the frogs.

Life was better, but it was still hard. August was hot and the hard beds were not forgotten in the breathless nights. In September the days were warm and gentle, the nights were cool and strangely fragrant with the subtle change of season. Now, when the coolness came, it was good to smell but it hinted of winter after the autumn. The peaches were hauled away to the canneries, and there was nothing left but the prunes. They stayed in the prunes, the Dunnes and Starwoods and others. Men wielded huge sledgehammers covered with heavy rubber so they would not injure the trees. Their wives and children stooped under the trees, gathering prunes all day, putting them in boxes. The boxes were big. They weighed thirty or forty pounds, and the pay was two cents a box. There was no other way. The whole family had to work in the prunes if they were to make even two dollars a day.

It was time for school and yet the children were needed to pick up the prunes. But school was important. It might give the children a weapon against this destiny that nipped at the heels of their parents in their desperate flight halfway across America, and up and down, down and up this long Pacific coast.

At school, after their parents put the new word in their minds, the California children addressed the farm worker boys and girls as "okies." Bitterness was a new taste in their hungry mouths and their wondering hearts, and they drew together in pride and accepted the barrier, but with a question. This question, this pain would live in their minds forever, insoluble. When they washed their feet at night, bending low over the small pans, seeing the toes come up clean through the brown water, clean for school, the remembered hurts flew in and out their troubled hearts like little birds wanting to settle. *"Okie." Okie? Okie! An okie. Something bad? An okie is me. Why does it hurt? It is only a little word, as little as my littlest toe. Why does it make me feel all by myself? And sad? "Okie" is a funny word, and an okie is me. Someone different. Someone not as good.*

Thirty-two

The first week in November they were on the road again. Their backs were sore from picking up prunes, and for the first time in her life, Mrs. Starwood mentioned guiltily that she might be getting old. When she caught the look of wonder and unbelief in her children's faces, she felt ashamed, but the burden of this thinking was too heavy in her mind to thrust aside at once. She spoke again, half to Frieda, half to the children, "This kind of life makes you old before your time. It ain't the work so much as the worry. When I'm too old to work, I'll be dead."

"What does she mean?" Pard asked Tessie, watching his mother's unsmiling eyes.

"I mean it's better to wear out than rust out," Mrs. Starwood said. "I mean there's a lot of work left in me yet." They looked at her face, which in repose showed the years more than her laughter permitted. They had never looked at her so closely before, and she suddenly looked like a stranger to them, a stranger who resembled their mother. If "the dickens" would only come back in her eyes. If she would laugh aloud, or scold them, they would know her again. If she would only "gape" and pat her mouth with her hand making a singsong noise.

"Get a move on now, before I skin you all alive!" She waved her arms at them. They turned, feeling better, but there was no place to go until they were settled once again.

Frieda drew her right hand from her faded overall pocket and smoothed it over her cheeks. She felt the firm line under her chin. Her lips were dry and she moistened them. Her blond hair was sunburned.

"Do you think I'm looking old?" she asked solemnly. "Look at me in the sun. Are there any big wrinkles yet?"

Mrs. Starwood snorted a laugh. "You look better'n before. What do you care for a few little crows-feet? If you meet the right man, he won't care two cents." Frieda would not have mentioned it, but now that Mrs. Starwood had answered her thoughts, she felt bolder.

"I wish I could get married before I'm too old to have some kids," she said. "I used to want to do something with my life, but now it seems if I could even get a husband, I'd be satisfied."

"What more do you want, child?" Mrs. Starwood asked in surprise. "You'll have your hands full getting a husband these days. One of the nicest things in the world is to have somebody to sleep by ever' night. Lord almighty, sometimes I feel so lonesome for Ned I don't know what to do. I get to thinking about him dead and gone forever, and when you think long enough about being dead, you run into nothing. Did you ever try to think what nothing is, just to imagine nothing? It's scary!"

"No," Frieda said, "but if I try to imagine next year or the next, that's scary enough."

"Well, Anna's married now. Someday you'll be too. She's lucky Max's got such good folks since they have to live with them for a time."

"Do you really think I'll ever get a husband?" Frieda did not want to leave the subject until she felt some assurance.

"Honey, God almighty hisself couldn't guarantee a husband now, I reckon. But if you can earn half the living I don't see why not."

"I don't mind it," she said, "if I can get the work."

"We got that settled, now all we got to find is the man! Wonder if the poor critters know how we have to scheme behind their backs to try to get a little love and affection." They both laughed a little.

"I hope I won't really have to scheme," Frieda said.

"Won't hurt to learn, it'll come in handy afterward, if you don't get a real good one."

Thirty-three

A silver airplane sparkled in the afternoon sky, flying lazily, slanting like an arrowhead down to earth, landing at the municipal airport. The breeze that fluttered the windsock gently westward blew into the car windows against their warm tired faces, cooling their cheeks, lifting them momentarily from their monotonous lethargy. They watched the plane. It bumped along the runway and came to an easy stop, not far from them. This was their first time to be close to a plane; it looked huge and wonderful and made their hearts beat harder almost as if they had come down in it.

"Not much farther, now," Milt said. "A couple of hours past the airport, the man said. See, there's already a small cotton field over there." They had eyes only for the plane, and he slowed the car and watched it too.

"Maybe if we could all fly away in that, we wouldn't have to worry about anything," Myra said.

"You can't get out of things that easy," Milt said, "but I'd sure like to get up in the air once."

"I wouldn't," Julia said. "I'm afraid of them."

"Would they take us, Papa, if we said we wanted to fly? It'd be like riding a big hawk. Would they?"

"No, Lonnie, it costs money," Milt told her.

"Gee." She said disappointed. "Everything nice costs money and everything bad just comes for nothing."

"That's about the size of things, Sprout," Milt said. He glanced back at her quickly. Her white brows were drawn together in a frown. A lane of trees came between them and the airport, and the silver plane was far behind. Buildings stood out a short distance ahead. They took the road that skirted the town and picked up the highway again outside. The Starwood truck rattled behind them.

A sign said, *For Repossessed Farms, See Within.*

The highway ran along the lush valley floor between small ranches with fenced houses of quasi-Spanish architecture. Round green trees weighted down with ripe oranges grew close around the houses, and stretching beyond were the bare-limbed peach, apricot, and cherry trees. Gray-leafed olive trees hemmed the fruit groves, making a shelter from the wind. Farther on, they passed strange prehistoric-looking fig trees, their low branches twisted as if by an old and tragic wind. The small houses disappeared, and gave way to a landscape of tumbled-down barns decaying in the fields, their boards long ago weather worn to a leaden gray, and light slanting through the sagging roofs where the shingles had gone. Beside most of these barns they saw old cars, and children moving about the clearing, and knew that workers were living beneath their dubious shelter. Sunday quiet lay everywhere over the land. Grape vineyards took the place of the fruit groves, and as they drove through them, Milt looked along their perfect rows, thinking of wine he had heard about from the slopes of Italy. His thoughts clung for a moment to the vague romance of faraway places, and he wondered if some grape picker in Italy dreamed of the new vineyards in the California valleys. He remembered the Italian names he had seen on the warehouses just outside the town back there. Did any one of these men ever walk among the vines, picking the grapes with his own hands, remembering when he came to America a worker? A worker perhaps who yearned away from the work he found here for the vines he had tended at home? Did he ever look at the men he hired now and remember himself in them? The name of one of the largest owners of the California fields came to mind. It was an Italian name, and Milt had never thought of it before as any particular kind of name. As he looked at the vines, thinking of the men in California and the men in Italy who picked the grapes, he knew it was not the name that made the difference. It was something else. It was money, maybe—money enough to hire another man. There was something else behind that, which let a man get money enough to harden his heart and forget the humanity of man. Well, it was a strange thing, and Milt was not a thinking man. He kept his eyes on the road and his thoughts turned away from the grapes, and the web of questions they wove in his mind.

Near the culverts in clearings were beginning to appear small groups of tents surrounded with a litter of tin cans, dried branches of firewood, and old cars. The tents sagged into the dirt. Now and then scrubby children peeped out the flaps at the passersby or played dispiritedly in the bare yards. All along the way, single tents were pitched under trees, and there was something fearful in their lonely, unshared poverty. In front of one of these sat an old woman sucking a piece of food wrapped in a rag, moving her toothless gums in hungry rhythm like a baby. She looked at them without noticing, deep in her own thoughts, as if she neither saw nor heard the noise of the car.

The sun was low in the sky when they came to the next town, much smaller than the one they passed earlier. Here there was a large squatter camp two blocks from the main street. They drove alongside and stopped, undecided whether to camp or go on to the fields at once. Men and women were moving about in clean clothes. Children were jumping rope. In the center of the camp a hydrant dripped into a mud puddle. Two ramshackle toilets leaned a few feet away. Behind them a row of battered garbage cans enticed a greenish-black swarm of flies. This was the only open space in the camp. Here the children played, the younger ones pursuing one another in and out the lane of cans, waving the flies away from their laughing mouths. A tiny white-haired girl swung precariously on a door handle and, losing her hold, sat down hard on the ground. From some place in the maze of tents her mother heard her crying and ran up to carry her away.

Julia looked a long time at the children playing and said nothing. The campground sloped low toward the center.

"This'll be a lake when the rains come," Milt said, "and there's already too many people for the ground." He started the engine.

* * *

Outside this town again, the surroundings grew more dismal. There were few trees, the cotton fields lay about them for miles. Over to the east the mountains made a wall around the valley. The tallest ones were crested with snow, the second range showed purple. The mountains looked impassable, inviolate, and made a barrier between California and home. They passed groups of corrugated tin huts bearing the Hayes and Berkeley company

169

sign, and a formidable board near the driveway that said, *No Trespassing*. Workers in clean shirts and overalls sat about the yards. Finally they came to one building with a sign out that said, *Men*. Milt slowed the car.

"Quick as they see my license tag they'll cut the wages in two. They know newcomers ain't wise and need something to eat in a hurry." He turned off the motor and got out. "Well, I'll try to stall a little."

"Don't stall so much we don't get a job," Julia cautioned him in a low voice.

"From the people we've seen around here it won't do much good anyway, unless they're too weak to pick." He crossed the ditch and went up the two steps into the land company shack marked Office. Mrs. Starwood and Frieda followed him. The people in the yard watched them quietly.

"Where's this?" asked Lonnie.

"Be quiet, just wait till they come back." The little girls began to whisper. Julia noticed with relief another dripping hydrant here. Through the open door of a hut, she saw a light bulb swinging from the ceiling.

After what seemed a long time, Mrs. Starwood and Frieda came out, then Milt. He got in the car without speaking and swerved the car into the drive and circled the camp coming up into a space beside one of the tin huts. Julia waited.

"Seventy-five cents a hundred, and six dollars a month for lights," he said without expression.

"Six dollars!"

"Six flat. You have to live in a shack, so you have to take 'em. Won't do any good to look around. Two companies, Hayes and Berkeley and the Harvey Land Company, they own the fields, and they both charge you for the lights. What can you do?"

"Nothing, I suppose, but it's robbery. This is worse than the other ways they get us."

"Well, that's life. We better get unpacked before dark."

"What about them?" Julia nodded toward the Starwoods' truck.

"They both got work. I hate to see a woman picking cotton. It's hard enough on a man."

"Where's the school?"

"They can catch the school bus at the corner quarter of a mile down."

"Well, that's something," Julia said.

"You know what that bastard said to me when I asked him about the school? He said that over in the next county they forced the government to build a school for the migrants, and the town people 'round here're trying to do the same. He said they don't like their kids mixing."

"What did you say?"

"I said 'it's too damn bad' to myself, but I just kept still. We got to have work." He was silent a moment. "They sure hate us."

"Frieda was telling about a bunch of club women who want to have us all sterilized," Julia said.

"Yow, they want to fix us like horses. Just good for work."

"It makes you feel queer being in a place where everybody hates you."

"It makes you desperate sometimes. I felt desperate when he said they don't like their kids mixing. I could tell he thought so too, the damned bootlicker."

"Let them talk. Our kids are as good as theirs, and they're clean when we have soap and water." They got too busy with putting up the tent to talk anymore. The cotton grew right up to the camp.

"When the cotton's all picked," Julia said, "I'll pick a little scrub at night for a new quilt, if I can. Our covers are all worn out."

When they had the stove up and the beds ready, Julia fried a pan of potatoes for supper, and soon after they went to sleep.

Thirty-four

They had just finished the third day of picking and were getting up from the supper table when someone knocked on the door. Julia hurriedly cleared the oilcloth and piled the dishes into a pan, while Milt went to the door. The camp manager stood outside in the heavy autumn darkness.

"Come in, Mr. Hinkle," Milt said and stood aside to let the big man in. Hinkle pushed his hat to the back of his head but did not take it off. Milt shoved a chair toward him and sat down on the bed. Julia nodded hello and kept on with her work. The children sat at the table still, not knowing what to do in the presence of this man. Milt was tired. He made no attempt to open the conversation. *Let him come to whatever he wants and go on about his business,* he thought.

"Just checking over your picking," he said. "How much you figure you can get up to?"

"First day," Milt said, "I only picked two hundred pounds, but I hadn't picked for some time. Next day two hundred fifty and today I got up to near three hundred. Pretty hard day though."

"Wife picked before?" He gave Julia a slow appraising glance.

"She ain't strong enough," Milt said, as if that ended the conversation.

"We got a rule here in camp, you remember? To live in the cabin, you gotta average nine hundred pounds a day. Women usually always pick with the men." He glanced at Julia again.

"Well, she ain't going to pick," Milt said. "And even if she could she wouldn't make nine hundred."

"That's right," Hinkle said.

"We offered to live in our own tent," Milt said, "but you got some kind of "sanitary" rule so's you can get the six dollars a month lights. That it?" Hinkle's face hardened, then he looked at Julia as if speaking to her.

"We want to give you something better'n a tent to live in. These houses ain't bad." He looked around the one room. Two beds. Stove. Table. Boxes. Clothes hung up wrapped in a sheet.

"It's all right," Julia said in fear.

"Sure." He stood up. "Well, mostly two or three families in the cabins. How about them two women both picking? They ought to make the nine hundred." He walked to the door and opened it, waiting for Milt to say something.

"I'll see 'em before I go to bed," he said.

"Okay." They heard him going to another cabin. Milt looked into a cigar box, finding his weight tickets, counting them again.

"These goddamn company camps!"

"Sh-h," Julia said, rolling her eyes toward the little girls. "You used not to talk that way, Milt."

"I know. I used to not live this way either. Why, all of us living in this cabin will be worse than Dad's dugout, and I thought that was about as bad as we could get without digging a hole in the ground."

Julia kept still, not wanting to raise his ire by any unlucky chance remark. He pushed his sweat-stained shirttail into his pants and went out. He went to the other cabin.

Mrs. Starwood opened the door only a crack and peered out.

"Milt. What's wrong?" He stepped inside. The children, standing about half undressed, stopped in their curiosity. Tessie leaped under the covers. Mrs. Starwood walked back toward the box she had left, leaving wet tracks on the floor, and eased her feet into the pan of hot water. Frieda sat on a box behind her rubbing her back.

"Sorry-looking bunch we are! Frieda and me's half dead; our backs are broke. I sure hate this cotton. Give me apricots." She sighed heavily. "Well, you look like the old nick yourself." Milt told her about the visit from Hinkle.

"Lord God!" she said, and her voice went low, empty. Her big shoulders slumped, and Frieda stopped rubbing. "Ain't we got enough trouble?"

"How do they expect us to sleep?" Frieda asked bitterly. There was no use to answer.

"That free rent is a minimum of nine hundred pounds to a cabin and six-dollar lights," Milt said. "Ain't nothing free but the air, and they'll figure out some way to selling us that before long."

"Well, I don't see no way out," Mrs. Starwood said, "'cept some of us living in the car, taking turns sleeping in the beds. Reckon we can put one of our beds in your cabin. I sure hate to crowd you folks more."

"That's all right," Milt said. "We got to stick together."

"I could kill that Hinkle!"

"That wouldn't do any good," said Frieda. "He's just a big piece of beef who enjoys his dirty job carrying out the rules from on high."

Mrs. Starwood winked at Milt. "The girl's getting her dander up." Frieda blushed.

There was a soft step just outside the door, and a slight rustling noise. They all stopped talking and looked toward the door. The children's eyes grew big and dark with fright. In the silence, their breathing sounded loud in the room and they tried to take long quiet breaths. What had they been saying? They all tried to remember the words in the brief moment they were waiting, suspended. All eyes watched the door. *Blame fool, I didn't latch it,* Mrs. Starwood thought. Quietly, a small green sheet of paper slid under the door, slowly at first, then sailed across the floor, catching on one of the wet footprints. Softly, the steps went away. They all relaxed, blowing their freed breath out fully. Milt picked up the printed handbill and saw it was written by a farm workers' committee explaining legal rights, the Wagner Act, other things, and calling for action. Mrs. Starwood stood up with her feet still in the pan, and they all gathered round her while Milt held the paper and read aloud. Suddenly he stopped.

"Better read to ourselves."

As they read, they smiled and mumbled part of it aloud. When they had finished and looked at one another in astonishment, Mrs. Starwood ran her worn finger along a line, and said in a low voice, "Better hours, better wages, better living conditions. All hours we can see, wages not enough to eat decent on, and two families in one shack! We got a *right* it says, made by the govamint.

174

The govamint knows about us." She beamed with her new knowledge. Then she took the sheet from Milt and looked it all over carefully, suspicion moving down her face. "You don't reckon it's some kind of trap?" Frieda and Milt laughed.

"No," he said. "See that D.F. 68 printed on the bottom? Well, I heard of the D.F. One of the government men started it mostly to keep the camps clean, and then so the camps would have self-government for their problems. Wherever there's some D.F.s in a camp, they have the people elect a camp committee, a women's committee, and the like. Finally, they got to putting out Educational Bulletins to tell the workers about the laws for them. This is number 3. This government man pays for 'em, just does it on his own hook to help the people. D.F. means Democracy Functioning."

"Now, where in the world did you get that mouthful?" asked Mrs. Starwood.

"A fella here in camp was telling me. He must be the one come to the door."

"What's it got to do with a union?" Frieda asked.

"Nothing, just hopes it'll educate the people to get in a union and protect themselves, I guess."

"Well, I never!" Mrs. Starwood had one foot out of the pan of water without knowing it. She sat down quickly. "Hand me the towel, Frieda." When she stooped to dry her feet she groaned for the soreness of her back. "Well, you can tell the world I'm gonna do something about my rights!"

"Now?" Frieda laughed.

"As soon as I can find out a few more things."

"Firing a single barrel won't help anything," Milt cautioned her. "We ought to ask for someone to help us get together before we say a word."

"That's right. But we can talk."

"Plenty of talk going on now, because of the nine hundred pounds and the wages. I've got to get back now. Don't leave that laying around. Goodnight."

When Milt went into his own cabin, Julia was sitting under the swinging lightbulb reading the handbill. He smiled but she looked up with worried eyes.

"You didn't do this, did you, Milt?"

"'Course not. I was at Starwood's when it came."

"People take such chances."

"It's the law," he said.

"You know the law here," she said scornfully. "Somebody will get in trouble for this."

"Well," Milt said impatiently, "we've got to do something sometime. People are getting desperate. If we don't stand up for ourselves, now, it'll be worse."

"It couldn't be much worse."

"That's what we said before, but you see for yourself."

"Well, just don't get into trouble, Milt, just be careful."

"You women are always worrying!" He caught himself a little guiltily. "You ought to hear Mrs. Starwood. She wants to do something." Julia said nothing more but started undressing and got into bed. Milt pulled his clothes off and flung them on a box and got heavily in beside her. The weathered rusty springs squeaked stridently as he turned over. Julia settled herself as quietly as possible, and in spite of her foreboding thoughts, she felt a deep weariness pulling her away into the great dark cavern of sleep.

Thirty-five

Lonnie and Myra were on their knees near the road absorbed in the determined journey of a small black-and-orange bug.

"Tease him," Lonnie said.

"I will." Myra shoved a blade of grass ahead of the bug, making stiles for him to conquer. He labored over the blades keeping firmly on his way.

"He must know where he's going. Or, do you think he just meanders and is stubborn?" The bug crawled onto a large leaf. Lonnie shook the leaf.

"Earthquake!" The bug stopped still, drawing his legs close to his body and waved his hairlike feelers tentatively ahead. The leaf was still. He waited. The quake came again.

"Oh, stop, now—you'll make him sick at his stomach!" The bug waited for the stillness and made quickly for the edge and onto the ground. They let him go his way unmolested, then they put more barriers in his path, each of which he patiently crawled over. They tired of this.

"Tickle his behind!" Myra twirled a small stem at his rear and he went under a leaf in fright. They felt ashamed.

"Come out, little bug, we'll let you go home. Come out!" The bug stayed in the safe dark of the leaf. Myra raised it and stroked his back gently but he was as quiet as a dead bug.

"We are giants and we've scared him half to death," Lonnie said sorrowfully.

"If he would tell all the bugs what we've done to him, they could hurt us, but he is just a little bug by himself afraid of us two giants."

"Do you think he'll tell them and they'll get us?" asked Lonnie in wonder. "If they will, maybe we ought to kill him. I'm afraid of him."

"Silly! He's only a bug, not a person. Let him go home."

Lonnie bent over him and whispered, "Go on, bug, don't be afraid. But don't tell the other bugs what the giants did to you." After a long quietness, the bug crawled away.

* * *

The little girls stood for awhile looking into the cotton field trying to find their mother and father but the bending, crawling figures under their flopping hats or sagging sunbonnets looked all alike. The sun was low in the western sky and the air was cooling.

"We'd better go in and start to fix supper," Myra said. "Mama won't feel good. Come on, Lonnie. You can peel the potatoes if you peel them thin—real thin. Tonight we are going to have a big meal. Pork chops. I'll make the corn bread and fry the meat."

"I wish we could have some meat every night."

"Don't be wishing that when they come in. Keep it to yourself."

"Do you suppose we can ever have a cake?"

"Not anymore. Maybe Christmas. The bad man will get you for wishing all the time."

"Who said that?" Lonnie asked.

"I did."

"You don't count. I wish a million trillion things to eat!" she said in defiance. They went into the hut. There were three beds now and only a path through the room to the stove and table. Tessie was sitting on a bed peeling potatoes. Her thoughts were far away and she kept her head lowered so that the younger girls would not speak to her. They went to work. The two Starwood boys came in, and Felix sailed his hat through the air onto Tessie's head. She looked up angrily.

"Want me to kill you?"

"I dare you," he said.

"Stay outdoors till supper. There's no room and we're busy." The boys paid no attention and lay down on a bed.

"You think you're something," Pard said.

"Shut up, you kids!" Mrs. Starwood said coming in the door. "You go to school today?"

"Yep, we all went to school," Felix said.

"Yes, we okies all went to school," Tessie said with scorn.

"Never mind, Tessie, never mind," Mrs. Starwood said tiredly. "You got high grades."

"Always never mind."

"Maybe not always. Things come hard for the poor. You have to learn it."

"I know it by heart. I could get an A-plus!"

"I'm awful tired now, child. Let it wait," her mother said patiently. She went outside and ran water into a wash pan, and they heard her splashing her face and blowing the soap away from her nose and mouth. Milt and Julia and Frieda came up, and Julia came in to hang the hats on the wall. Her face was streaked with sweat and dirt, and there was a bright place on her dress where the cotton strap had kept off the sun. She smiled wearily when she saw that supper was almost ready and stood a moment rubbing her back, then went outside to wash.

When the nine of them had seated themselves around the table and on the beds with plates on their knees, there was no other sound in the room than the sound of contented eating, with the final soft swoosh of bread over the plates gathering the last morsels. Even the children opening their mouths with some remark of the day almost slipping off their tongues glanced hastily around at the remote thoughtful faces and subsided into silence. Their eyes looked into restful nothingness; their shoulders sagged with the hard-earned peace of hunger momentarily appeased. The women's hands were as worn as Milt's, the skin dry and cracked, the nails thickened and broken, with ridges running lengthwise into the ragged flesh. Julia was more tired than the others, but her blue eyes, bloodshot and heavy, were clear of the pain that burned across her back. When he finished, Milt pushed his plate away, shoved the box under the table, and got his hat from the back of the door.

"I'm going around to the store before it shuts."

They scraped their plates of the small leavings for the dog, and the women carried their boxes outside to sit for a while in the autumn evening while the girls washed the dishes. Milt returned from the store in a little while, driving the car close to the shack. When he got out, Julia knew by the way he walked toward them that something was wrong. He sat down on his heels leaning against the wall and rolled a cigarette. He smoked it out to the thin twisted end before he spoke.

179

"Here," he said to Julia, handing her the coupon he had received from the company store in exchange for his weight tickets. "You can't even draw your own money down there till Saturday. Chances are there won't be any left. Half the stuff's twice as high as it is in town."

"I heard that," said Mrs. Starwood, "but I didn't pay it no mind. It's no joke, huh?"

"I reckon it is at that," Milt said. "Some of the fellas told me they get in debt to the store. They say they do the poor Mexicans that way all the time and add stuff on they didn't buy. We'll put down everything we get and the price and take our list along on Saturday."

"You were just growling about the Mexicans the other day working for nothing," Julia said testily.

"Oh, well, I reckon they work for nothing for the same reason we do. But what makes me mad is those rich bastards can't make enough sweating the blood out of us, they got to overcharge and cheat us out of our own money. It ain't how you save pennies that makes you rich, it's how you steal pennies. Pay 'em out and steal 'em back before a man even gets to feel his own money. I respect a bank robber more. He's got a gun in his hand and he don't pretend to be anything but a crook."

"That's what I say!" said Mrs. Starwood.

"Well, I don't," said Frieda. "I hate them both. The crook is more honest, maybe, but they're both parasites. Sometimes I think we're all a bunch of ninnies to let them live on us. That's the way it is, but they like to say it's the other way round. I used to think it was till I heard them talking and then I didn't have sense enough to know how hard it was on the other end. My Papa's just like these men only not as powerful yet."

"Sh-h-h, Frieda girl, let the past lie buried," Mrs. Starwood said.

"Well, it's so. I don't ever intend to go back there again."

"It's your own life," Milt said.

"What there is of it."

"You can't tell what will happen," Julia said, looking at Frieda through the dusk, knowing her thoughts.

"Well, I wouldn't go far wrong guessing," said Frieda. "Let's go to bed. It must be eight o'clock."

180

"Heavens!" Julia said. "I was going to do some patching."

"Too late now, if we're to get up before the sun," said Frieda. "Want me to rub some liniment on your back?" Julia gave her a grateful pat and they went in. Mrs. Starwood stood up, stretched, and gave a loud contented yawn.

"Button, button, who's going to get a bed?" she called out.

"Why don't we try sleeping three in a bed?" Julia asked.

"Pard and Felix don't mind sleeping in the truck, do you, boys?" Mrs. Starwood said bumping into the table. "Soon's it's colder, we'll have to anyway."

"We don't like to sleep with an old girl, do we, Pard?" said Felix.

"Naw," he said, putting down a *True Story* magazine he had found around camp. "But I'm gonna sleep in my clothes. It's cold in the night." Mrs. Starwood looked worried for a moment, then she saw the magazine and snatched it up, glancing quickly through the pages.

"Where did you get this trash?" Felix looked at the quiet little boy, who still missed following his father, and who worked hard like him at any chore he could find to do.

"He just likes to read a story at night," Felix said, his dark serious eyes reproaching his mother.

"Well," she said, and she stuffed the magazine into the stove. When the boys were outside, Felix tried a promise, which he wondered soberly how to fulfill.

"If you could have a book, what kind would you want?"

"Adventure," Pard said promptly.

Thirty-six

"Four people working and $6.75 a day together!" Milt said. He was sitting at the table adding up the weight tickets. "Nine mouths and eighteen feet. Nine backs." Julia was sitting under the swinging bulb making Lonnie a coat from another old one some people had left at the camp with a sack of clothes. Milt went over the tickets again, mumbling, and swearing under his breath. She no longer heard his words with surprise although she cautioned him about the children. There were times when the words came impatiently into her own thoughts but she bit them back. "Six dollars for lights. Cotton sacks dollar ten apiece. Groceries. Fuel. Work shirts. Kids' shoes. Four bellies."

"Oh, Lord, will you stop muttering! Do you think I don't know we have four bellies to fill, feet to shoe, backs to dress? Do you think I get anything fancy out of my dollar and a half a day? Looks like you could figure to yourself when you know I'm thinking about the same thing as it is."

"That dollar and a half must be making you feel your oats," Milt said, not looking at her.

"Oh, shut up! What can I feel about something I've never even seen? You make me tired."

"Well, it's not my fault you don't see it. All I get is my smoking tobacco extra. I sure as hell don't see mine."

"Stop swearing. You've lost your respect for me." He looked up from the tablet and did not say anything for a long time.

"No, I ain't."

"Listen at you," she said embarrassed. "You just talk any old way now. *Ain't.*"

"I ain't," he said stubbornly. "I've been going to tell you when I got around to it about feeling proud of the way you took to the work. I don't want you to have to do this picking again, though."

"I don't mind," she said quietly. He shoved the box back and put his hand on the back of her neck.

"By God, I'd like to live with my own wife again," he said, getting up.

"Don't show it, Milt. They all feel bad about it."

"Reckon they feel worse about themselves—a widow and a young girl wanting to come alive." Milt let his hand move gently down Julia's back and he felt her stir almost imperceptibly. He bent over her and bit her gently on the back of her neck and heard her breath quicken.

"Does my hair smell sweaty?" she asked, pulling herself forward a little, continuing to sew.

"You can't help that right now," he said, cupping his hands under her breasts and pressing against her. She felt him and felt the warmth moving in her belly and through her legs and centering. He hurried in the narrow aisle of space and hooked the door. Julia laid her sewing on the box. He switched off the light and held her, pulling her onto the bed beside him.

"We'll have to hurry," she whispered. "The kids . . . " The everyday of her life drifted away in the pulsing dark, and they lay buried deep, yet high and secret, in a moment of wonder, indefinable and incomprehensible. For a moment some captured wholeness seemed within their reach, but before it could be held and kept, it fled, fled into peace that flowed over them more gently than sleep.

Steps came round the house and someone tried to open the door, then shook it briefly. They forced themselves back to awareness, and suddenly then, they knew they had fallen asleep, and they struggled up quickly, feeling for their clothes, putting them on in the darkness, smoothing their hair. Milt switched on the light, and Julia went shyly to the door and opened it.

Thirty-seven

In spite of the time of year, the sun beat down, hot on their stooping backs, and the cotton sack dragged up a thin dust from the ground and the drying plants, already stubborn and catchy to walk through. Autumn comes gently in the easy temperate climate, with none of the pungent smells of decaying leaves or the sharp fragrance of a changing year. Seasons slip from one to the other with scarcely a natural sign. The landscape is always green, with here and there a grove of deciduous trees leafing and shedding bare according to their temperate habit. The midwesterners knew the month and the crop of every valley, and they knew that the mountains were green in winter and brown in summer, and they marveled at the fabulous land sheltered from the violences of nature they had fought at home.

Milt moved steadily along the leafy aisle, picking with precision and speed, his eye on the next boll before his hand had left another. He knew every way to save his strength, every move to cut short the time, and yet if he stood up a moment, his back would break like a green bough toughly refusing. His shirt was wet, and the cotton strap, which Julia had padded to keep from blistering, was rubbing the sweat in a stinging hot band on his shoulder and back. Julia was picking a few rows over, ten yards behind him. He could not see Mrs. Starwood but she picked like a man, weighing in with the best of them. Frieda, like Julia, picked around one seventy-five, but there were hard days when they weighed in two hundred, and they joked tiredly at supper about their speed. A tall Negro worked alongside Milt keeping the same pace. Someone worked close behind him on the other side of the row. Two rows over, keeping up with them but leaving cotton if he fell behind, was Seff, whom they all suspected was a stool. He tried to talk to the men and women next to him, but the warning had gone out, and no one exchanged more than civilities about the weather, careful even then not to sound complaining.

Sometimes he worked as if his thoughts were far away, but they knew he was listening for any chance word he could take to the boss when the day was over.

The man close behind Milt worked up even and wanted to talk. You could always tell when a man was trying to act natural.

"Whaddya say, Dunne?"

"Not much. Hot day." Milt knew the man's face but could not remember his name.

"Yow. Ain't no changes a year in this country. A man don't feel right." The man suited his speed to Dunne's.

"What'd you say your name is?" Milt asked.

"Snow." He spoke lower when he gave his name. Milt looked up at him, and Snow made a light gesture with his head and his eyes toward Seff. Milt glanced at the Negro beside him, who nodded his head once downward and kept on picking. Milt picked awhile without talking.

"Whaddya think of the seventy-five?" Snow asked.

"Can't make much at it," Milt said, not looking up.

"Either of you hear the fellas talking?"

"Powerful lot of talking over'n that end of the field," the Negro said.

"What's your name?" Milt asked him. "Mine's Dunne."

"Garrison."

Milt waited automatically to hear the "suh" and when it did not come, he was relieved. He had been wondering how he would say it, tell him not to. *We're both picking cotton for the same hand-to-mouth wages. I'm no better'n he is; he's no worse.* The memory of being called a white nigger in Imperial Valley lay in his mind unforgotten, sore, like an exposed nerve. Milt looked at him. Garrison looked back, his eyes straight, and there was no difference.

"Man, don't be talking too much 'round here. I worked here for three years. I know 'em."

"You're not in camp?" Milt asked.

"No-o," Garrison said smiling in a way that Milt did not understand. "We got a camp of our own three miles away."

Milt understood the implication then, but he dared not voice his sympathy in the face of this man's dignity.

"Say," Snow said, still in a low voice, "there's a lot of talk in the field. The men are getting sore as hell about the light bill and no cash till Saturday and then like as not they don't draw nothing. And the seventy-five. Whaddya think?"

"What do you figger we think?" Garrison asked.

"What's it matter what we think?" Milt asked.

"That's just it. I ain't just asking fool's questions looking for fool's answers." Snow stopped and picked silently for some time. "That sonofabitch cocking his ear over there. You'll get yours, buddy, ain't room enough in this man's world for a skunk that shaves. Whyn't you get a little ambition and go be a pimp?" Snow was talking to himself.

Garrison smiled. "He gets het up."

"Well, as I was saying," Snow went on sarcastically, "the men were talking about setting down around the field some morning. All setting around so's they can't bring nobody else in. It's easy as rolling off a log, if we all do it. We'll set there till we get ninety cents or a dollar."

"Jus' as e-easy as rolling off a log," Garrison drawled.

"Well, why not?" Snow demanded, picking fast.

"Not so loud," Milt said.

"Who'll take charge and kind of lead us 'case things don't go right?" Garrison asked, very low.

"Any of us. If we all set down we don't need to worry about no leader. It'll be over before your ass gets tired."

"He's long on strong talk," Garrison said to Milt.

"How many will do it when the time comes?" Milt asked.

"Ain't a man here satisfied with being robbed of his labor," Garrison said. "But most of 'em'll be afraid, and you can't blame 'em. Got to be *somebody* responsible. These poor men and women ain't gonna foller a lot of wind." Milt felt himself drawn to Garrison's logic, and still, the other fellow was right: if they all sat down, they'd get more like what was coming to them, and it wouldn't take long. Day after tomorrow he might be making $2.70 or even $3.00 instead of the top $2.25.

"What do you say, Dunne? Gonna hold out for a captain with brass buttons?"

186   "Not that," Garrison said unperturbed.

"Well," Milt said, feeling confused, "I'd sit down if the rest of 'em will."

"You gotta say yes or no; we wants to know, so's we can figger."

"Who's we?" asked Garrison, never forgetting to keep his voice low.

"Just some of us fellas. We was all talking nearly ever' night, and finally we agreed to find out which way the wind blow'd with the rest of you."

"These people ain't letting it go so easy, I'm telling you," Garrison said. "We oughta be prepared. I ain't agreeing without we have somebody to advise us. I need this job powerful bad."

"Okay. We'll set down with you." Milt looked at Garrison and saw his face was serious, worried. He glanced sidewise at Milt and shook his head slowly, then he went on down the row picking with deft quick moves, hardly looking at the cotton. When Garrison was ahead of him, it seemed to Milt he could guess by the tired stoop of the man's burdened shoulders that he was disappointed in him. Milt felt sorry. Somehow he wanted this man's respect, and suddenly he was not ashamed to acknowledge it to himself.

Thirty-eight

A strange white gleam shot full into an early morning sky and scattered the gray flocks of lingering night into vast wastes of air. Back of the Sierra Madre Mountains, the great red sun was climbing and suddenly, into the lonely monotones of dawn, a fiery glow dusted the crest, poured the wide valley full of warm light. They came out of the shack and stood for a moment looking at the clear lines of olive groves, grape vineyards, and orchards to the north, awed, secretly reverent of the splendor of the morning and the fruitful world. This was a part of life that was never old. The sun wheeled up over the rim and fast into the sky. The pure clarity of everything visible soon lay under waves of tepid autumn heat. Milt glanced around the camp. Workers were coming out of their shacks, walking quickly, feeling good in the freshness of the morning. There was a sound of doors banging in the quietness, and the smells of coffee and frying bacon.

"I could eat more than I got this morning, Julia," Milt said, smiling. He winked at Mrs. Starwood.

"Well, you may eat less before the week is out," Julia said, her face sober and thoughtful.

"More, you mean." Milt was watching the others. "You can tell there's something in the wind."

"'S your imagination," Mrs. Starwood said. "They act like lambs."

"That's just it," he said.

Frieda was trying to suppress her own excitement. She had almost forgotten the money it might mean in the emotion she felt at approaching a new experience.

"I'm scared," Julia said quietly. "I can't help it, I'm scared."

"You been through a lot worse things than this, honey," Milt said.

"It's not that. It's maybe we won't have anything for the kids to eat in a few days, living the way we have to from one day to the next."

"It's no joke, partner," he said to her, "but that's the reason we have to do it. Time to go to work."

"Well, it's a big day," said Mrs. Starwood seriously. "I hope and pray the Lord is on the side of the needy. Funny how we rambled around through all these crops and never missed a one so far—even counting some of the things they did to us. I reckon it's kind of the last straw with all of us."

"It won't be long," Frieda said gaily.

"You featherhead!" said Mrs. Starwood indulgently.

* * *

When they reached the field, men and women were still on their way, others were shouldering their cotton sacks, but by the time they were supposed to be in the field, they were all ready. The usual guards stood about. Milt looked at them for a sign of suspicion, but they appeared no more or less vigilant than they were any day. Then as the workers were ready to take their rows, they stepped back to the edge and sat down. Men and women sat down all along the field, and across the huge square of cotton, heads disappeared on the other sides. The fields felt suddenly and quietly deserted. Some of the men and women did not sit down but stood up looking at the others then went into the field. They walked to their rows and started picking. A murmur went all along the line. A man rose from among the sitters and not looking at the others went slowly into the field. A woman shamed him. He kept on down the row, his eyes on the cotton in his hands. A few straggled after him. As Milt rose on his knees and looked over the fields in every direction, he could see workers moving into the cotton, not many but a few. A guard came up in front of the men near him.

"What the hell you guys think you're doing? Been reading about set-downs and want to play set-down?" he asked sarcastically.

"Go tell your boss we want to send a committee to talk to him," one of the men said. The guard snorted and walked off.

"Those fellas are worse'n the bosses," a man said. "They don't love nobody or nothin'."

As the guard walked away, a woman began to sob loudly and ran into the field, dragging her cotton sack after her, running far

189

down the row, crying and stumbling. As she began to work, slowly, the others saw her stooping shoulders jerk with the uncontrolled weeping they could no longer hear.

"Matty! Matty!" a man's voice called after her. "Come out of that cotton! Matty!"

"I can't," she wailed. "I can't!" The man rose and started after her. A guard hurried over to him.

"No you don't!" he said and grabbed his arms holding him fast. The man's poorly fed strength was no match for the guard. He stood still.

"That's my wife," he said.

"None of my business," the guard said. "She's got a right to work if she wants to."

"You ever hungry?" one of the farmers asked the guard in a friendly voice.

"How can you work if you're starving?" the guard asked.

"We ain't," a man called out. "See?" The guard walked away.

Milt looked at Julia. She was still and waiting, her eyes counting the figures in the cotton. Someone beside her got up. It was Seff. He looked around at the men in a sad way.

"Fellas, I got a living to make. Something tells me there's gonna be trouble."

"Something tells you, eh?"

"We all know what kind of living you got to make, friend. Go right ahead. You ain't gonna hear nothing fit for listening setting here." Seff strode into the field as if he were sorry to leave them.

"He's a movin-pitcher actor."

"Handsome as Robert Taylor," a woman giggled. "Ta-ta, Robert!" Seff hurried along the row out of hearing.

"What do you figure a man like that's made of? Reckon he's actually got a mother or was just washed ashore?"

"Hard to tell."

The men looked into the cotton quiet like Sunday. The full white puffs hanging still on the brown plants needed picking. It was good to go down a row, filling your sack, reaching the end, starting on a new one, weighing in, knowing how much you could do in a day.

190

"You know, I can only pick two hundred pounds at seventy-five cents," a man said, "but if I could get a dollar a hundred I could pick two fifty or three. A man feels like working when he gets enough to eat and get along on. He likes it then. Yessir, I could pick three."

Along the line a way Milt saw Garrison. He waited to catch his eye. Garrison nodded and turned away again, busy with his thoughts. He felt cheered now that he had seen Garrison. They must have a good chance. No one else was going into the field. All they had to do was wait. Some of the men got up and walked around. They sat or stood in little groups and talked, but they had to be careful of what they said because they did not know the spies. All of them were not as easy to figure out as Seff.

Thirty-nine

Next morning notice was served on all workers in camp to move off the property or return to the fields. About half of the men and women went back to work. The others waited. Before the crop season, on the basis of stricter health rules, an ordinance had been conveniently and quickly passed prohibiting all squatter camps in the county. This meant that most families must live in private camps on the owners' places. It meant there was no place to go except the public road, and moving on the road called for gas. The women were urging the men to go back to the fields; the odds were too great. Before noon a rumor came that several hundred workers had struck on the Harvey Land Company. Hayes and Berkely controlled the cotton district; if they could keep their men in the fields, the others may as well go back. This was just one of the H & B camps, but over two-thirds of the workers in their other camps had come out. The men were cheered, but already those who believed it was "easy as rolling off a log" were beginning to realize the monster proportions of their move. Men suggested contacting a union. They wanted to be organized. They knew they needed advice and direction. They wanted a symbol to hold them together to meet the tightly organized farmowners. "Why didn't we think of this before?" someone asked. *'Cause no one tried to organize us; 'cause it would have been so simple, so easy if everyone had come out.* They remembered the spies they had joked about and scorned. Well, it was too late now. Something had to be done and quickly or they would lose. If they went back now, it would be worse for them. The prices in the company store might go up. Many of them were sure to be fired. They would be afraid to talk at all. There was no turning back. When the women saw this, they grew bolder, because each one saw herself or her husband fired.

"It's like walking between the crick and a prairie fire," a woman said, "and not knowing how to swim. We could go back to work but we might get fired. Might as well stay on the ground and fight the blaze."

"Who got us into this anyway?" someone joked.

"Our dern bellies, I reckon."

"Well, they're gonna have to get us out. How far can you tighten your belt, Monroe?" Monroe was tall and skinny, his belt always slipping over his sharp hip bones.

"My old belly," said Monroe dryly, "is already gnawing on my backbone, gnawing and growling."

"Well, we'll stay out today and maybe by nightfall we'll know something more. We got to talk to the ones that went to work today. We can get a raise yet, maybe ninety instead of a dollar, but something, if we can keep our feet warm."

* * *

That night after dark, Milt and four other pickers drove four miles east to meet the organizers. They drove past an unpainted shack that blended into the night except for a dim light coming through the cracked blind. They parked the car in front of another house and walked back. They went through a sagging wooden gate and up a cinder path to the door. One of the men knocked and the door opened promptly. Milt went in last, and back of the door holding the knob was Garrison.

"Evening, folks," he said, and closed the door, slipping the bolt across. He smiled slowly and pointed his open hand to the woman sitting at the table with her heavy arms folded above the red-and-white checked oilcloth cover. "This's ma wife, Phoebe." And he named the men. The woman smiled and nodded.

"You folks're welcome to our house," she said. "These're our friends here." Two men came forward and shook hands with the pickers. One of them was thin and stooped and ill-looking.

"This's John Lacy." The other was a short, stocky Filipino. When he smiled at the other men, Milt saw how his white teeth glistened and his small brown eyes danced over their faces in friendliness.

"This's Pedro."

They sat down around the table. Milt had a queer feeling filling him up, both exhilarating and sober at the same time. He was in the presence of something new, a part of something he could

193

not name. He was responsible to the men waiting back there in camp; he was under obligation, and the obligation stirred a great warmth in him. He looked at Lacy's bony face with the reddish whiskers sprouting along his pale jaw. The man looked dead tired. He wore no tie and his worn sweater needed darning in two places in front. He was smoking a cigarette and his roughened hand shook. He looked at the oilcloth and traced the checks with a little finger, holding the cigarette quieter. Mrs. Garrison looked at him sharply and started up.

"I forgot and lef' your milk in the kitchen," she said. He put his hand on her arm and pushed his chair back.

"I'll get it," he said. "Thanks."

"He's got an ulcer of the stomach from eating any ol' thing," she said quietly. "Besides being gassed in the wah. Those po' boys live something terrible. 'Bout like us an' worse sometimes I reckon. Union's broke too." The Filipino boy smiled at her, and she stopped and shook her finger at him. Milt noticed how neat he was in his cotton tie and work shirt under the leather jacket.

He seemed to be waiting for Lacy to come back into the room, then he said as if filling up the silence, "It is our opinion—the office—" he looked at them, watching their faces, his eyes serious and stern now, "that it may have been a mistake to strike now, but if we work hard and keep the men together, we can get the raise and a few other things—like light meters on the cabins so you pay for what you use." His English was precise and clipped quick by his accent. "We can expect to win, but we must face the facts that are against us if we are going to get anywhere." Lacy came back into the room and sat down.

"The first thing we've got to face," Lacy began, "is getting hold of some land. They won't let you stay in camp much longer. If we have a place to go, the rest of them won't be so scared to stay out. We're working on something now, but this whole country is controlled by H & B, and it takes a little time." He coughed, and while he was resting Pedro continued.

"The next thing is to talk to the men and help them understand what we have to do. We have to make a plan and try to run smooth, and know what they're going to do before they do it. Now let's get down to tacks." He began to question the men,

194

and in a few minutes they were all talking in turn, suggesting, questioning, explaining, planning. Sweat broke out on Lacy's forehead, and Pedro took off his leather jacket. Smoke lay above the table like a fog bank. Garrison talked in his slow, sensible way, and sometimes Phoebe spoke, reminding them of something they had forgotten.

"Yes, Madame Chairman," Garrison said and smiled. Finally she began to yawn and sat back in her chair trying hard to keep awake.

"Won't be much longer," he told her.

When they finished, the organizers left first, and after a few minutes the five men walked singly up the road to their car. It was eleven o'clock. They did not speak until they had started back toward camp with the motor to cover their voices.

Forty

Julia was fastening Lonnie's dress and giving her a final review before she and Myra left for school. The house was filled with the last minute chaos of children getting ready to leave. The boys stuffed their meager lunches into their overall pockets and yelled at the girls.

"Hurry up! We'll miss the bus!"

A loud knocking shook the door. Mrs. Starwood pushed the boys aside and opened it. Two strange men were standing outside. One of them shoved himself into the room. "We got orders to move you out right away," he said, and he appraised the crowded room.

"Well!" Mrs. Starwood said and looked toward Julia, who was staring at the men.

"You should of been out yesterday, so we're helping you." He glanced at the other. "C'mon, gimme a hand. We ain't got all day." He handed out a chair and the small things that stood in his way. Lonnie began to cry and buried her face in her mother's skirt. The other children stood back frightened. Mrs. Starwood seemed to come to herself.

"Go on, you kids, go on to school now."

"Where will we come home to?" Felix asked her.

"I don't want to go!" Lonnie cried.

"Sh-h!"

"Where will we come home to?" Felix repeated.

"The Lord only knows," his mother said, looking belligerently at the two men as they gathered up the bedcovers and carried them into the road. She went to the door and watched as they dumped them into the dirt.

"You dirty excuse of a man!" she yelled at him. "Don't you touch another piece of my things!" The men paid no attention. It was as if they were deaf and dumb.

"Go on to school," Julia said to the children. "We'll pick you up at the corner this afternoon."

"You sure?" Myra asked.

"Yes. Now, go on, you'll be late." She wiped Lonnie's face dry and gave her a gentle push toward Myra. Myra took the younger one's hand, and they all went out. The men came back into the room and, after stripping the beds, began to knock down the bedsteads and toss them into the road. Julia took the dishes off the table and put them in a box. One of the men reached for the table just as she cleared it. The three women took down their clothes quickly from under the old sheets on the wall and folded them into the battered suitcases. The stove was still warm. One of the men tried it.

"We'll go next door and come back after the stove," he said. "Got everything?"

"Yeah." They went out, and the women soon heard them in the next shack. They picked up the bags and boxes left on the floor and carried them into the road.

"Look at this mess," Frieda said sadly. "Everything will be full of dirt!" She began to shake and fold the quilts, piling them on the bedsteads lying by the road. Julia looked in the house to see if they had everything.

"Well, we'll just have to wait for Milt," Julia said.

"I'll back the truck out and we'll load what we can," Mrs. Starwood said. "I ain't got too much gas left either." While they were working, they heard a woman a few shacks away pleading with another couple of men. They stopped to listen.

"He's sick, I tell you," the woman protested in a thin voice. "He's got the flu, he's been in bed four days. He'll catch his death."

The men seemed abashed, but finally one of them said, "I guess there's nothing we can do. We got orders to move all you strikers out, sick 'er well. Only way is, I guess, if you want to go back to work, you can stay."

"No," the woman said simply.

"Well, then—"

"Can't you leave 'im till tonight till I could find a place to go? I'll move out tonight. I'll get help tonight. My sons'll be back in a little. Please mister."

"Sorry, ma'am, we can't waste any more time. This is our job."

"He's got a raging fever," the woman persisted. The men were tired of it. One of them went in, and she withdrew into the shack, and the other man followed.

"Poor old couple," Mrs. Starwood said, shaking her head in disbelief. They waited to see what would happen.

All the household goods came out first and were dumped in the road not far from their own. Finally, covers and a bedstead. Then more covers and a wire davenport. The old woman hurried out into the road and dragged the davenport to the side and raised up the wings quickly. One of the men backed out the door carrying an end of a heavy pad. The long thin body of an old man lay under the quilts. He kept his eyes open looking from side to side. The other man held the pad at his head. They carried him to the road and laid him on the cot. The old woman hovered around him, fixing the covers, piling more quilts on, tucking them around his shoulders and under his chin. She was subdued now, saying nothing more to the men, not even looking at them. They closed the door and walked back to another shack, not raising their eyes as they passed the women at the Dunne shack.

"Shame!" Mrs. Starwood said in a low voice. The men said nothing.

By this time, the men had heard what was taking place, and Milt came hurrying up with the others. There was nothing they could do, so they began loading their belongings into their cars and trucks. They stood together a little while when they were ready, wondering where to go. The health ordinance would not permit them to camp on open land. They had no money to rent a space in town.

"We can't do nothing but stay on the highway," one man said. "We ain't got much gas and can't keep moving much, but if we don't get too close together maybe we can kinda stop alongside the road till morning."

"I see some of our friends decided to stay," another man said.

"I almost stayed too," a woman said. "It's not easy just moving into nowhere. I'm sure sick of being on the go."

They loaded the car and once more they were on the road, this time with no destination. Other families were loading up, not talking, just loading. Cars chugged by from other fields piled high with hastily gathered belongings. The men who decided to stay in camp went into their shacks and closed the doors. The women did not come out to bid their neighbors goodbye. Everywhere was quiet and looked unlived in, but not like Sunday. The quietness was wound up tight like the alarm spring of an old clock.

Forty-one

Hundreds of families lived on the highways for three days, then protests forced the county to permit the use of a space in the country several miles from the cotton fields. The men who selected the small plot were careful to find sunken ground on the level valley floor, which would fill with water as soon as the winter rains began. This was just a precaution, a kind of suggestion that nature would make. Of course, there were other means of preserving the migratories as such. One of the most effective was a particular system of bookkeeping, ordained to keep migratory workers from registering and voting. All members of an organization of big farmers kept a record of their workers' car license numbers and the date they entered into the state. When a worker had been in a county for six months, by law, he could register. If convenient for the crop at hand, the worker was let out just before that time. As he moved on asking for work from other farmers, their records showed he should be on his way to another county. Unless he was fortunate enough to get work from a small independent farmer who had no such record or no reason for keeping one, he found the county an unwelcoming place. This discovery was no discovery at all; it was so commonplace as to appear unquestionable.

As the families pitched their tents close together, driving stakes, setting up housekeeping once more, the continuous walking broke the dry surface of the earth and left deep fine dirt underfoot, which rose up in a mist and settled in the tents. The floors of the tents also became soft and dusty; there was no water to spare for sprinkling them down. The health authorities put up two toilets in the yard, and little children were standing about waiting to use them. Mrs. Starwood was asked to head a camp committee to look after sanitation, and her problems increased.

Word came every day that the company men would not see the strike committee. Word came every day that the four hundred people still in company camps were being intimidated and would never find the courage to leave as long as there was no place to go. They would be driven out of the county, and what else could they find near but cotton? Winter was coming on, and in the winter the rains came, and there was very little work; and even if there was no snow, you could get very cold in a tent. So—there were still four hundred scabs, and it was painful to think of them as scabs because they were just like the others, but they were frightened. They were frightened because they were hungry now, but if they lost their jobs they would be hungrier, and winter was coming. Winter haunted them all because there was only scrub cotton to pick for awhile, maybe a few oranges now and then, maybe not anything. There were colds and flu and pneumonia, and babies being born and unborn, and school, and shoes wearing out. There were old men and women dying, and sometimes the young died before their time. Babies died. Life was just a little thing to them: a shrunken breast, a colorless tent wall in their curious sight, hunger without name and explanation, pain, and the dark. Sometimes in the short winter days, the mothers looked at old magazines and saw ads for milk and pretty blankets and lacy pillows, and insurance for your baby's education, and sometimes they found articles about how to care for a baby, and they knew why their babies died. They knew anyway. Often they wondered why their babies did not die, how they could survive without all the things necessary to babies in the outside world.

They had come now to think of the rest of the world as the outside, because they had lost all the things that connected them with other people. Well, almost all the things. They still had their work, which made a link between them and the outside—but the people who hired them wanted them to feel they were not needed. They all knew if they ever believed this, they would be lost, because not to be needed is to be isolated, displaced and drying up, a dead root. If they looked at the fields they knew this was untrue. The cotton was standing in the fields unpicked. And four hundred people could not pick it all before the fogs started rolling in at night from the Pacific, making it damp. Already the cotton was a little damp in the early morning before the sun warmed it, and workers could not pick as much as when it was dry and came fluffily into their quick hands. In a little while, if they did not give up and go back to work for seventy-five cents, the company would round up some hungry people in another place and bring them in trucks with guards, and the guards would have guns. Maybe the four hundred people would not come out with the others because they were afraid of being hungry, but they were also afraid to speak about it, to find out if enough were willing to let them win. Among the four hundred were many spies, and these spies were careful. They had worked before and knew how to act like real workers. Everyone was afraid to trust anyone. Everyone worked solemnly now, as if he had nothing to say at all to anyone else. No one had a toothache to talk about, no woman told another woman about her female trouble that plagued her in this new life, no man told another how he lost his farm back home. There was a great silence in the fields. The people were ashamed. At night they thought of their neighbors living in the dirt, without coupons to use at the company store, and they were ashamed. They wondered how those folks could live on nothing but they were too ashamed to ask one another. It was a bad time. It was a meager miracle how the strikers lived from day to day. It was a painful humiliation the others felt who held their fears in a glum silence.

But somehow it went on: one week, two, three, four weeks, five. The outside heard about the strike, and strangers came with old clothes, with food, with money—not much. These they left at the union office in town, a small dark room off an alley, and the young girl there gave a few men money for gasoline to take the things out to camp. If they could get to town, they picked out what they needed most, but the young girl was careful that everyone had a chance. They heard about people in other towns holding meetings for them, collecting money, so they would not starve—but most of all, so they would not have to give up their right. Maybe the strike was a mistake at first because they did not act with enough caution, but the workers would not give in now because they had suffered too much, because they had been threatened, arrested, jailed, and beaten for wanting enough to eat, and taking the only way left them to get it. All they had to sell now was their labor—this was all they had to withhold.

Would a businessman sell his goods below cost? they asked one another. Then, how could they sell their labor below cost? And what was the cost of a man's life? Enough to feed him and his family, to clothe them, enough for a shelter over their heads. Nothing more. And that was not much was it? Was it, really, here where shelter was only a tent and food less than enough? A man could want more, of course. But in these years, they said to one another, a man was lucky to eat and sleep. But less than that? No. It was better to sit here and wait. It was better to starve than to become the shadow of a man on this earth that could give him a full, whole life. It was better to starve than to become a sullen thing who fed his belly and slept in his sweat and forgot about his heritage. Such a man would forget his dream. And everything new was begun in a dream. Man's destiny suspected and unsolved would crash in the darkness because he was too puny to assert his soul. These words may not have been on their tongues because the stirrings in a man's mind can be wordless. The man with words is not the only man who thinks and weeps with the deep question of his being. Let no one ever think himself apart in this. Let him sit down and talk to any man and feel his shame; the unsayable things come out as clear and simple as a bell at night in every word he speaks. He wants more than bread and sleep; he wants himself—a man to wear the dignity of his reason.

Forty-two

Milt was in jail. Garrison. The two organizers, Lacy and Pedro. Frieda. The young girl leader at strike headquarters. And eighty other workers. At one time or another since the strike, at least half the men had been picked up for vagrancy or any kind of convenient charge and held in jail overnight or sometimes for a few days. It was getting to be a joke except when the men were beaten. In the first weeks of the strike there was an attempt to pass an ordinance to arrest any "loafer" who did not have the imprint of cotton-sack straps showing on his clothes and soil on his knees. But these intimidations, along with others, failed to break the strike, and the growers' vigilantes finally picked up the two organizers, beat them badly, and dumped them out at the jail, where they were arrested for disturbing the peace and locked up. Next day, when over eighty workers were at strike headquarters, two stool pigeons started a fight in the street outside. When the vigilante-deputies arrived—with questionable promptness—the workers retreated into the small office and crowded others into the dead-end alley. The deputies shot tear gas into the crowd and then into the packed headquarters. Some women escaped, but the whole thing was so well arranged that most of the workers were herded off to jail. This was a successful move—the strike was almost wholly beheaded of its leaders. Men and women would return to work for seventy-five cents, with no faith in the union, and no precedent would be set for the next season. Women were discouraged by the hunger of their children, and they went to work on their men in jail. This was one of the easiest strikes the companies ever won, because the workers did not have sense enough to join the union before they struck and to lay a plan. Monday morning they would all be back in the fields. The H & B men got drunk Saturday night in the Golden Valley Bar and told the Harvey Land Company officials how to break a strike.

"Next year when we get that cotton chopper out of Fresno, and in a few more years when we begin picking cotton by machine, we won't need these damned okies. There's not much a man can do that we can't get a machine to do. No back talk, then. Boy! What a load off my mind. I can drive up to Frisco for a little fun without worrying about the pickers wanting something they haven't got."

"Streamline farming incorporated, eh? How much you figure this strike has set you back?"

"Plenty, to break it, but it's worth it. These people've got to be discouraged from wanting too much. I figure we'll come out 'way ahead with that 40 percent reduction bonus we get from the government on cotton."

"It's the goddamn government encouraging these okies. Look at these federal camps around. Flowers in the yard, bathhouses, playgrounds, pretty little dollhouses to live in, washing machines! Pretty swell, eh? But who pays for all that?"

"Who puts California on the map?"

"You said it, who does?"

"Aren't we entitled to something? What I say is, these damned okies have never been used to anything but working and starving back where they came from. Now they come out here and they think they can put the screws on us because we got thousands of acres of crops and they're sore. It's a free country. Any of 'em might have had the same."

"You can't get around it, there's a class of people made for that kind of work the world over. Put them up and they'll be back down again."

"Yeah, but we have to look out now. They're trying to climb up, and those damn unions are trying to help them. We can't get to feeling too cocky because we're winning a strike."

"Let's drink to the mechanical cotton picker and forget our troubles, eh?"

"Yeah, let's drink to something. Everybody's against the big man now, even the government. Sometimes I wish I was a working man with nothing to worry about except how to eat and sleep. What do we get out of all of this anyway?"

The waiter set a round of fresh drinks on the table, gathered up the empty glasses, slid a towel over the wet rings.

"On the house," he said, and walked noiselessly away on his rubber soles. When he put the glasses on the bar, he looked back at the round table. One of the men gave him a wink and nodded toward the phonograph. The waiter fished about in his pocket with the tips. He walked over and studied the names of the records. He placed the coin in the slot and pushed the button on his selection. Soon the bar was filled with the loud and swaying beats of "Dipsy Doodle."

Forty-three

"I could smell the orange blossoms on my shirt when I took it off at night. Sometimes I just rubbed against 'em a purpose in the orchard so I could feel 'em and smell 'em deep. I love flowers—any kind of flowers." Mr. Burdick sighed and Julia looked at him. She smiled at the clean blue-and-white striped overalls and the clean shirt he had darned himself where the shoulder was wearing. She wondered how old he was. About fifty, maybe not quite that. "Yes'm, I always loved flowers, and when I had this little orange ranch just outside Visalia, I planted ever' kind I could lay my hands on, but there was never anything like an orange blossom. The sweetest smell in the world."

Julia thought, *I wish he would go,* but instead she asked, "What happened to your ranch?"

"Oh, I was repossessed. I hung on as long as I could, but it wasn't much use. I told Frieda all about it. She knows."

He's getting around to it now, Julia thought. The steam was rising off the pan of water into her face. The smell of the water made her feel a little sick. She sat down on a box by the stove and listened to Mr. Burdick. He told her all about losing his farm, losing the flowers, and the orange blossoms.

"Frieda is a fine girl," he said finally. "Sensible and clean as a pin. I like a clean woman, one that smells nice." Julia smiled and he was encouraged. She smiled to keep from talking because she was tired. He told her all about the fine trailer he built when he knew he was going to lose the ranch. "I used to be a cabinet-maker by trade, but no place for my handwork now. Well, I built everything right in my trailer. It's like a little home, pretty as a picture inside. Just needs a woman to set it off. I carved all the frames and I made the prettiest door you ever saw. I enjoyed using my hands again. Now, you take a girl like Frieda," he said.

"She'd take good care of it," Julia said.

"That's what I mean exactly," he said.

"You'll have to wait till she gets out of jail," Julia said.

His plump shoulders drew up slightly and down again. He scratched his knee a long time as if it helped him consider the problem. "No use joking, it worries me. That's no place for a woman. She didn't do a thing, and by gorry, here she is in jail. It's disgraceful. Not to her, mind you."

"This probably won't be the last time, either." Julia watched his clear blue eyes. She thought they looked as clean as his shirt, and kind of innocent, for a man.

"What's that?" he asked, perking up.

"Well, Frieda's got a lot of new ideas since the strike. She says if she's going to work she wants to know as much about her business as the people who hire us do about theirs, and that she can't sit in a grandstand seat and do what she wants to now."

His face puckered with seriousness, and Julia hoped she had not said too much.

"She can do anything she wants to, I reckon. I ain't one to argue with a strong-minded woman. Do you think she could like an old duffer like me?" he asked, almost fearfully. "I'm a pretty good man yet." It was dusky in the tent but Julia saw his ears redden. "I can work like a mule and try to make a living for her, such as we make nowadays," he added quickly.

The water began to boil. Julia got up and put a lot of pepper and salt in it. Burdick watched her intently. She let it boil and stirred the condiments through the water.

"What's that you're fixing to make there?"

"It's made." He looked puzzled. "Pepper tea," Julia said. "Didn't you ever hear of pepper tea?"

"No. You never either."

"Oh, yes, I have."

The canvas-covered screen door opened, and Lonnie and Myra stepped over the wallboard and came in. They were quiet. Julia looked at their faces and asked them about school. Lonnie's face was getting very thin. Myra was strong but she had dark shadows under the eyes.

"Do you like to go to school?" Burdick asked them.

208   "Yes, we do," Lonnie said shyly.

They helped each other off with their coats and hung them on a nail on the tent pole back of the mirror. Then they both lay down on the bed. Lonnie closed her eyes and Myra stared at Burdick. She made him uncomfortable. He did not know what to say.

"Don't you kids go to sleep, now," Julia said, "because you can both have some pepper tea as soon as it cools." They both sat up, waiting.

"Isn't there any bread to soak in it?" Lonnie asked.

Burdick got up. "I've got a little bread left, kind of hard," he said. "I'll get it."

Just then Mrs. Starwood rushed into the tent, her face flushed and her eyes angry.

"I caught her!" she said. "It was that Mrs. Westly all right. I gave her a piece of my mind she won't forget in a hurry!" Burdick hesitated since she was blocking the door and he wanted to hear what the trouble was. Julia tried to get Mrs. Starwood away from the door so he could leave, but the angry woman stood still.

"As if I ain't got enough troubles already with this strike, the kids hungry, Frieda in jail, and then this sanitation business, and one woman breaking the rules ever' single day. I set my mind to catch her today, and I sure did. Standing on the seat, says she's afraid she'll get something. 'We'll all thank you for that,' I said, 'but if y'er too nice to set on the toilet, then y'er too nice to have to.' I said, 'I'm the head of the camp committee,' and I just stood right there and made her clean the whole toilet. 'Don't you think I'm responsible for the whole camp?' I asked her. She just scrubbed and bawled out loud like a baby, but I wouldn't budge an inch." Mrs. Starwood puffed and sat down where Burdick had been. As soon as she was away from the door, he went out in a hurry without a word.

"He'll be afraid to come back now," Julia said.

"Poor soul," said Mrs. Starwood. "I mortified him, didn't I? Well, I declare, I was so upset." She glanced at the steaming pan of water, and then at the children, and got up.

"I've got to go see about my younguns. I declare, it's all I can do to keep from going to work if it wasn't for betraying ourselves."

"Me too," Julia said quietly.

"Not after they put Daddy and Frieda in jail!" Myra said. "We can wait."

"Well, I never!" said Mrs. Starwood and went out.

Burdick came back in. He brought the end of a loaf of bread wrapped in a cloth. He sat down without being asked, but he said nothing. Julia poured four bowls of pepper tea and broke the hard bread into two of them. One side of the table was near the bed, and the two little girls sat there and ate their soup. Julia and Burdick drew their boxes to the table. She removed the cloth from the counter but there was nothing under it but spoons in a glass, a bowl half-filled with sugar, and a pitcher with a little syrup in it. They ate without talking, blowing on the hot water and sipping it very slowly. Once Burdick coughed when the pepper burned his throat. When they finished, Julia filled the bowls again. She saw the tablets and pencils on the bed for the first time. She looked at Myra with a question in her eyes.

"We're not going back to school. I wish we could have brought the books home but they belong to the state," she said, explaining this last to Burdick. He nodded and looked down into his soup before her steady gaze.

"Why not?" Julia asked, just to be saying something.

"Because we're hungry," Lonnie said suddenly.

"We can't study when we're hungry, we can't play with the other kids at school who aren't on strike because we're weak and sleepy. We decided."

"Who's we?" Julia asked her.

"Tessie and Felix and Pard and us. We talked it over walking from the bus, and we made a solemn pact. We're going to talk to the other kids here."

"What do you aim to do?" Burdick inquired. Myra finished her soup and looked straight at him, then at her mother.

"Tessie says they're trying to starve us all out, and they think 'cause we're kids our folks will go back to work. She's going to organize us to quit school and people will hear what they're doing to us. She wants to be like Pedro, and Lacy, and that girl at the union office," Myra ended importantly.

Julia did not know what to say. Her thoughts were all on their hunger and what she herself could do. She thought of Milt in jail with the others and knew she could not return to work with nothing gained after all this suffering. Burdick was looking at Myra and Lonnie in amazement. Myra blushed and lay back down.

"Sounds pretty good to me," he said and nodded sidewise with a wink.

"That's the way Konkie used to do," Myra said. "I wish he was here. Mama, why don't we get a letter from Konkie?"

"He's getting old and he doesn't like to write letters anymore, I guess. When we can buy some stamps, you'd better write him."

"I will," she said soberly. She imagined her grandfather approving her now. She looked at Lonnie, who had fallen asleep. She got up and reached for her coat.

"Where are you going now?" Julia asked. "You'd better save your strength."

"With Tessie," she said simply and went out the door. Julia and Burdick looked at each other and laughed.

"This pepper tea is some idea," he said. He stood up and wiped his mouth. "I was proud to have it. I'm gonna try to catch a ride in town before it gets late and see what I can hear. If there's any news, I'll drop in and tell you so's you won't have to worry about your husband." He picked up his hat and dropped it on his head, gave the top a pat, and went out. Julia sat at the table a long time, looking at Lonnie asleep. *I do not know what to do,* she thought. *We have done everything we can think of, just trying to live till now. There isn't anything else I know.* She could not stay here in the tent just looking at Lonnie. She spread a coat over her child, put an old sweater on, and went out. She walked along in front of the tents and she did not hear anyone talking, no one at all. None of the children were out playing. The whole camp was quiet, quiet and still like—she could not even think of it. She felt afraid. At the far end of the camp, she saw Myra and Tessie come out of a tent and go into another. But they were too far away— she could not hear their voices. It was hard to believe that people could use hunger against one another. It took a long time to believe it.

Forty-four

The old man wrote about the first snow, the planting of the winter wheat, and his loneliness. He said he could not get used to the farm anymore without the little girls, and that he was letting Rusty sleep in the house because winter was coming along, and he knew he was an old man. He had taken to leaving the door unlocked and Rusty knew how to pull it open by a leather strap—just in case anything happened to him. "So," he wrote, with uncertain curly-cues festooning his words, "you can set your minds at ease. Max and Pete look in when they pass. A man can't live forever, but he can want to." He wrote that life was as hard as ever with them all, but the country was coming out of the dust. "Did I tell you the first snow fell? Some of the fields around us are showing green. It may take years to restore the soil in places but it appears that nature can right her wrongs quicker than man." He said that he better close and stand at the gate to stop the mailman because the flag on the box was broken and the mailman seldom ever had reason to slow down there anymore.

The little girls listened while Julia read. She put the letter away for Milt, and Lonnie and Myra wrote the old man and gave the letters to Julia to keep until they could buy a stamp.

"I'm tired of pepper tea," said Lonnie, who had been sleeping and was lying down again, feeling drowsy with the monotonous sound of the tent roof flapping tautly as if it would jerk free.

"Us kids should of quit school sooner and not waited till we're so weak," said Myra. When the truant officer comes we've got to be ready to tell him why. We'll get something else to eat then, Lonnie—maybe."

"You'll have some bread in the morning, honey," Julia said. She had made up her mind to go down to the store at the filling station early in the morning before they opened and watch for the bread delivery and take a loaf from the basket. She hoped the milk delivery would be left under the porch roof too, but that would be too much to expect. If she was not careful she might not even get the bread. Her heart beat fast to think of taking something that was not hers, to think she might be caught, and here her thoughts were lost in a frenzy of what Milt would say if she got into trouble, what would the children do, and what was the law for stealing a loaf of bread? It was shameful to steal from that poor storekeeper who did not have much more than they did. But the company store was always watched since the strike. She dreamed for a moment of taking the basket and bringing it back for the camp; she smiled to herself and tasted the bread for all of them. The fear was gone—the law was far away. Then she remembered old lady Kirkland's son. He stole four scrapped radiators from a junkyard and sold them in the next county for three dollars. He was arrested on his way back to his mother, who had not eaten for four days. He had a box of groceries in the old car and a few gallons of gas. When the FSA man happened by, she was almost crazy with worry about her son. She was weak with hunger and lying on the bed, the floor of the tent was mud, but she was crazy strong with worry and he had to hold her until she fainted. That was the day the famous writer and the photographer from the big picture magazine were along, so they went to the judge at his house and told him how hungry the old woman was. The judge thanked them and said he thanked them again because it was the first time he had thought of these okies as human beings. The writer and the photographer and the government man felt happy that everything was understood, and the people in camp felt better. When the boy came up for trial right away, the judge sentenced him to eleven years in San Quentin. Breaking into, stealing, transporting to another county. But most of all being an okie. But the judge remembered the visitors. He went with two more men to see the mother, and they took her a basket of groceries.

Julia was frightened, remembering how the old woman howled at the men and chased them away, how she shook her fist and fell down in the mud. She could hear her howling, far away in her mind, and the tears started to her eyes in awe and fear. They took the old woman away before they sent her son to San Quentin. But there were worse things she remembered, things that did not end quickly, things that went on silently, timelessly, eating away at their lives. It would be easy to take the bread. She would take it and anything else she found, and it would not be wrong. It was only wrong to suffer in silence, and wait—the way she had always done, erasing herself and waiting, believing, believing in what?

The tent was so quiet she looked up from her thinking. Myra was asleep at the table with her head on her curved arm, her face toward her mother. Julia thought she had probably been watching her as she watched everyone with intent and open interest. Her brief eyelids, closed over those searching eyes, gave her willful face a gentler look. Lonnie's pale fragile face was tense even in sleep. Her thin, innocent mouth was open slightly and her breath came through her lips. There was a shadow of fear and pain disturbing the childish expression. Julia looked at her children and she knew she did not understand them beyond her love. She would follow them in silence and waiting, and look at their lives as they made them in the hard and tortuous ways they seemed already to comprehend more clearly than she. And this gave her an ornament of comfort, a grave and tremulous spring of joy.

Forty-five

It was deep dusk when the men came together in the small camp clearing. The strike was broken. It was all over and done with, until next crop. The workers had been released from jail, all except Garrison and another worker named Barth. It was they who had called in the union when they saw the men were going to strike without being organized. The Filipino organizer, Pedro, and the war veteran organizer, Lacy, were still in jail. They would be released when their beatings had faded. The young girl leader would be out tomorrow, provided she left town. Scabs were picking cotton under guard.

"Any of you fellas ever see the old stockade that the big guns built over around Salinas for breaking strikes?" There was a mumbled no. "Well, I declare, it's like a war relic. High walls with places for guns and sentries and barracks inside, where they would herd the scabs in an' out. We're all the time saying what does a bank 'er a railroad know about farming, but that's where we're wrong. They know more'n we do 'cause their business ain't farming, their farming is business. I been studying it over in my mind a lot lately and I reckon I'm 'bout ready to draw a few conclusions." The men waited expectantly, but the speaker had finished and wiped his mouth with the back of his hand. It suddenly occurred to Milt, who was standing next to him, that he meant he was "about ready." Several of the men had soiled bandages on their heads and held their backs gingerly in their coats. Milt had a healing bruise over his right eye at the edge of his hair, and one of his hands was swollen badly.

One of the men grinned at the others and they laughed. "You shore leave a fella hanging by his toes." The speaker paid no attention.

"The way I figure it," Milt said, "is ever' one of these big valleys is a factory to those big fellas, and if it's a factory to them, it's a factory to us. We ain't farmers anymore'n a man who works in

215

a shoe factory is a custom boot-maker. We're like the fellas on the belt manufacturing automobiles only we're making food—mile-long refrigerator trains full of food, cross-country highway trucks full of food. We're a lot of parts that can't stand alone because we haven't got an acre of our own to keep our feet on. We're manufacturing food and our bosses that we never even see are selling it to the world. We're littler than we used to be, and they're kicking us around while we got our tails down so's we won't remember ourselves—but we're bigger too. What these big companies got is power. I've been reading the papers whenever I can find an old one laying around, and everything in the world now is power: countries trying to get more power than the next one, and they're mean getting it, like our bosses're mean getting theirs and keeping it. You can laugh if you want to, but I figure these bosses of ours, they might as well be outsiders for all they care about the people that do the work. They're looking out for the Almighty Dollar, and if they have to starve us to get more'n they can count, they can do it because there's more where we come from; they can do it because they never have to look a poor man or woman in the eye. We ain't human, we're figures on the books." He took a deep breath. He had not meant to talk so much, but now he was started, he just went on. These thoughts had been stirring blindly in him since he left his own field, churning and taking shape in these hard months, grown clear and strong in the days he sat in jail and had a chance to think them through. The men were still, listening, nodding assent. Milt laughed once. "Not long ago some of the fellas were having an argument about who were our real bosses here. One of 'em said the banks, another one said the railroads, one said the power companies, one said the big land companies, one said the farm machinery companies. Nobody knew. These names don't mean much, we don't know who's behind 'em. I can't get it out of my head that whoever owns us makes no difference, it's that they're powerful enough to do it. Plain ordinary horse sense'll tell us that we need some of the same medicine if we're gonna get strong enough to keep 'em from pushing us down to brutes. There's people like that in these valleys; we've all seen 'em. Maybe they were proud once, maybe their parents were, but someplace along the line they got stepped clear into the earth. They'll do the same to us if we don't use our own kind of power, and they'll do it easy because they won't ever think of us as people like themselves with stomachs, and brains—maybe not so big yet—and feelings, feelings as big as they make 'em."

The man who spoke first turned his head and spat far out into the dark and drew the back of his hand across his mouth again. "I reckon I won't have to go about drawing them conclusions now. Milt here's done beat me to 'em."

The men were quiet, thinking. Milt was quiet, but he was not thinking. He had a great clear space inside him that had been as hard as a rock for a long time. He breathed in the air that smelled damp and fresh as it seemed to go all through him, blowing away the little webs of old thought that had tattered his being. He felt as if he had just been born, and he laughed for thinking it, but he believed it with all his heart. He made up his mind to talk to Julia about the bread she had taken. He would talk to her in a new way, and she would be able to talk to him. They had been hard-pressed for a long time, or maybe they had never really known each other very well. It startled him to think like this. He stood there in the dark thinking about his wife with pleasure—thinking how they would talk things over, thinking how still she was and a long time getting riled, thinking how nice she felt in bed, how nice. The men's voices came in on him and he had not heard what they were saying since they had broken their own thoughtful silence.

A drop of rain spattered on his swollen hand. Another and another plopped softly on their shoulders. The men looked up. There was no sky. Clouds drifting loosely above their heads dropped down low, trailing the earth with their shapeless ends. One of the men looked toward his dark tent.

"We could go there," he said,

"We can go to mine," Milt said. "It'll be warmer." They followed him down the ragtown street. The rain fell lightly. His tent was glowing darkly from the fire and the oil lamp within. He opened the door and the men stooped and went in, stepping over the board and onto the ground again, powdered dry and fine from the many steps.

"I want you to know my wife," Milt said. "Anybody who doesn't." Julia came out from the gloom of the corner bed. The men crowded in and stood in the small space looking tall and uncomfortable. She did not smile but she welcomed them with her eyes.

"You're welcome to sit down," she said, "but we can't offer any place but the beds and a few boxes." Milt kicked the big lard can gently out from under the table and offered it to one of the men. They sat down, on the edges of the beds, careful on the one not to disturb the little girls asleep. They sat on the boxes, and on their bended legs. The room smelled only of warm dry earth, but as the rain fell harder, beating a strong tattoo on the tent, the air turned chill and damp and smelled of canvas. Julia sat down on the bed and listened without moving or speaking. There was a knock on the tent pole, and Mrs. Starwood and Frieda ducked in quickly dropping their sweaters they had held upturned over their heads.

"Good evening, folks," Mrs. Starwood said and Frieda nodded and smiled at them all. There was a low-voiced round of howdys. Two men moved to let the women sit down. On her way to the seat, Mrs. Starwood leaned toward Milt and poked his ribs. "We was listening to you, you rascal. Both me and Frieda'll vote for you." They all laughed and Milt laughed too. "Some committee we got here now," she said, settling herself.

The rain fell hard. They looked at one another.

"Raining on the cotton," someone said very low, as if to himself.

"Well, folks," began a man named Nelsen. "I think we better get down to business so's we can get out of this camp before we're flooded." He stopped and looked around the tent, and he rested his eyes on a tall thin man with big blurry features and gentle eyes. "We hardly ever move off together like this, but we're thinking about it now, being's we all been together through some pretty tough sledding these last few months, and I reckon we feel kind of like brothers and sisters, as we say in the union, and can stand each other a while longer. All of us're broke, as you may well know, and we can get where we're going better together. Mr. Hightower has a little something to say to us." He looked at the man again. Hightower locked his fingers together, resting his elbows on his knees, and looked at the others. He was a stranger.

"Folks, I haven't got much to say for myself so I won't make up any fancy excuses. I been working. You can see my knees are muddy. I was on a Harvey Land Company place. We were all afraid to come out unless all the Hayes and Berkeley men struck. Harvey ain't as big as H & B. I knew I was doing wrong, but lot of the other fellas didn't understand what they was doing. My wife was having a baby and she's the kind of woman just has to have a doctor, no two ways about it, and I just got scared of my job and worked. My conscience weighed on me heavier than that cotton sack, and I ain't gonna do no more scabbing. I quit yesterday and took out my union card. I saved a mite of money working." He looked down at his hands and said nothing more. Nelsen peered at him through the faint gloom.

"Brother Hightower saved eighteen dollars and he give it to us." There was a kind of mumbling thanks in the moment of stillness, and Hightower knew they did not hold anything against him.

"Well, now," Nelsen went on, "we got something else. Brother Burdick over there in the corner mortgaged his sweetheart, that purty trailer he made himself, mortgaged it for fifty dollars and he give it to us." There was an unpreventable intake of breath around the room. Nelsen put on a new air. "We shore all hope Andy Burdick gets work enough to pay off the mortgage, or else we can get enough to help him because he'll be needing a home now. We're gonna have a wedding in our midst. Our young jailbird over here has flew the coop."

Everyone looked at Frieda and then at Burdick, and then they smiled and laughed and questioned them. Frieda blushed and hid her face behind Mrs. Starwood's broad back, and then she got up and ran out of the tent into the rain. They could hear her steps running toward the Starwood tent, and after a while they all got quiet again.

"Among us all we collected four dollars and some odd cents, so we're putting it all together for gas and food, and tomorrow we're packing up, and leaving at daybreak next morning." Nelson unfolded an old eviction notice—

To John Doe and Mary Doe, whose true names are unknown:

You and each of you will please take notice that you are required to vacate and surrender up to me the premises now occupied by you; said premises being known as the California Lands Unit 20.

This is intended as a three day's notice to vacate said property upon the grounds that you are in unlawful possession thereof, and unless you do vacate the same as above stated, the proper action at law will be brought against you for the restoration of said premises to me.

Manager, Hayes and Berkeley Company

—and turned it over. "I got a letter here on the back wrote tonight by one of the committee and if you like it we aim to get it to that little girl tomorrow when she gets out of jail. She's mighty worried about us. Hank Todd's out gettin' everybody to sign." Julia and Mrs. Starwood leaned together and read the penciled letter.

Dear Sister Martha Webb,

Don't you worry yourself none about us now and don't get discouraged. We was just practicing. You might say we're in about the same boat we'd of been at this time if we'd of worked. No money, but I reckon we might of had a little something more sticking to our ribs. All of us folks know you people done your best.

It's raining wild cats out here in camp and we're all fixing to move north aways and see if we can't pick some grapes and later some scrub cotton. They say Jan. Feb. March there's no work anywhere so we got to try to get hold of something before then. We all thank you and hope your none the worse for being the guest of the county awhile.

The rest of the page was filled with "Mary Doe" and "John Doe," written many times in as many different handwritings. They each signed in the same way and passed the letter on.

"Now wouldn't you think they'd be ashamed of themselves putting a girl like that in jail for trying to help working people?" a man asked. They all laughed at him. "I glory in her spunk," he said.

"When you just get to thinking about it, it shore seems kind of funny the things these big ones do. They got blacklists. Our fingerprints is made when we get our auto license if we don't say no.

220

They got guns and clubs and tear gas and vomit gas and them vigilantes paid to fire the guns. It shore seems kind of funny them acting like that before a man even has a chance to make a living. 'Pears they could use the money they spend for gangsters and guns to raise our wages. It'd be a power more right," Hightower drawled.

"I never seen anything like this strike myself," Nelsen said. It seemed the men could not let it go. They kept chewing it over like a dog his bone. They would be digging it up in the future and chewing it over and over again.

"When a man works and makes a good wage and knows he's taking care of his family," Milt said, "I tell you, he feels mighty good. He don't want trouble."

"When a man's got a clear conscience, he don't carry a gun," Julia said quietly. Milt looked at her and she felt somehow warmed and pleased. She wondered what had come over him.

They spoke of their plans. They spoke of the past, and the changes they had seen. One man said he had lost his wife—they had had to take her away. It was the ever'day worry. Mrs. Starwood remembered her husband and began to talk about the rain so she would not remember too hard. One of the men—whose father died of pneumonia when he was moved from camp, and who with his two brothers took care of his mother and her old sister—leaned back on the bed and spread his arms out in a stretch that looked like a wide embrace.

"Gee, it's a good feeling to be together. It's sure good to feel the love of one another." The word *love* lay in the warm air of the little tent for each of them to feel in the unashamed and simple truth of his knowing. No one spoke for a long time.

"Well, Julie," Mrs. Starwood finally said, yawning, "maybe you'd better go to bed so these folks can go home."

Still they sat. The rain beat hard on the tent and the fire died in the stove. Water trickled in, making rivulets in the dust. By morning the floor would be mud. One man stood up and made a move to go. The others sat unashamed with their silence. One man whistled an old tune, low, for himself to hear. It was as if these men and all the men they knew had been standing alone in the wide valleys, dwarfed beneath the western sky, and over to the east the dark Sierra Madres bristled with hidden guns, and over to the west, farther than they could see beyond the fields, the ocean made an end. South to north the valleys curved in a long green flowering bowl, filled with food enough for a nation, while hunger gnawed these workers' bodies and drained their minds. An old belief fell away like a withered leaf. Their dreams thudded down like the over-ripe pears they had walked on, too long waiting on the stem. One thing was left, as clear and perfect as a drop of rain—the desperate need to stand together as one man. They would rise and fall and, in their falling, rise again.